BLEU MURDER

BLEU MURDER

BRIAN MILLER

authorHOUSE®

AuthorHouse™
1663 Liberty Drive
Bloomington, IN 47403
www.authorhouse.com
Phone: 1-800-839-8640

Published by AuthorHouse   07/30/2012

ISBN: 978-1-4772-1894-5 (sc)
ISBN: 978-1-4772-1895-2 (hc)
ISBN: 978-1-4772-1896-9 (e)

Dedication

I dedicate this book to my mother, whose love and support has always sustained me.

I am also grateful to my friends in France for their help in bringing *Bleu Murder* to life. Without their support and insight this book would have been impossible. *Merci bien!*

CONTENTS

Dedication v

Chapter One 1

Chapter Two 5

Chapter Three 11

Chapter Four 17

Chapter Five 25

Chapter Six 32

Chapter Seven 37

Chapter Eight 41

Chapter Nine 45

Chapter Ten 53

Chapter Eleven 58

Chapter Twelve 62

Chapter Thirteen 66

Chapter Fourteen 72

Chapter Fifteen 80

Chapter Sixteen 93

Chapter Seventeen 104

Chapter Eighteen 111

Chapter Nineteen 113

Chapter Twenty 118

Chapter Twenty-One 124

Chapter Twenty-Two.. 129

Chapter Twenty-Three.. 137

Chapter Twenty-Four 147

Chapter Twenty-Five.. 156

Chapter Twenty-Six... 162

Chapter Twenty-Seven 169

Chapter Twenty-Eight 176

Chapter Twenty-Nine 180

Chapter Thirty.. 185

Chapter Thirty-One... 192

Chapter Thirty-Two 200

Chapter Thirty-Three 208

Chapter Thirty-Four.. 221

Chapter Thirty-Five 228

Chapter Thirty-Six 239

Chapter Thirty-Seven 249

Chapter Thirty-Eight... 261

Chapter Thirty-Nine.. 266

CHAPTER ONE

"**B**UT IT'S IMPOSSIBLE!"

Domestic bliss had lasted all of three weeks before the universally divisive subject of money raised its ugly head. Bob Hunt had been nervously anticipating this day since he and his wife Kate had moved to the idyllic French village of St-Sébastien des Vignes in the heart of the rural Vendée. It had taken them nearly twelve years to summon the courage to turn their *maison secondaire* into a permanent home and it seemed to Bob that a decade of planning had unravelled in the space of less than a month.

"We don't have any choice," Kate said calmly.

They were stood at the end of the narrow alley that passed between their house and the neighbouring property. Bob, with over twenty years' experience behind him, could tell that Kate's evenness of tone would last about as long as the gate that they were arguing about. And that had already fallen off its hinges. Twice.

"You can't just prop this," Kate lifted the loosely connected planks of wood and shook them, "between two posts and expect people not to comment."

One of the planks chose this moment to desert the structure entirely, splintering onto the fragmented tarmac road that passed for the main thoroughfare in St-Sébastien.

"It's been there years," she continued. "Certainly as long as we've owned the house. It was blue then. Look at it now."

Bob picked up the fractured limb and took the rest of the frame out of Kate's hands before she could do any further damage.

"Everything in the Vendée is blue. This, err . . ." Bob searched his mind for an appropriate description. "This russet colour makes a pleasant contrast."

"But that's how it should be," Kate countered. "The whole of France is blue."

"I suppose so." Bob admitted defeat quickly. He had never quite understood how it seemed possible for there to be so many shades of one colour. He had been amazed the first time they visited the *brico*, their local DIY store, at just how many different blues there were. One dull afternoon, while Kate was obsessing about cushions, he had counted 151 different varieties. There was Atlantic *bleu*, Brittany salt *bleu*, Cote d'Azur *bleu*, Provence *bleu* and, of course, Kate's favourite the Vendée *bleu*. Any wooden protrusion from every house and every piece of street furniture adorning the département was doused in the regulation colour. *Bleu!* It was just like blue but with a Gallic shrug.

"Anyway it's not russet it's just plain rust," Kate complained.

"It isn't that bad. I could give it a lick of varnish if you really wanted. Otherwise I don't see the problem." Bob had a simple motto where household chores were concerned; why do half a job when you can get away with doing no job at all? "Frankly I can't see why we need anything here anyway. People never shut it properly when they go through it." He propped the frame against the wall.

"Because . . ." Kate's voice had reached a pitch that most people would describe as shouting. Bob, however, knew that there were at least another two levels to go. He yanked her down the passage, through the back door and into the kitchen.

"You were saying?"

"People don't shut the gate because they're afraid that they'll break it."

"They won't need to worry now. You've already done it for them."

"We need a new gate and we need it now."

Bob was certain that their elderly neighbours, the Poussins, could have heard the last word. In fact probably the entire population of

St-Sébastien des Vignes had heard it. It was a good job that none of them spoke any English.

"Well, I suppose I could start looking round for something. Start pricing it up."

"Don't you listen to anything I say?"

Bob looked around guiltily. "Exactly what thing?"

"I told you yesterday that I'd already found a gate—a nice tall one with closed boards that Monsieur Poussin can't ogle at me through—and I've had a quote from a company in Luçon to fit it."

"How much?" Bob guessed that it would be more than they currently had in their French bank account.

'Fifteen hundred euros.'

"What?" Bob bounced up in horror and banged his head on the ceiling beam. Madame Poussin was about four foot two, short but positively Amazonian for the Vendée, and it appeared that all the houses in the village had been built by her ancestors.

"Plus tax," Kate added.

"We don't have that sort of money."

'We do in our English account."

"But that's my lump sum," Bob grumbled. He had been a professor of English and taken early retirement from the University. "It's supposed to be a nest egg for us."

"There are a few chickens coming home to roost already," Kate insisted, thrusting a small chunk of brown-stained wood into Bob's face.

"But that money has got to last us until your pension comes through." Kate had worked for an ambitious marketing company, whose policy on retirement had been optimistic to the point of actuarial bondage. "And it's already taken a hit."

"How?"

Bob swallowed. It was time for a few—rather uncomfortable—home truths.

"Well, we do seem to be living beyond our means at the moment."

"Beyond our means?"

3

"Just a smidgeon."

"Please quantify smidgeon for me."

"About a hundred a week."

"A hundred. Shit!"

Bob conceded that the residents of St-Sébastien probably had understood that word.

"How is that possible?"

The upside was that Kate seemed to have forgotten about the gate. The downside was . . . At a rough estimate Bob expected the downside was going to be his life for the next four days.

"You remember that I said that my pension would be nine hundred a month?"

"OK," Kate tapped her foot on the tiled kitchen floor.

"You seem to have assumed that I meant pounds."

"Yes?"

"And . . . I didn't."

"You told me your pension in euros?"

"I didn't bother translating it into Bulgarian Leva for you." Bob picked sarcasm as his defence mechanism of choice. It was a bad choice.

"You lying, cheating, lazy . . ."

"It's good to vent."

Bob ducked as a coffee cup flew over his head.

CHAPTER TWO

I F YOU HAD to fall in love with an idyllic French village then
St-Sébastien des Vignes was a wise choice. The locals called it a
village perdu; a lost village. In other words it was so far off the beaten
track that even the normally inescapable Napoleonic road numbering
system hadn't caught up with it. There was a Greco-Roman church
whose bells could be heard at unreasonably early hours from the
Hunt's house at the other end of the village. There was a traditional
Loire-style chateau, now owned by Germans who had converted it into
a chambre d'hôte. But most importantly, from Bob's perspective, there
were vines. And lots of them.

Wine-making in the area dated back to Roman times but had been
for local domestic consumption until 1972 when the French viticultural
association recognised the *Fiefs Vendéens* as an official *appellation
controllée*. Since then the growth of tourism in the département and
the lack of anything much else to do had led to the proliferation of
wine production as almost every resident of the commune turned over
their land to vines and created their own label. Along the main road of
St-Sébastien the observant traveller could count at least twelve separate
wine *caves*, the traditional place for wine tasting and drinking. And
all of them were—apparently—closed to visitors. To the persistent
traveller, however, there are ways and means of getting access to these
dens of inebriation. And where alcohol was concerned Bob could be
very persistent indeed. It didn't take him long to discover that his
nearest *cave* was, in fact, next door.

"She told me to find a job." Bob had been 'next door' for half an hour before he broached the subject with his fellow drinkers.

"A job?" Jerome Gautier, the owner of the *cave* looked puzzled. "But you've retired haven't you?"

"Yes, but well . . ." Bob exhaled into the ancient wood-wormed beams of the former stable that had been equipped with two large vats and a trestle table to become an officially licensed drinking establishment. "She thinks we need more money."

"Women always think they need more money," Thierry growled from the darkness at the other end of the table and slammed his glass down on the table to emphasise the point.

"Another?" Gautier asked the question out of politeness. He always gave you another drink.

In return for unlimited free wine in the *cave* all that he requested was a gift towards the operation of the retail side of the business. Thierry—an odd-job man as far as Bob could tell—had supplied the barrels in which the wine was allowed to mature. Poussin, Bob's neighbour on the other side, had donated the entire back seat of a 2CV, complete with safety belts, which was laid out along one side of trestle table.

"For the comfort of my patrons," Gautier had explained one evening. "And as a reminder of the importance of our drink-drive regulations, without which you'd all be down at the chateau drinking their over-priced swill."

Bob's contribution had been enough corks to float the entire fleet of Brittany Ferries.

"But what can I do?"

"I thought you said you'd been asked to give a conference paper?" Gautier had the perennial optimism found in every barman and professional counsellor.

"Yes, but I only get paid expenses and a modest attendance allowance, so there's not much money in it. Unless I win the prize for the best paper. But that won't happen."

"You never know. I'm sure your work is very good."

"I doubt it," Bob sighed.

Shakespeare was not his strongest subject. He had been relieved enough when his original conference abstract was accepted. It had been a rushed job merely committing him to identifying the central theme in King Lear. Thank goodness the deadline wasn't until the following July; over nine months away.

"No jobs round here," Thierry grumbled. "And if there were they shouldn't be given to the English."

Thierry stared at Bob, who took no notice. It wasn't personal with Thierry—he just hated everyone.

"I don't know," Gautier said amiably. "During the tourist season there's always a demand for English-speaking workers."

"But that's not until May."

"There might be some Christmas work in the shops."

"Kate says I have to get a job straight away."

"You could always try Rogier up at Longchamp. He always needs help on the farm. There's only him and his girl live up there now."

"But I've never done anything like that before. Not even when I was a student—and I did some desperate things in those days."

"You'd have to be bloody desperate to go up there," Thierry grunted. "They say there's dead bodies half buried in the fields." He raised his head towards Bob and scratched at a copious growth of stubble. "It's no place for a soft English tart like you."

The three sat in gloomy silence. Bob contemplated his dilemma—how on earth was he supposed to find a job? He swirled the dregs in the bottom of his wine. No two glasses in the *cave* were the same style or size. Like the furniture they appeared to have been begged borrowed and otherwise appropriated from a multitude of sources. Bob had never been invited into the Gautier house, but he imagined it to be full of three-quarter sets of chairs, cutlery and dinnerware.

The stable-door creaked open revealing a shaft of autumnal bronze light from the fading sun.

"Ah, here's Poussin. He'll know what to do."

"Good afternoon gentlemen. How are we all?"

Monsieur Poussin was eighty-one but still hadn't completely retired. He kept a smallholding at the back of the Hunt's garden with chickens, goats and the obligatory half dozen rows of vines. He had the face of a walnut and the handshake of a vice. And he was tiny. Even smaller than his wife, Poussin must have been the shortest man that Bob had ever seen.

"Bonjour Pierre." In the *cave* Bob was allowed to call him by his first name. But only in the *cave* and absolutely never—under any circumstances—in Madame Poussin's presence.

"Ah Bob, how's the gorgeous Kate today?"

"After money." Thierry slammed his empty glass down.

"She wants Bob to get a job." Gautier passed freshly charged glasses to the three guests before filling his own.

"Good thing too. Young man like you needs something to do with his time. What'll it be? Harvesting?"

"Bit late for that now." Bob tried to conceal the relief from his voice.

"True, true. How about tanker driving? There's a dairy down the road that always needs drivers."

"I don't have a French licence."

"No, no, I've got it! Road mending. The crews'll be busy from now until April."

"Oh yes." Gautier thought this was a good prospect. "It's coming up to the time when they strip all the displays off the roundabouts and plant the bulbs and so on for next year."

The French are very strict about decorating their roundabouts. Themes are changed annually and rigorously applied, except in Road Safety Week when it was normal for the *Police Municipale* to abandon a couple of wrecked cars on each roundabout as a warning to new and aspiring drivers. Bob's experience was that the young motorists were far less dangerous in practice than their octogenarian counterparts who encouraged overtaking on blind bends from the safety of their tortuously slow 'sans permis' vehicles.

"I suppose it's a possibility," Bob conceded reluctantly.

"You remember to tell that lovely wife of yours that it was my idea," Poussin said. "You can earn about twelve euros an hour. Not bad for this part of the world."

"Before you get taxed by this thieving government." Thierry cleared his throat in preparation for hostilities.

"Not now," Gautier fussed. "You know the rules. No politics."

Cave etiquette was concise but rigorously enforced. You could talk about almost anything—as intimately as you wanted—but it never went outside the *cave*. Most men seemed to regard it as far more secure than the confessional. There were only three topics that were off limits; politics, religion and food. It was accepted that everyone was entitled to their predilections on these issues and that discussing these contentious topics could only disunite the otherwise fraternal conviviality of the *cave*.

"I suppose I'll have to go to the *Pôle d'Emploi* to see what they've got."

"No, no," Poussin argued. "Word of mouth is the only way to get a job round here. Man's work." He had a mischievous glint in his eyes. "Kate'll thank you for it when you've built up your muscles."

He flexed his arms. The three other men shrank back into the shadows of the *cave*.

"At least I don't have to get a stepladder to change a light bulb," said Bob in self-consolation.

"I'd change Kate's light bulbs any day." The old man's face split into an adolescent grin. He gave birth to a sound that was somewhere between a wolf-whistle and a foghorn. It all ended in a phlegm-filled fit of coughing. Bob had never been surprised that the Poussins had nine children and thirty-four grandchildren. Pierre had enough life force within him to populate a small département.

"I told Kate that thinking is my *metier* so thinking about work is my ideal career. I really don't understand why she thinks I need to get a job. She just needs to spend less."

"She's only trying to do her best for you both." Gautier was a model of fair-mindedness. "After all you wouldn't want end up back in England, would you?"

"I suppose not," Bob agreed. He was sure that none of the suggestions he'd heard would meet Kate's financial requirements and feared a frosty reception. But this was France, and she couldn't expect to recreate their easy English existence in the Vendée. *Demain*, he decided. It was a problem for another day.

CHAPTER THREE

BOB FLAPPED OPEN the screen of his laptop. A defiant screech of plastic confirmed his worst fears about the state of the computer. Perhaps it was time to buy a new one? Bob shook his head. It was out of the question. Their financial position was even bleaker than he had revealed to Kate. If things carried on deteriorating at their current rate there was a real danger that their French dream would be as short-lived as a mouse in a cattery. They would have to go back to their old lives in the UK and Bob would have to go back to marking students' work. It really didn't bear thinking about.

At least Bob had the conference to look forward to. He would earn a small amount from the attendance allowance and possibly extract some visiting lecturer opportunities if he networked effectively. And then, of course, there was the conference prize. Five thousand pounds and the chance of a book contract for the best paper. It wasn't a huge sum of money, but in the circumstances it could make all the difference—and the boost to his profile would surely open a few more doors for him. All he had to do was write the damn thing.

King Lear. Not one of Bob's favourite plays. All that gloomy stuff on the heath; madness and badness. It wasn't going to be easy to find a theme to hang a conference paper on. There was almost too much to choose from. A beep from the laptop prompted him to enter his password followed by a long period of inactivity while the system dredged up his programs and files.

"*Enfin*," Bob muttered as a blank document dazzled the screen with white.

Where to begin? He typed the title of his paper and his own name into the computer and felt a little better for having made a start. Then he felt a lot worse: he didn't know what to write next. How had Shakespeare managed to do it—to take the whole universe and squeeze it into poetry that had resonated with humanity for generations? Surely it was impossible to do justice to such inspiration in a conference paper of several thousand words. Bob began to wish that the laptop had been slower starting up. That would have given him time to think through what he was going to write and would have saved this humiliating white hiatus.

And, after all, wasn't that why they had been so keen to come to France in the first place? For 'time to think'? That had definitely been one of the main attractions. Living at a slower pace gave them time to enjoy simpler things. Time to savour life itself. He thought back to their lives in England. Kate had spent most of her time racing round the country satisfying the fickle needs of her clients, which were always immediate. They had sometimes joked that she was too busy to have children—only it hadn't felt very funny at the time. The odd thing was that when you were young everything needed to be done quickly—as soon as possible. It was only as you got older that you valued the importance of taking your time, and bizarrely that was just as the time available to you was getting increasingly limited.

Lear had discovered that. He had come to a point in his life where he needed to plan for his future—and that of his realm—and he had rushed into a decision. Instead of taking the time to reflect on the merits of the claims of his three daughters he asked them to recount their love for him. When he didn't get the instant response he wanted from his youngest daughter Cordelia, he simply reallocated her inheritance to the other daughters. It was only later, amidst the bickering and backstabbing of his two remaining heirs, that he found the time to regret his hastiness. Bob reflected that perhaps he and Kate would come to regret the hastiness of their move to France. If they needed to return to England would they be as unwelcome as Lear had been in his own country?

He looked down at the laptop and began to type.

'King Lear is one of Shakespeare's most complex plays but its central theme is the concept of time.'

It was a start. Now all he needed was a second sentence. Bob meditated for a moment, trying to draw grand ideas from the well of inspiration. It was empty.

"Time for a coffee," he declared as he stood up at the desk and slammed his head into the overhead beam—again.

He put the battered tin kettle on the range and waited for it to boil. There was a note and a grubby piece of newspaper on the kitchen table, tucked between the pewter salt and pepper pots. It looked suspiciously like a task. After twenty-one years he could just about translate the spidery hieroglyphics that passed for his wife's handwriting.

'Found this in local paper. Call them today. Love you. Kate.' There were some scrawlings at the bottom that could have been a sketch of the Taj Mahal. Bob was in a good mood and interpreted them as kisses.

He picked up the ragged-edged newspaper cutting and read it. As he had suspected it involved work.

'Reliable person required in South Vendée. English import/ export business needs an honest and dependable person to clean and maintain small house in Vendée village. Excellent rates of payment for the right candidate. Immaculate references essential. Would suit retired professional person.'

There was a telephone number at the bottom of the advert and he was surprised to note that it had a Parisian dialling code. Bob sighed. He might as well get it over with now. After all, he could tell Kate that he had tried and that the vacancy had been filled. That would be one less thing for him to do. He went to the lounge and picked up the phone. And, when he came to reflect on what happened next, Bob realised that this was probably his first mistake.

Over the years Bob had just about got used to the delicate purr of the French dialling tone, almost feline in comparison to its brittle British counterpart.

"Hambleton's of Paris. How may I help you?"

The brisk English voice took Bob by surprise.

"Oh, um. Well, I hope that I've got the right number. I read an advert that you placed in La Roche-sur-Yon looking for someone to maintain a property in the South Vendée."

"Yes, that would be the summer cottage. I do believe that Mr Charles placed the advertisement."

"Would it be possible to speak with him?"

"Unfortunately not. Mr Charles is presently out of the country. However, I do recall that Mr James expressed an interest in the subject. I shall enquire whether he is available to speak with you. May I know your name?"

"Of course. My name is Robert Hunt."

"Please hold the line."

The phone went silent for a minute. Bob could feel his pulse racing away. It had been years since he'd put himself through a job application.

"Are you still there Mr Hunt?"

"Yes."

"I'll put you through to Mr James now."

There was a brief clicking in the earpiece.

"Mr Hunt?"

"Er, yes."

"It was ve'y good of you to call us about the advertisement. My name is James Hambleton. I am one of the joint Managing Directors of Hambleton's of Paris. I fear we may have forgotten to place the name of our business on the notices." The voice was as rich and plummy as thick jam. Not a single vowel went unlengthened.

"I must admit I hadn't noticed that."

"Nor should you, old boy, nor should you. Our oversight entirely. Anyhow I'm awfully glad you took the time to give us a call. You see, we've got ourselves into a bit of a tizzy with this summer cottage business and we'd be terribly grateful if someone would keep an eye on the place for us." There was a pause, as if an offer had already been made and an immediate answer was expected. "I do hope that I haven't put you off." The last word rhymed with dwarf, which was how Bob felt in the presence of the awe-inducing voice.

"No, not at all. Where is this cottage?"

"Ah! Now I should have guessed that you would ask me that. Do you know—I haven't got a blessed idea what the place is called. Lovely little town though. Bridge across the river with one of these huge churches and a sandstone chateau overlooking the whole lot. Pretty as a picture but I'm damned if I know the name."

"Is it on the coast?"

"Good lord no. Too many tourists on the coast. Wanted somewhere a bit more peaceful. There's a very good restaurant there, if that helps."

"I find it usually does."

"Ha-ha, yes. It's called La Petite Bus or some such thing."

"La Petite Bourse?"

"Yes, that's the chap! Little tables on a terrace by the river. Accordionist usually, too. Excellent selection of wines. Ve'y good value. Do you know it?"

Bob certainly knew it by reputation. At a hundred euros per couple for a meal even the *hors d'oeuvres* would have required a small mortgage. He couldn't work out whether the name was ironic; a small stock exchange would have been more likely than a little purse.

"Sort of."

"Perhaps you know the owner there? Gorgeous young gal. Lisette, I think, or Lizzie. Something like that. Built the place up from scratch she told us. I said it was just like Hambleton's. D'you know my dad started this business in 1952? Handed it on to Charles and me in the nineties." Bob discerned a change in James' tone; the lightness was gone, replaced by an almost missionary earnestness. Business was obviously a serious matter. "We're brothers you see. Dad didn't want us fighting over the business after he'd gone. Poor old sod died a year later. Dad that is, not Charles." Hambleton's former conviviality returned. "He's still well and truly alive—somewhere in the States at the moment I think. Anyway, what do you think about the cottage?"

"I think it must be in Marieul-sur-Lay." The small market town was about ten miles away from St-Sébastien.

"Hmm, might be. Name rings a bell. Point is—we've recently bought this place for the business so that members of the family can use it for breaks and holidays and such like, but hardly anyone uses it. It needs someone to keep an eye on the cottage, tidy it up before guests arrive and do any jobs that want doing."

"Is there a garden?" Bob asked suspiciously. He'd been caught out that way before by Kate, for whom all gardens were low maintenance—principally because he'd done all the work.

"There are some lawns, but they're all maintained by the manoir."

"The manoir on the hill?" The grand old building sat at the top of cliffs facing the chateau on the other side of the river. Bob imagined great rivalries had been played out between the two dynasties over the years.

"That's the one. The cottage is just on the edge of their grounds. Must have been a lodge at some time I imagine. So they maintain the lawns and the lake and all that . . ."

"Lake?"

"Oh yes, at the bottom of the hill. Links up with the river."

"I never knew that the grounds were so big." Bob had assumed that there were just houses behind the manoir. In his mind he couldn't quite work out how you would get there.

"Tell you what, old boy, why don't I arrange for Charles to meet you there and show you round? He's popping down there when he gets back from America, probably the weekend after next. It was all his idea in the first place. Typical, really, he's the brains behind the outfit. I'm just here to make the place look pretty. Ha-ha!"

"That sounds like a good idea."

"Splendid. I'll get Maureen to take your details and pass them on to Charles and he'll be in touch directly. I don't think we'll bother with anyone else—you're just the right chap for us, I'm sure. See you soon, no doubt. Toodle-pip!"

"I can't wait." Bob said, mainly to himself, as he was transferred back to the switchboard.

CHAPTER FOUR

THE TOWN OF Mareuil-sur-Lay sprawls in a cross along the twin axes of the main road between Luçon and Les Sables-d'Olonne and the meandering River Lay. At its centre is the Pont Neuve; a stone-built bridge of three arches topped with black-painted ironwork, from which the Romanesque church and the sandstone chateau frame a picture postcard image of traditional French tranquility. Anyone who stands on the bridge for any length of time, however, will find it anything other than tranquil. Luçon and La Rochelle beyond are home to major producers of mobile-homes and luxury yachts. Consequently, the road through Mareuil has become a rat-run for every conceivable form of *convoi exceptionelle*.

Bob joined the traffic jam just beyond the boulangerie and eased the Clio into first gear. They had agreed to buy a local car, complete with the department's '85' number plate, as an essential investment from their lump sum. Having an English vehicle would mark them out as tourists and it made sense to buy a diesel car because the fuel was so much cheaper in France. The salesman told them that it had had one owner but it obviously hadn't been a careful one. There were three separate dents on the driver's door, a scratch that ran the length of the passenger side body and a dubious-looking stain on the rear seat. The light in the boot compartment didn't work either. Otherwise it had been a bargain.

Bob chugged over the bridge and turned sharp left at the traffic lights before climbing up the steep hill towards the manoir. About halfway up the hill he saw the narrow alleyway which, he had been promised by the Hambleton's receptionist, led out of the town and around the manoir's grounds to the cottage. The instructions had all been very precise and businesslike. He was to attend an interview with Mr Charles Hambleton at the property itself and was to furnish him with a written testimonial from a former employer and three means of proving his identity.

The turn was sharp—effectively into a blind corner—and Bob gritted his teeth as he swerved the Clio into the unknown. A double hairpin bend followed and the car crunched into a mechanical grumble as the gradient started to take its toll. A green Citroen C4 sprang out of the turn, its downhill momentum carrying it onto the wrong side of the road. As the vehicles passed Bob was sure he could see the colour of the other driver's fillings. To his relief the road widened out as it ran alongside the grounds of the *manoir*. At the brow of the hill a lane to the left marked 'Domaine' led through an open gateway to a small cottage. Bob pulled up on the gravel drive next to a top-of-the-range BMW and, feeling more than a little inadequate, stepped out of the Clio. This is stupid, Bob thought as a figure approached him from the front of the cottage, my first interview in over thirty years and I'm as nervous as a kitten.

Charles Hambleton was a middle-aged man of medium height and average obesity for an Englishman living mainly in France. His hair and eyes were a dull brown and his nose and mouth were distinctly nondescript. As he approached the only outstanding feature of the man was that his crisp navy jacket and black trousers were offset by a pair of brown shoes. It was an ensemble that Bob had been expressly and unambiguously forbidden to combine.

"Mr Hunt?"

"That's right. Please call me Bob." He was not surprised by the limp handshake, but the estuarine English accent was certainly a contrast to his brother.

"I'm very grateful that you were able to meet me today. In fact we're all very grateful that you took the trouble to answer our advertisement.

I believe you've spoken to James about our 'requirements'." He emphasised the final word by twitching his index fingers in the air.

"Well, only briefly. He told me a bit about the house and that the company used it as a sort of holiday home."

"That's it—more or less. To be honest, although the cottage belongs to the business we tend to treat it more as a family crash-pad. Generally we take in turns to use it at the weekends and occasionally we entertain clients or suppliers who want to experience something of the 'real' France." He sketched some more air quotation marks with his fingers. "Mainly, though, they prefer to stay in Paris to take in the sights. You know—the Eiffel Tower, Moulin Rouge, Notre Dame—that sort of thing."

"I know what you mean. Although it's been ages since I was there."

"Oh. You should come and visit us sometime. At the office I mean. That is, of course, if you take the job. It might be helpful for you to meet some of the staff and see exactly what we do."

"What does the company do?"

"Import and export basically. We take traditional French favourites over to England for the Francophiles and bring back Marmite, Christmas puddings and baked beans for the ex-pats. Amazingly lucrative really, although the market has been getting increasingly competitive as the larger supermarkets have caught on to it."

"And it was your father that started it all up."

"Yes, yes. Back in the fifties before there was a 'Common Market'." Charles scratched the air again for emphasis. "Dad was a bit of a visionary. He loved France—it was where he met my mother—but he could never quite bring himself to leave England. He'd fought in the war and was a great patriot but because he'd seen something of the world he caught the travelling bug. He drove all over France picking up some *foie gras* here and some vintage wine there and bring it home for us. *Brie, Champagne, Cognac*—you know the sort of thing. Naturally as time went on people would ask him to get particular things for them and before he knew it he had to drive across the channel in a van. The whole thing just grew from there."

"So why is the business called Hambleton's of Paris?" Bob resisted the temptation to air apostrophise.

"Marketing."

"I'm sorry, I don't understand."

"Think about it. If you're buying French bread are you really going to be tempted by 'Croissants of Croydon'?" Charles' fingers flicked into the sky again.

"I see what you mean."

"The only problem was that having established the name he had to set up an office in Paris, although most of the work was still done in England."

"You grew up there?"

"Oh yes. James and I had a fairly traditional British upbringing. Public school, Oxbridge educations, professional qualifications." The final upward inflexion made the list sound like a menu from which Bob had to make a choice. "Of course you were in that line yourself weren't you?" This time it really was a question.

"Not in that league I'm afraid. I'm a professor of English at a fairly unknown University."

"I thought you'd retired."

"More or less. I still do a bit of casual teaching and write the odd article when I can." Or if I can, Bob thought to himself. He still hadn't got round to doing much about his conference paper. "Professorships are like war wounds—they stay with you for life. What did you train as?"

"I'm an accountant. James is a lawyer. I'm not sure we chose our professions—I think Dad just encouraged us to take up careers that would give him free advice."

"And now you run the firm together?"

"After a fashion. I run the operations and James does the 'front of house'. It works surprisingly well really. I enjoy getting on with the logistics, the planning, the making-it-all-work side of things." Bob ducked away slightly expecting an imminent apostrophisation, but it never came. "And James does the publicity, marketing and schmoozing. He does a lot of schmoozing." Charles looked down, as if noticing for the first time his dreadful footwear *faux pas*.

"You don't get jealous?"

"Oh no!" Charles looked up at Bob as if deciding whether to confide in him. "I can't stand all that kind of thing—it makes me too nervous. I prefer to just melt into the background.' Bob believed him.

"So, about the house?"

"Of course. I'd nearly forgotten what we were here for. Let me take you in and show you round. I've got the keys here." Charles produced a neatly labelled set of three keys from his breast pocket and gestured to Bob to follow him.

The cottage was a squat two-storey building running along the side of the gravel track which Bob assumed must lead up to the manoir. It had been rendered in a pale peach skin with the traditional wooden shutters painted in blue and a red-slated roof. Charles led the way through a short hallway into a lounge stuffed with the largest collection of soft furnishings that Bob had ever seen.

"We've made the place as cozy as we can. The family uses it as a place to relax so it's all very informal."

"How many members of the family are there?"

"There's James and me, of course. And then there are our children who are all employed by the firm. James has two daughters, Jasmine and Rose. You won't be surprised to learn that he likes flowers, although I seem to end up doing all the gardening."

"I know the feeling."

"Jasmine is married to one of the company's 'rising stars'. They have a young son called Marc who loves coming down here—they spend nearly all the time on the beach and in the sea. That's one of the reasons why we bought the cottage. Of course we bought it in the spring and have only just realised that we need someone to keep an eye on it over the winter."

"Do you have any children?"

"Yes—Louise. She's seventeen and works in the office doing all our web-based stuff."

"Does she come to the cottage much?"

Charles smoothed his hand along the top of the sofa.

"No, never. I don't, er . . ." he looked away from Bob and plumped up the cushions on one of the three armchairs. "She's still very young and I'm afraid that if we let her use the cottage she might take advantage of the situation. I know that I'm bound to say this as her father, but she is a stunningly pretty girl and quite naïve. She's had a few boyfriends lately and I don't really want to encourage her to have any more." He hugged the last of the cushions to his chest. "Since her mother died it's been a bit of a juggling act, I'm afraid. So far her only vice seems to be the occasional cigarette. At least while she's in Paris I can keep an eye on her." He looked up at Bob. "Do you have any children?"

"No, no," Bob said. He gazed down at the thick oriental carpet and decided that they should move on. "So you need someone to look after the house?"

"Yes," Charles seemed as relieved as Bob. "We need it cleaning every week and also for the fridge to be stocked up before someone comes down on a visit. I can get the girls at the office to call you in advance. To be honest, at this time of the year hardly anyone stays here—there's too much to do in Paris—and the winters here get surprisingly cold."

"Oh, I don't know. They beat English winters hands down." Frost in the Vendée was such a rarity that it had been known to bring the traffic to a halt in Mareuil.

"I suppose so." Charles led him into the kitchen. For an old cottage it was a travesty in style. A microwave oven and dishwasher stood cheek by jowl with a traditional French dresser and a selection of silver cheese knives. "Obviously we'll pay you a float to buy the food and so on and there'll be a monthly retainer of three hundred euros. If you work more than twenty hours in a month we'll let you have an hourly rate of thirty euros on top. The girls will go through all the paperwork with you. Shall we go upstairs now?"

He gestured through the hallway to a steep wooden staircase that turned back on itself to reveal four doorways.

"There are two bedrooms on this floor and a bathroom. There's a cupboard here," Charles pulled at a handle which opened up to reveal a janitorial treasure chest. "If you just buy whatever equipment you need and then charge it back to us that will be fine. Similarly, if you need to get someone in to do repairs or replace furniture then the easiest thing is to get it charged to our accounts department. All the utilities are paid directly by us from Paris."

"It all seems very well-organised to me." Bob tried to control the smile that had appeared on his face the moment he realized how much money he would earn, but found that he couldn't. The amounts involved were beyond his wildest expectations.

"Good. I hoped we'd be able to sort all this out today. All I need to do is see your references and ID and I can let you be 'on your way'." Dust moved through the air where Charles' fingers twitched. There would be work involved, Bob reflected, but it would be a quiet place to think away from Kate.

"I thought there would be an interview."

"You seem ideal to me. The only requirement that we have is for the place to be kept together and clean for when we visit. Someone to keep an eye on the place. A sort of representative in the Vendée, if you like."

"Excellent," Bob replied and couldn't help rubbing his hands together.

"Oh! I nearly forgot. There is another bedroom. If you wouldn't mind standing back a bit." Charles raised his arm to the ceiling where there was a short piece of cord and pulled sharply. Bob ducked reflexively as a trap door in the ceiling opened and an aluminium stepladder tumbled out in front of him.

"Sometimes it sticks," Charles said and indicated that Bob should climb up the steps. At the top was a long thin room that had obviously been the attic originally.

"There's a light switch just on your left."

Bob felt for the button and a neon strip buzzed into life. A small single bed and a chest of drawers sat in the centre of the room, which was very Spartan in comparison with the rest of the house.

"We don't use it very often but occasionally someone has to sleep up here. I wouldn't worry about cleaning it unless you know that it will be used. I imagine that getting a hoover up here is a bit of a nightmare."

"Not too bad," Bob was feeling generous. "I think I'd probably do it every week. If it gets left I expect the dust will just build up and make it harder to clean the next time." He ran his finger across the chest of drawers and held it up to demonstrate the point.

"Whatever works for you." They stepped back down onto the landing and Charles closed the doorway with a firm push. "It can be a bit tricky at first, but you'll get used to it. Now if we go back down to the lounge I'll have a look at your paperwork and we can do 'the deal'."

The final set of air apostrophes seemed to settle the matter and Bob spent the whole journey back to St-Sébastien beaming at himself in the Clio's mirror. It was easy work, he reflected, but someone had to do it. Besides, Kate would be so proud of him.

He had no idea that 'the deal' would include the dubious honour of becoming the prime suspect in a murder.

CHAPTER FIVE

BOB STOOD ON the pavement and looked up at the faded white tower which, if his geography was correct, housed the offices of Hambleton's of Paris. He had to admit to a sense of disappointment. The building was one of those anonymous, utilitarian, could-have-been-built-anywhere structures that dominate commercial architecture across the globe.

He yawned. It had been an early start. Kate had dropped him off at the railway station at La Roche-sur-Yon before seven in the morning and he had arrived at Montparnasse three hours later. He had drifted through the busy streets of Paris, grey and damp in the January drizzle. His route had taken him past the classical symmetry of les Invalides, between the imperial eagles guarding the river crossing at Pont d'Iena and through the understated grandeur of the sixteenth arrondissement before arriving at the office. It was a prestigious enough location—had there been any sunshine the building would have sat in the shadow of the Eiffel Tower—but it lacked either the gravitas or the flair for which the city was renowned. In fact, Bob concluded, it looked rather sleazy.

He pressed the relevant buzzer on the doorframe and the intercom bristled into life immediately.

"Hambleton's of Paris. How may I help you?" Bob recognized the brisk tones of the receptionist from their ongoing conversations about the arrangements for the cottage.

"Hello Maureen. It's Bob Hunt."

"Bob—at last I get to meet you. I'll open the door for you. If you would make your way up to the third floor I'll meet you there."

The door clicked open and Bob entered a dingy hallway that looked as if it hadn't been dusted for about half a century. There was no sign of a lift so Bob started to climb up the old wooden stairway. White paint peeled away beneath his fingers as he held onto the bannister at the top of the first flight of steps. He began to wish that he'd stuck to Kate's diet over Christmas rather than tucking into the complimentary hamper that Hambleton's had sent them.

Eventually, breathless, he reached the third floor and was greeted by a well-dressed woman in her late fifties, whose immaculately styled white hair and steely grey eyes reminded Bob of a talk he had once given to a WI branch deep in Cotswold countryside.

"Mr Hunt, what a pleasure to meet you."

"Likewise," Bob urged the word out of his bursting lungs.

"If you would care to follow me I'll take you into Mr James' office directly."

Maureen set off through a glass-panelled door onto which the words 'Hambleton's of Paris' had been stencilled in an old French script style. She set a rapid pace across the creased linoleum that flapped loosely over creaking floorboards. Bob followed with difficulty as she bustled through a reception area, down a corridor and rapped her knuckles against a door marked 'Mr James Hambleton—Joint Managing Director'.

"Come in, come in." Hambleton's stentorian voice was unmistakable.

"This is Mr Hunt." Maureen motioned at Bob, turned quickly on her heels and disappeared back up the corridor.

Whatever expense had been spared on the offices that Bob had seen so far had obviously been lavished on the room into which he now entered. From the plush oriental carpet to the leather banquette lined up behind a mahogany coffee table the room exuded affluence. Sat at its centre, in a grand regency armchair alongside an elaborately-marqueted walnut escritoire, was a large man stuffed into a broad pinstriped suit sporting a pink carnation from his lapel button. He sprang up and pumped Bob's hand as if he were some long lost friend.

"Bob, my dear old thing. I may call you Bob, mayn't I? I feel I know you so well already."

"Of course."

"And can I just say that we're all most grateful for the way that you've kept the cottage in such pristine condition."

"It hasn't been very difficult. So far only you and your daughter Rose have stayed there."

"Yes, well, the Vendée in the winter can be rather quiet. And the firm has been so busy."

"That's good to hear."

"It appears that France is *á la mode* in London at the moment. It goes in phases you know."

"We were always attracted to the Vendée—the pace of life suits us perfectly."

James gestured for Bob to sit down on the banquette before returning to his own chair.

"And we're going to move into the American market now. I'm off to the States in a couple of weeks to sign a deal to ship crates of Champagne over to them. They do seem to have got over their aversion to French foreign policy—not before time. All splendid news for us, of course."

James rubbed his hands into a small ball in his lap and grinned widely. Bob thought that he looked like a contented toad about to go a-wooing.

"How long are you away for?"

"Oh, I'll only be in New York for ten days, but I intend to fit a lot in. I've never known such a place for non-stop entertainment. Culture on every corner—it knocks Paris into a cocked hat. How does the song go? I want to wake up in a city that never sleeps . . ." James opened his arms as he crooned the line, jowls trampolining in delight at the prospect.

"Will you be taking your wife with you?"

"Good lord, no! She'll be far too busy with her own work to come with me."

"You must find it difficult to get time together."

"Not really—I see her virtually every day at the office."

"She works here? Will I get to meet her?"

"You've met her already, old boy."

"Have I?"

"Of course. Maureen, maid of all work, is the light of my life."

"You're married to Maureen?"

"Don't sound so surprised—she's a marvellous woman. Very efficient, you know. A tad bristly on occasions; but then that's the gentler sex for you."

"I'm sorry," Bob felt his face flushing. "I didn't mean to imply anything."

"My dear fellow," James stood up and planted one of his big fleshy hands on Bob's shoulder. "How quaintly old-fashioned you are. Maureen has always been the receptionist here. In fact she was the first person my father employed in the business who wasn't a member of the family. Well, it didn't take me long to change all that, you know. I fell in love with her the moment I set eyes on her." He paused. "It's a small failing I have." He smiled wanly. "Women—one of life's irresistible pleasures. Talking of which—how is your good lady?"

"Oh, very well, thank you."

"An enjoyable Christmas?"

"Our first since moving to France. Very relaxing. No need to make excuses to various bits of the family about why we couldn't visit them. Not a problem that you face I imagine."

"Don't be deceived by appearances." James plumped himself down next to Bob. The banquette dropped noticeably in response to the additional weight. "The fact is that although we work together as a family it's purely a commercial arrangement. Business is thicker than blood, as my father used to say."

Bob was just about to ask James about his daughters when the door burst open and a woman in an unseasonably low-cut flower-patterned dress flounced in.

"Daddy, Rose says I won't be able to go to the cottage in June because she's already booked it. Tell her not to be so wretched. I've promised Marc he can go swimming and I wanted to do it before the schools break up."

"Jasmine, this is Bob Hunt." James slapped his hand back onto Bob's shoulder. His daughter ignored him.

"Tell her she can't have it. Please."

James sighed. His worn expression suggested that he'd been in this position before.

"I'll talk to her about it."

"Oh, thank you, daddy." Jasmine, who Bob reckoned to be in her mid-twenties, wrapped her arms around her father and kissed his cheek.

"I'm not promising anything, but you know I'll do my best for you." He gave her a big theatrical wink. "Now come and be a nice girl and say hello to Mr Hunt. He looks after the cottage for us."

"Hello, Mr Hunt." She gave Bob's hand a limp shake and turned away from them, her dress swirled out to reveal bare knees. Bob shivered. "I'll go and tell mum to change the booking. See you."

"I said that I can't . . ." But James was wasting his breath. His daughter had already swept out of the office. He turned to Bob. "You don't have children, do you?"

"No."

"Sensible move, if you ask me. They are, of course, a miracle and a delight but sometimes you just wish they would start behaving like adults and take responsibility for themselves." He rolled himself off the banquette and back into his armchair. "Now then, old boy, let's get down to business. What do we need to do to help you with the cottage?"

They talked about the cleaning and maintenance arrangements for a while and Bob had just come to the conclusion that—as far as jobs went—he had landed on his feet with this one when they were interrupted by a tentative tapping on the door.

"Yes. Come in." James shouted.

29

The door was opened by a woman in jeans with a very pale complexion, whose long, jet-black hair hung lankly over a knitted sweater. As soon as she saw Bob she shrank back as if he were a mad axe murderer.

"Rose, my love, do come in and meet Mr Hunt."

Bob stood up to shake her hand but she backed away from him.

"Pleased to meet you," he said simply.

"I'm sorry, I didn't mean to disturb you. I mean I didn't know you were with anyone." Her voice was tentative but her dark eyes were animated, darting between her father and the visitor. "I'll come back later if you prefer."

"I'm sure that Mr Hunt doesn't mind. Of course, you know that he looks after the cottage for us."

"Actually, that's what I wanted to talk to you about." She looked at Bob and paused, as if weighing up whether he could be trusted. "I've just been told by my wonderful baby sister that I won't be going to the Vendée in June after all."

"No, no, that's not what I said . . ."

Rose flicked her hair away from her face. "I just wanted you to know that it's OK with me."

"It is?" James sounded dubious.

"Oh yeah. I don't really mind having to change all my arrangements to accommodate your precious little Jasmine."

"But I haven't made up my mind. I was going to talk to you about it first."

"Like—when?"

James looked at Bob and then back at his daughter. "Later." He raised his arms in a vague gesture of helplessness.

"It's funny really." She stared back at him. "My father always brought me up to believe that when you agreed something you should stick to it."

"Darling, that's very unfair. I never promised anyone anything."

"You said I could stay in the cottage in June. You know you did. Mum even wrote it into the book."

"Yes, but Jasmine's got little Marc to think about. It isn't easy for her and Alain."

"Sure. Anyway I thought I'd let you know that it's cool with me and I'll just have to go in July instead." She started to leave the office but paused in the doorway. "And that means I won't be able to attend your wedding anniversary party—the highlight of the Hambleton social calendar. What a shame."

"Rose! You can't do that," James blustered, his face reddened with anger. "You know very well that I expect you all to turn up to that."

"But I won't be able to. I have to take my holiday sometime." She held her index finger against the corner of her mouth. "And if I can't go to the cottage in June then I'll have to go later on in the year. Such a shame."

"Don't you threaten me." He wagged a chubby index finger at her. "If you don't come to our anniversary party then I'll make sure you lose your job and your allowance, young lady. And that's a promise that I will keep."

"Yeah—you do that!" Rose practically spat the words at him and slammed the door so hard as she went out that plasterboard walls of the office trembled in response.

"You see what I mean?" James turned back to Bob, who felt embarrassed for him. "You really can't win with the children. Anyway, I'm terribly sorry that you were forced to sit through that. It's really most uncivilized and I can only offer you my most humble apologies."

"Don't worry," Bob replied. "I'm sure I was just the same with my parents." Actually he was quite sure that he hadn't been anything of the sort. His father had been a strict disciplinarian and had brooked no dissent, not that Bob had ever offered any.

"In return I will treat you to the best lunch that Paris can offer. How does *L'Ambroisie* sound to you?"

"It sounds very expensive."

"It is," James harrumphed. "But it's on expenses and we've earned it." He stood up and motioned that Bob should follow him. "And if we're quick we'll be just in time for their first serving."

CHAPTER SIX

"FRANKLY I'M AMAZED at how quickly it's all taken off, darling."

Kate leaned down to kiss Bob, who was sitting on one of the armchairs in the *sejour*, the lounge in the cottage, gazing at the empty grate in the huge fireplace. Her long blonde hair tickled on his bald pate.

"Well, it's a start I suppose."

"Yes, and we can put the money aside for a new gate in the spring."

"You and that bloody gate," he growled. "Will you ever stop going on about it?"

"Unlike some people I care what the neighbours think of our house. If we're going to spend the rest of our lives here then we should at least have a gate that doesn't fall apart as soon as a visitor touches it."

"You do exaggerate. It's not that bad."

"Oh no?" Kate's voice had risen to an ominous pitch halfway between irony and derision. "So why is it that the last time Monsieur Gautier came round he brought his own screwdriver with him to tighten the hinges?" She flung herself into the armchair opposite him, the dim January light from the window reflecting the anger in her eyes.

"He likes to help," Bob replied calmly.

"I'm fed up of it. In fact I'm fed up of the whole thing. Cutting corners here, making do and mending there, living life on the cheap like a couple of tramps. Everything we do seems to cost us more than we can afford."

"I'm doing something about it, Kate. After all I am earning us an extra few euros a month from the Hambletons."

"A few euros doesn't really do it for me. I was almost a Director, if you remember, before you dragged me out to this place and into a life of poverty."

"But you said that you loved France; that this was your dream house and all you wanted to do was live here forever."

"Huh! I didn't mean living here like a peasant." She favoured Bob with a final glare before adding "Anyway, I'm going shopping." Then she stomped off into the kitchen slamming the door behind her.

Bob knew she was right. As time went on their financial position seemed to go from dwindling to deficit without much relief in between. The money situation was placing a stress on them both. He and Kate had been through their ups and downs when they lived in England, but never anything as stormy or as regular as this. He'd have to work harder than ever at finding a new revenue source for them—and that meant that he needed to get on with his conference paper. He retrieved the laptop from the top of dwindling stock of firewood and propped it up against the side of the armchair.

Shakespeare—he'd had financial troubles of his own hadn't he? Bob tried to recall. Wasn't there something about keeping his wife Anne Hathaway in her house in Warwickshire whilst he lived it up in London with his theatrical friends? It was hard enough keeping up one home without trying to fund two of them. Poor Kate, he thought, I really should have planned this all out much more carefully. They had gone into the situation blind, and he was behaving like a fool.

The words fused in his mind. Of course, it was obvious! He pushed the power button on the machine. Eventually, the laptop completed its electronic warm-up exercises and Bob found the file with his conference paper on it. He highlighted the entire text that he had written and flicked the delete key. Onto the fresh blank screen he typed 'King Lear is one of Shakespeare's most complex plays but its central theme is the concept of folly.'

Bob felt the creative adrenalin course through him and flexed his fingers in anticipation of the muse. Then the phone rang.

"Hold on, hold on." Bob called as he extricated himself from the laptop. It really was time that he updated to a wireless machine, he decided, as he unwound the cables from his legs. At which point the phone went silent.

"Bloody phones," he cursed as he went back to the chair. "Bloody phones, bloody laptop, bloody France." He would have continued with his litany except that the phone started to ring again.

Bob stared at it—daring it to stop. It didn't, so he answered it.

"Allo, Bob Hunt."

"Hello Bob, is that you old boy?" Beyond the crackle, Bob could make out a plummy English accent on the other end of the line. It sounded as though the caller was at the bottom of a very long tunnel made out of greaseproof paper.

"Yes, yes. Who's that?"

"It's James here. James Hambleton." Bob finally recognized the distinctive elongated vowels.

"You sound as if you're the other side of the world."

"Yes, I am." Another bubble of interference spat across the conversation. "I've just got into New York. Marvellous journey over you know; got a superb glass of claret with my meal. Very rare these days you usually just get . . ." A huge roaring sound blasted down the receiver forcing Bob to hold the phone away from his body.

"Sorry, only a plane taking off." There was a pause. "Is that any better, old boy?" It was—marginally.

"Yes. You sound in good spirits."

"I'm in New York—what more could a man want?"

"Can't think of anywhere I'd less like to be," Bob replied. "Anyway what can I do for you?"

"I am sorry for calling you, but I just remembered that I promised someone that he could use the cottage tomorrow. The trouble is I'm going to be holed up here for at least a week; presentations to give, clients to schmooze, bars to visit. You know the deal. Could you pop up there and check that it's all tidy and clean for him?"

"Yes, of course."

"I'm awfully sorry that it's such short notice but he's a terribly sweet man and I wouldn't want to let him down."

"That's alright. I'll go up there now for you." The crackling on the line increased again.

"You are kind. I'll be sure to bring you back something special from the old duty free place. What's your tipple?"

"Don't worry—it's all part of the agreement."

"Nonsense dear boy. I insist. What'll it be—would a seventeen year-old single malt suit you?"

"I leave it entirely to you." Bob could just about make out a tannoy announcement in the background. "What's the guest's name?"

"Oh!" There was a brief pause at the other end of the line. "Sorry about that, slipped my mind for a moment. Must be my age, what? His name's Timmy. Timmy Wells. If you wouldn't mind awfully just giving the place a bit of a sprucing up and restock the provisions. Make sure there are a couple of bottles of red there—the old chap drinks like a fish. Leave the key under the doormat, I'll let him know where it is."

"Will do."

"Thank you. You really are too kind. But a word to the wise, old boy."

"Yes?" The line was getting more indistinct, like a radio going in and out of reception.

"Be very discreet. Timmy's a man of . . ." There was the briefest of pauses. ". . . exotic habits. He enjoys indulging himself."

"Indulging himself?" Bob thought this sounded ominous.

"Best to just let him get on with it, I'd say. Each to their own, what!"

"Oh, I won't get in the way. I'll just leave the key."

"Good man." The tannoy blared again and was quickly replaced by crackling, like interference. Something registered in Bob's mind. Something out of place. "Anyway I'd better get going before we lose this connection completely."

"Hope it all goes well in New York."

"I'm sure it will. I've got a jolly good feeling about all of this." It was a feeling that Bob didn't share. He couldn't work out what was wrong, but he had an instinct that not everything was quite right. "Anyway, must dash now," the booming voice continued. "There's a taxi rank approaching. See you soon, old boy. Toodle—pip!"

The phone went dead. Bob stared down at it absently. There was something niggling away at the back of his mind—if only he could remember what.

Suddenly he was back in the present.

"Oh no. Kate's got the car!"

CHAPTER SEVEN

BY THE TIME Kate returned the afternoon was slipping away and the light was fading into the sunset beyond the Atlantic coastline. She'd been spending money that they hadn't got—on replacement secateurs of all things. If she kept losing them then she should do without as far as Bob was concerned. The pair exchanged a quick sentence before he grabbed the car keys out of her hand. No doubt Kate would accuse him of being sharp with her but he would make it up to her later—if he could be bothered. The way their relationship had been lately he wasn't sure that he could.

The Clio grumbled its way through Mareuil and up the slope towards the manoir. As it rose towards the sharp right turn the engine coughed, harrumphed and stalled—straddling the road like a stranded tortoise.

Bob swore. He quickly double-twisted the key in the ignition and the car jumped forward narrowly missing a passing cyclist who was freewheeling down the hill. The Clio died again as if in response to the angry fist shaken in Bob's direction. "Damn, damn, damn!"

Three more attempts to start the car failed before a tractor launched itself out of the bend and clunked to a halt millimetres away from Bob's door. The tractor driver was close enough for Bob to see his grey-white moustache quiver in annoyance and to lip-read the agricultural expletives that issued from beneath it. The tractor reversed back up the passageway and then burst out of the junction at a different angle, charging towards the side of the Clio before swinging around at the last moment to pass by. Bob breathed a sigh of relief. Then the tractor reversed at full speed towards the car.

"No, no," Bob cried as he braced his body and squeezed his eyes shut, anticipating the inevitable crash.

It never came. Instead the tractor stopped dead as it touched the Clio. The driver jumped out of the cab and ambled round to Bob. He was seventy if he was a day, and his walk was unsteady. It looked as though he'd been through a hip replacement operation that had been aborted at the halfway point.

"Broken down?"

"It seems to have stalled. I can't get it going again."

"Shame. Nice car." A pause. "Once."

The tractor driver looked the Clio up and down as if examining a former lover who had gone to seed. He spat onto the road and turned to look at Bob more closely.

"English?"

"Yes." Bob tried not to sound too guilty, but he couldn't help feeling out of his depth. The tractor driver seemed to regard him with pity.

"Tow?"

"That would be great. Are you sure?"

"Where to?"

"I'm just going up to the cottage at the back of the manoir."

"Brake off," came the brief instruction and the old man hitched the Clio behind the tractor and pulled him up the hill to a small lay-by about two hundred meters from the gateway to the cottage.

"Can't turn." The driver pointed to the narrow gateway that led through to the manoir's drive. "Best here." He unchained the tractor.

"Thank you so much for your help. How much do I owe you?"

"*Cadeau.*"

"Well, thank you *monsieur* . . ." Bob offered his hand and the old man grasped it firmly.

"Rogier. From Longchamp." Bob quickly withdrew his hand. Wasn't that the farm that Thierry had been so afraid of? "*Bon courage.*"

With a cheery wave the old farmer left Bob on the side of the lane as the sun disappeared beyond the tree-fringed horizon. Bob shivered and zipped his old gardening fleece up to the top. He pulled the cleaning equipment, some baguettes, cheese and two bottles of something expensive from the Gironde out of the Clio and threw them into a battered old suitcase that had been in the boot for ages. He would worry about the car later. He trudged along the lane in the dwindling light up to the gateway and the cottage beyond. It had been a while since anyone had stayed and there was a sense of damp isolation that hung about the place like forgotten washing.

Putting the lights on didn't make things better. A couple of spiders had woven a lacy web along the hallway ceiling and the light magnified its shadow into a malevolent matrix. Bob switched a couple of the electric heaters on in the lounge to air the place and immediately regretted the decision. He reckoned that the electric system of the cottage predated Ampère. In order to have more than two appliances turned on it was necessary to turn off the fuse switch in the cupboard at the top of the stairs.

Bob sighed. Everything seemed to be against him today. He turned the light switches and the heaters off and felt his way up the creaking staircase to the cupboard. He opened the cupboard door and flicked the fuse back into action.

Bang. The front door of the cottage slammed shut.

While Bob had been pre-occupied with the electrics someone had entered the cottage. Had Timmy Wells arrived early? He didn't have a key. Apart from Bob only Charles and James did—and he'd only just spoken to James who was in New York. It must be an intruder. Bob decided that he would have to defend the property and looked around for an appropriate weapon. Surely he was still too young—just—to die. The only thing he could lay his hands on was an extendable feather duster. He held it out in front of himself in an aggressive manner and shuffled behind the wall at the top of the stairs where he could look down into the hallway.

Bob could see two bodies silhouetted by car headlights from outside. He shrank back along the landing as one of them touched the light switch, bathing the hall in a low watt glow.

"Welcome to my lair." It was a young woman's voice, followed by a giggle.

"I expect a warmer welcome than that." The second voice was masculine and deep—and suggestive.

"Then follow me."

The woman started to climb the stairs and Bob quickly ducked into the main bedroom. The couple had reached the top of the stairs and the footsteps stopped. Bob could hear the sound of kissing followed by another girlish giggle. What the pair were up to was clear enough but who were they? Perhaps they were part of the extended Hambleton family. If so it would be very embarrassing to have to confront them in these circumstances. Bob reminded himself that this was the only regular income that he and Kate had between them.

One feature puzzled Bob. The couple had spoken in French, whereas the Hambleton's normally spoke English together. Before he had time to work out what it meant the couple were on the move again. They were heading his way. In the darkness of the bedroom Bob fumbled with the lock on the wardrobe. It was the only place large enough for him to hide. The lock seemed to be stuck and the footsteps on the landing were rapidly approaching the bedroom door. They stopped abruptly.

"Here we are." The woman's exotic accent would have left Bob weak at the knees, but they were too busy knocking together in panic. "The moment of truth has arrived", the woman purred as she pushed her conquest through the door, flooding the room with light.

Bob took the only remaining refuge—and dived underneath the bed.

CHAPTER EIGHT

"Y OU LOOK AS if you could with a drink Bob." Gautier almost ran to the wine vat as he welcomed his neighbour into the *cave*. There was a howling wind blowing up the street and the old wooden door slammed shut behind the professor.

"He's English. He could always do with a drink." Thierry was as amiable as ever.

"Actually I've had a bit of a shock." Bob threw himself onto one of the wooden chairs in the *cave*, which responded with an ominous creak and an alarming redistribution of his weight.

"Here you are, *mon ami*," Gautier passed him a tumbler. It was late, even by *cave* standards. Bob could see at least a dozen empty wine bottles lined up neatly beside the door.

"Ah, the *pineau*? Just what I need." Bob swigged the drink down in one and Gautier raised his eyebrows at him. "Another one? Don't mind if I do actually."

"It must be bad," Thierry grunted. "Wife trouble?"

"No, no. I've just been forced to watch sex!"

"*Quelle domage!*" Bob was aware of a distinct lack of sympathy.

"I didn't mean watch. That isn't quite right. I never saw a thing. It was all very bizarre. I suppose you could say that I had to endure a couple having sex about ten centimetres above my head."

"I think something has got lost in translation." Gautier placed the replenished tumbler straight into Bob's outstretched hand. "Endure isn't the right verb to use when discussing sex. We French tend to

41

use the word enjoy. I know the English terms are very similar but you ought to try to get it right."

"The English don't enjoy anything," Thierry snorted. "It's all that rain."

Poussin chuckled from his chair in the semi-darkness. "Let's hope you've learnt a thing or two to get your Kate going. I've been in training for her."

He winked at Bob, who looked away. The church clock bell chimed. It must be eleven and he was conscious that he hadn't been home yet to let Kate know what had happened. She could wait. Right now his nerves needed calming.

"It's like this. I went up to the cottage at the *manoir* to get it ready for a guest and a couple of people came in. I wasn't expecting them and so I panicked and hid under a bed."

"Very sensible," Thierry interjected. "A cupboard is much less fun!"

"I didn't have time for a cupboard. Anyway, it turns out that they were looking for a place to . . ." Bob flushed. He blamed it on the drink—and his natural English reserve, which seemed to be returning by the bucketful. "It went on for ages . . ."

"It's how we like it on this side of the Channel," Gautier added genially. "It's why we have two hour lunch breaks."

"Eventually they'd had enough and disappeared as quickly as they . . ." Bob chose his French vocabulary carefully. ". . . arrived."

"Who were they?" Thierry's interest was piqued.

"I don't know?"

"They must have been the guests you were preparing for." Gautier passed Bob another full glass.

"But he's not due until tomorrow. And anyway the couple didn't stay, they just had their fun and left."

"Burglars?" Thierry sat up and stared at Bob.

"No, no. Whoever they were, they had a key."

"It must be friends of the owners. What are they called?"

"The Hambletons. It's possible—there seem to be hundreds of them."

"Yes, well one of them probably gave the key to a friend in return for a similar arrangement the other way." Gautier's argument seemed very plausible to Bob.

"And you saw nothing." Thierry hadn't taken his gaze off Bob.

"No, nothing. Well, except for the legs."

"Legs?" Poussin was suddenly interested.

"From where I was lying it was all I could see. Not that I was looking, of course," he added quickly. "But yes I did see her legs." He drained the tumbler, conscious of the three pairs of eyes staring at him.

"And . . ." Gautier encouraged.

Bob sighed. It was a long blissful sigh—the sound of a memory of lost love.

"They were . . ." he paused. How could words do them justice? ". . . intoxicating."

"So is tractor diesel but it doesn't make me sigh like that," Gautier said. "Describe them."

"They were long and slender and perfectly smooth. The shape of the stem of a champagne flute and as firm as ripe peaches."

"You could tell all that from under a bed?" Poussin sounded doubtful.

"I promise you that I would recognise those legs again. There was something indelibly perfect about them. Something exotic, illicit and yet tantalisingly tangible. D'you know what I mean?"

They nodded. A collective sigh breezed across the cave.

"I am going to dream so well tonight," Poussin said happily.

"I'm not,' Bob said. "I think I'm going to get a terrible telling off from Kate."

"Just tell her you kept your eyes closed the whole time," Gautier advised. "She can't be offended at that."

"But that's the normal English approach to sex," Thierry argued. "She'll think he was enjoying himself anyway."

"No, no. It's not that I'm worried about." Bob emptied the contents of his glass and Gautier responded as quickly as if he were a *Fiefs*

Vendéens vending machine. "It's the Clio. She broke down and I've had to leave her up at Longchamp."

"Longchamp?" Gautier passed the fresh glass to Bob. "That's old Rogier's place isn't it?"

"I wouldn't go up there if I were you." Poussin exchanged glances with Thierry. "It's too creepy. I get goosebumps every time I go past the place." He pulled his quilted coat tighter around himself.

Bob was surprised. He couldn't imagine anything scaring his neighbour. He was such a straightforward person—a traditional man's man. The farm must hold some dark secret if Poussin was afraid of it. The rain drummed down on the *cave* roof.

"Pissing like a cow, by the sounds of it." Poussin said eventually.

"*Pineaux* all round," Gautier announced suddenly. "After all we have something to celebrate." Gautier poured the pale liquid straight into the drinkers' glasses regardless of whether they were empty or not. "Your grandson's getting engaged, isn't he Poussin?"

"Is he?" The old man scratched his head. "Which one?"

"Dominic. He's marrying a girl from Talmont-St-Hilaire."

"I suppose he might be. I always wait until Madame Poussin tells me what's going on. He's a good-looking lad—takes after his grandfather. Anyway, how do you know?"

"Oh, she's a distant cousin of mine. Sandrine. She works in the travel agency on the main road in Talmont."

"I thought Dominic was seeing an estate agent, but maybe that was another grandson. So many of them."

"Anyway, good luck to the happy couple," Gautier concluded.

They all raised their glasses

"To the happy couple!" Bob toasted, and wondered how on earth he was going to explain his evening to Kate.

CHAPTER NINE

"WHERE'S THE CAR?" Judging from the tone of Kate's voice it was going to be another difficult breakfast conversation.

"Uh?" Bob was nursing a firmer than usual hangover. "Car?"

"Yes. You know one of those things with four wheels that one uses for getting around—especially when one lives in the back end of bloody beyond." Kate had her back to the wood-burner in the kitchen.

"Ah, you mean the car!" Bob's vision glazed over.

"Yes, that'd be why I asked where the car was. Car, *voiture*, automobile . . ."

"Mmm." He wiped the remaining flakes of croissant from his lips and thought carefully. Where was the car?

"Only I was planning to go out in it." Kate efficiently demolished a yoghurt pot with her fist, while he gave it some more thought. "Preferably this side of the next millennium."

Bob prepared himself for his wife's inevitable eruption. He'd just remembered the previous night's events. He slurped a long draught of coffee. The peppery aftertaste cut through to his brain.

"Well, it wasn't my fault, but basically the Clio didn't make it back."

"It wasn't your fault . . ."

"Er, no. It just sort of . . . stopped."

"Stopped?"

"Is there an echo in here?" Humour, Bob thought, was the last refuge of the guilty.

"No. There's just a half-sober man with a hangover who can't answer a straightforward question."

Kate pushed his coffee mug to one side and drew her face down level with Bobs.

"Where. Is. The. Car?" She separated each word carefully, her piercing blue eyes never once leaving his face.

Bob rubbed his head, scuffing at the thin fronds of hair that still remained around the crown.

"Longchamp."

"Longchamp?"

"There is an echo, you know. I told you we should have had this ceiling replastered."

"Shut up!" she yelled at point blank range. Bob could smell the rhubarb conserve on her breath. Suddenly he felt queasy. "What the hell is the car doing at Longchamp?"

He folded his arms defiantly.

"Bob, don't mess about. I need to go out to fetch some threads for the tablecloth I'm working on. This means I need to use the car."

Bob lifted his chin imperiously and glared at her.

"Why is the car at Longchamp?"

He pouted at her.

Kate picked up his mug and slowly lifted it above his head.

"You've got precisely ten seconds to tell me what's going on or else I'll pour this coffee all over you. Ten, nine, eight . . ."

"You told me to shut up."

"I didn't mean it. Seven, six, five . . ."

"You shouted at me."

"That—I did mean. Four, three, two . . ."

"You wouldn't dare."

"One . . ."

"Alright. I confess. I confess."

Bob prostrated himself across the kitchen table in mock supplication. Kate replaced the coffee cup on the table and folded her arms. He lifted his face, conscious of the bits of eggshell and croissant that had nestled in his stubble.

"Basically the Clio broke down and while I was sorting out the cottage Monsieur Rogier towed it back to his farm at Longchamp."

Bob carefully omitted the part of the story involving legs and beds. He was in far too delicate a condition to go through that again.

"How did you get home?"

"Well, I cleaned up at the cottage which took a bit longer than I expected. When I came out the Clio wasn't where I'd left it. I panicked for about twenty minutes, running around like a headless chicken up and down the roads around the manoir. Eventually a car pulled up and the driver asked me if everything was alright. Turns out he was a nephew of Rogier and knew all about the breakdown. He told me that his uncle had towed the Clio up to Longchamp. Then he offered me a lift back to St-Sébastien."

"So, he brought you back here? Why didn't you invite him in—for the obligatory glass of whatever's-in-wine-rack?" Kate was not placated. "After all, it couldn't have been that late by then, could it?"

"It wasn't exactly back here." A piece of muesli fell from Bob's chin. He tried very hard not to look at it. "He dropped me off at the *cave* first."

Kate's gaze was unremittingly hostile.

"Well, I had got rather a shock with the car breaking down and . . ." A pair of legs entered Bob's mind. ". . . Everything."

"How do you," Kate emphasised the word very carefully, "get it back?"

"Ah, yes, good question. Rogier's going to arrange for one of his cousins who's a mechanic to fix it for us and then he'll give us a call and we can go to their garage and fetch it. I'm sure Gautier will give us a lift up there."

"And when will this reunion take place?"

Bob gave an exaggerated shrug.

"No." The tone of Kate's voice was on the rise. "When did he say it would be ready?"

"That was what he said." Bob replied steadily. He shrugged again, lifting his shoulders higher this time as if to emphasise the imprecision.

"Oh, my God. You've left our car—our only means of transportation—in the hands of an unknown relative of a maniac farmer who lives halfway to Luçon, and you don't know when we're going to get it back?"

"You can see why I needed a drink." Bob wiped a slug of conserve off his forehead. "Is there any more coffee, darling?"

The call from Rogier about the car came the following day. The parts that were needed to fix the Clio had been located in assorted barns and out-houses within a three kilometre range of his cousin's garage. The most difficult item to acquire had been a rubber belt which ran between the camshaft and some other mechanism that was beyond Bob's skills of interpretation. Conjugation he could cope with, but automation was beyond him. The problem had been resolved through the strategic use of a trimmed waistband cut out of Rogier's late mother's knickers—and that was as much detail as Bob wanted.

"Great," Kate was in a brighter mood immediately. "That means you can take me into Luçon and I can get those threads I needed."

"You mean you want me to traipse along behind you whilst you do a tour of the shops."

Bob hadn't made any progress on the Lear paper because of the atmosphere between them. He really needed to knuckle down and get some writing done.

"I've been cooped up in here with you for days . . ."

"A day," Bob corrected her. "It's only Friday."

"It's felt like months, the mood you've been in. Hell, it's felt like years. So the least you can do is humour me for a couple of hours while I sort out a few bits of shopping that I need."

"Such as what?"

"It's spring," Kate replied simply. "When a young woman's fancy lightly turns to thoughts of clothes." Her face dared him to argue.

"And who I am I to stand in the way of a young woman's fancy?" He set off to alert Gautier of their impending departure.

Luçon was busy. There were two coaches in the main car park, disgorging tourists into the cathedral. Built and rebuilt in the gothic tradition, with a classical nave and triforium, the Cathedral

Notre-Dame of the Assumption has one principal claim to fame. In 1606 Armand du Plessis de Richelieu was made bishop of Luçon where he developed his political and religious philosophy before becoming, in effect, the first prime minister in France. The cathedral had, as a consequence, become a place of political if not religious pilgrimage for tourists from around the world. This was ironic because Richlieu had described Luçon as 'a mud-caked backwater'. It now presented itself to the imaginative tourist in its alter ego as 'Cultural Capital of the South Vendée'.

"Are you sure you've been into every shop?" Bob meant it ironically. They were walking past the front of the cathedral. For the third time.

"I think so." Kate hadn't spotted the humour.

"Oh I don't know. Surely there's some little alleyway tucked at the back of the cemetery that we've missed. I bet there's at least a hundred boutiques down there that we could waste a couple of hours in."

"I know someone who'll be visiting the cemetery very soon if he's not careful."

Bob kicked away at a line of gravel that had detached itself from the road. The strong February wind had reminded him of the storms in Lear, and he was keen to get back to work.

"Anyway, what was wrong with that pink, flowery miniskirt thing we saw in the first shop?"

"You mean apart from the fact that it was pink, flowery and a miniskirt? Well, for one thing, it wasn't my size."

"I thought it was quite chic."

"You would! You're colour-blind and have the dress sense of a . . ." She paused and looked Bob up and down appraisingly. ". . . Of a University professor."

"Monsieur Poussin would have appreciated it."

"I rest my case!"

"Damn!" Bob stopped mid-scuff. "Damn, damn, damn!"

"What is the matter with you? Have you forgotten something?"

"Damn, damn, damn." Bob had just remembered something.

"Or are you just suffering from a very polite form of Tourette's?"

"The case."

"What case?"

"At the cottage. I took the wine and bread and stuff up to the cottage in the only thing that I could find out of the back of the Clio."

"Well?"

"We promised to lend it to one of Poussin's grandchildren for their holiday. I can't remember which one."

"You promised, you mean. Probably while you were in a drunken stupor in Gautier's *cave*."

"But they want it tomorrow. Oh God! You know what this means."

"What?"

"We'll have to go up to the cottage on the way back home to see if I can find it."

"Fine! It's not the end of the world."

"Yes, but Timmy Wells will be there. And judging from what James Hambleton told me he might not be best pleased to be disturbed."

"Alright," Kate conceded graciously. "But honestly, of all the poor excuses I've heard for cutting short a shopping trip this must be one of the lamest."

Kate pulled the Clio into the empty gravel driveway outside the cottage. Timmy Wells must have brought a car with him, so Bob concluded that the property must be vacant. He was a little puzzled to find the key still under the mat where he'd left it on the Wednesday night. Perhaps Mr Wells hadn't arrived after all.

That theory was scuppered the moment that they entered the kitchen.

"He's already got through both bottles of wine," Bob remarked as he saw the kitchen dustbin.

"And enough vodka to bankroll three Russian oligarchs." Kate prodded the collection of bottles with her foot.

"Strange about the key, though. Why would he leave it under the mat?"

"Perhaps he thought he'd lose it and so it was better where it was."

"Sometimes, you're infuriatingly logical for a woman."

"And sometimes you're perfectly patronising for a man."

"Maybe he's finished with the cottage, so he put the key back when he left." Bob had been checking in the downstairs rooms and although there was evidence of someone having been using the cottage there were no personal belongings anywhere.

"I expect he's left all his bits and pieces in the bedroom. That's what I'd do. Hang everything up properly. Now where's this case? Let's find it and get out of here. All that shopping's made me hungry."

"I left it in the kitchen, before I was interrupted by the 'loving' couple." Bob caught himself air-apostrophising. "It must be this place," he muttered and smacked his own hand.

"It's not down here," Kate said, re-entering the hallway from the lounge.

"I'll look upstairs."

"You be careful, Bob. You don't want to catch any more lovers at it." It had become a joke between them. "You might learn something." He pretended not to hear her.

The case didn't seem to be in either of the bedrooms. In fact nothing seemed to have been moved in them at all as far as he could judge in the half-light. The beds were still made exactly as Bob had left them. Judging by how much Timmy Wells had drunk, he probably couldn't have made it up the stairs. He must have slept it off on the sofa in the lounge.

"Nothing up here."

"It must be somewhere." She started climbing up the stairs. "Aren't there any lights up here?"

"Ah!" Bob remembered the cupboard. "I bet he threw it in here out of the way."

He opened the door just as Kate got to the landing. There was an enormous clattering sound and they both jumped backwards, colliding into each other.

"Scared of our own shadows." Kate said. "Look, there's nothing but buckets and brushes in here." She lifted up a couple of brooms that had fallen out of the cupboard and a mop-bucket that had tumbled against the doorframe.

"No, but someone has been in here moving things around. They've even forced the door shut. That's why the stuff fell out." Bob re-organised the cleaning equipment and closed the door. "Still no sign of the case, though."

"What's up here?" Kate indicated the cord dangling down from the ceiling. "Is it a light switch?"

"No!" Bob pushed her away as she pulled the cord. "Look out!"

The trap door in the ceiling fell open and the aluminium stairs unfolded out of the top bedroom.

"I wasn't expecting that!" Kate said, rubbing the top of her head where the edge of the trap door had caught her.

There was a loud thud. A large and heavy weight tumbled out of the trap door and crunched into the landing between them.

It was a body.

Kate screamed.

Bob looked at the blood-stained hole in the back of the suit jacket.

It was a dead body.

He heaved the crumpled mass over.

It was the dead body of James Hambleton.

Chapter Ten

"It must have been a terrible surprise for you, Monsieur . . ." The police cadet referred to the sheaf of papers on the small wooden table that sat between them.

"Hunt," Bob completed. He had never been inside a gendarmerie before—and the experience was more than a little unnerving.

"*Bien sur*. Monsieur 'unt." The cadet looked up at Bob with appraising brown eyes. "You are English, *non?*"

"*Non*, er *oui*." Bob was flustered. An image of James' lifeless slack-jawed face came into his mind.

"Which is it? It's a simple enough question surely." The cadet switched language. "Are-you-Ingleesh?" The words were drawn out very slowly.

"*Oui*. But we live in the Vendée now—for our retirement."

"Ah! One of those." The cadet scribbled away on the papers.

"My French is normally very good but I'm afraid that finding the body has been something of a shock to the system."

"Certainly, I can understand that. It isn't every day that a corpse drops out of a cupboard onto you."

"No."

"Assuming, of course, that it did." The papers were examined and shuffled.

"Pardon?"

The cadet stared at Bob.

"We only have your word for it that the body was, in fact, dead, when you found it. The stab wound looked very fresh to our forensics expert."

"My wife was there as well."

"Ah, yes, Madame 'unt. Kate.' The cadet wrinkled his nose as he spat out the name. "In this country we prefer to use the full rendition—Catherine. We find it more pleasing to the ear."

"Well, she can vouch that we both discovered the body together and that Monsieur Hambleton was definitely dead when we found him."

"I'm sure she would vouch for you, Monsieur. Unfortunately, however, here in France it is not uncommon for husbands and wives to collude in criminal activities. So, for now at least, we must treat you both with a certain amount of—er—caution. You are currently the only witnesses to the crime scene and, consequently, the prime suspects."

"But that's ridiculous," Bob snorted. "Why would we want to kill James Hambleton?"

"Ah! And that is also a curiosity, is it not? Of all the people in the Vendée who might have discovered the body of an unknown foreigner it is, in fact, you that fall upon the corpse."

"I think it was the other way round—the corpse fell on us!" Bob replied, trying to lighten the situation.

"Levity is not appropriate in these circumstances, Monsieur 'unt. This is a very grave investigation and I would appreciate it if you treat it as such. You should consider your position extremely seriously."

Bob had to admit that things didn't look too good for him and Kate. They had found a body, they knew the victim and they had the keys to the body's location.

"What about the couple having sex?" he asked suddenly.

The brown eyes focussed back onto Bob.

"I have warned you already about levity . . ."

"No, it's true," Bob protested. "When I was at the cottage a few days ago a couple went into the bedroom and made love there."

54

"It's not so unusual. In this country." The cadet did not seem to be impressed.

"Don't you see? It means that someone else must have a key."

"And where were you when they had sex?"

"Oh, I was under . . ." Bob paused as he realised that this wasn't going to make his case look much better. "I was underneath the bed. But there was a good reason for that."

"I can't wait to hear what it was, monsieur."

"I didn't want to intrude."

"You didn't want to intrude?"

"No."

"So you hid under the bed where the sex was happening?"

The tone of incredulity in the cadet's voice confirmed Bob's worst fears.

"Well, yes."

"And you don't know who these people were?"

"No."

"So they were—at the very least—trespassing?"

"Yes, but they definitely had a key. I heard it turning in the lock."

"Mmm."

The cadet seemed to be taking Bob seriously now. This was encouraging.

"So, of course, you reported the situation to the police?"

"Yes. No!"

The cadet's eyebrows arched in annoyance.

"No, I didn't report it because it didn't seem very important at the time. I thought maybe she was a relative of James Hambleton who had a key and just wanted to make a brief use of the cottage."

"And would that be normal in England?"

"No—not at all."

"And yet you seem to think it is perfectly common in this country?"

"Well, not really. I just didn't want to make a fuss . . ."

"Until now. When it becomes suddenly convenient for you to be able to refer to this unknown couple who performed an uncorroborated act at a murder scene where you are the prime suspect." He pursed his lips. "Convenient seems an understatement in the circumstances."

"Where is my wife? She can explain all of this to you."

"As I said, she is being questioned separately, to ensure that your stories agree."

Bob was getting exasperated. He'd had enough of a shock discovering a dead body, without being treated as a murder suspect as well.

"Is there anybody else I can speak to?"

"You're talking to me." The brown eyes frowned. "That's good enough for the moment. Eventually a higher authority will wish to question you."

"A higher authority? You mean a superior officer?"

Here, perhaps, was hope.

"I mean an officer of a higher rank," was the indignant reply.

The shuffling of the paperwork became markedly more aggressive.

"I think I'd like to speak with your superior officer now," Bob said with a new-found confidence. "I'm sure they will be able to see the bigger picture and view my situation a little more sympathetically."

"I doubt it."

"Why?"

"Capitaine Fauconnier is not renowned for his sense of sympathy, or humour, or anything else for that matter. He is—as I think you say in English—a tough old bird."

"Great!" Bob muttered under his breath. "Just what we need."

"In fact . . ." The cadet checked his watch against the giant wall-clock that adorned the witness room. "He should be here at any moment. I'm sure he'll be delighted to put you through a superior form of questioning."

"Perhaps it won't be necessary for me to see him, after all."

"Oh no. He would be terribly disappointed not to hear your stories of bodies in cupboards and I don't doubt that he'll want to check every

fact most carefully for himself. He's very . . .' The cadet paused as if selecting the *mot juste* for the occasion. "I think the word is thorough, if you know what I mean."

Bob feared that he did.

"He won't need to question Kate as well will he?"

"Oh, he'll especially want to talk to her. He is a great believer that the woman is always the weakest link. But he'll start with you."

A door slammed in the outer office and a gruff voice barked a command. Chaos seemed to ensue next door.

"That'll be him now. I'll make sure you're not kept waiting."

The cadet jumped out of his chair and through the door into the main office of the police station.

Things didn't look good, Bob had to admit. Was it illegal in France not to report a suspected break-in? Was there a special law here that the person finding a dead body was presumed guilty until found innocent? He knew that the French justice system had an inquisitorial approach and that the chief investigation officer had significant influence over the choice and prosecution of suspects. Capitaine Fauconnier could hold a lot of power over the English couple if he took a dislike to them early on in the investigation. Their only hope was that he would understand the shock that they had suffered as a result of discovering the body. From the description that the cadet had provided it didn't sound as if that was very likely. Nobody could really be that bad, Bob concluded. The cadet was just laying it on thick to wind him up. Fauconnier was probably a pussy cat really.

"Stand up," the cadet shouted as he burst back into the witness room. "This is Capitaine Fauconnier."

"Monsieur Hunt," the Capitaine said as he entered the room.

Bob's stomach churned over as he recognised the senior gendarme. This was even worse than he imagined.

"Or may I call you Bob?"

It was Thierry.

Chapter Eleven

"*OH, MERDE!*" KATE rarely swore. When she did it was usually in French.

"I think the word that you're looking for is *meurtre*." The couple were washing-up after their supper. They'd returned from their five hour interrogation at the gendarmerie, exhausted and hungry.

"This is no time for jokes, Bob. Can't you see we're in real trouble here? Murder is a bloody serious business and if we can't find an alibi pretty soon then we'll be in a cell for the rest of our lives." Thierry had given them a stern warning that if they tried to leave the Vendée then they could expect a lengthy incarceration for ignoring police instructions.

"Bloody serious. Ha-ha very funny."

Bob flicked the gingham tea-towel at her. Kate span around, fury blazing in her eyes.

"One of these days I swear I'm going to murder you—and that isn't a joke. How the hell did you get us into this mess?"

"Me? Now it's all my fault?"

"It's your lah-di-dah James Hambleton that's got himself killed and his mate Timmy Wells that's done it. And we're the ones that are going to take the rap. Also thanks to you."

"How do you work that out?" Bob narrowly avoided being prodded by a fork.

"Because, my unfortunate husband, the time of death turns out to be within a twelve hour window beautifully framed by your sex-under-the-bed extravaganza."

"They never said anything to me about the time of death," Bob grumbled. "Anyway, I explained to them that I cleaned the attic bedroom after the couple had gone. There was no dead body in it then."

"What you don't seem to appreciate is that they don't believe that there ever was a couple copulating in the cottage."

"But I told them about it at the *cave* and Thierry was there at the time."

"Which they think is rather handy from your point of view."

"You mean—they don't believe me?"

"Of course they don't believe you. You're a murder suspect!"

Kate threw a plate onto the draining board, which Bob rescued as it crashed into a saucepan.

"Careful, darling, that's our best china."

"It's our only china."

"And that, my dear, is how we got into this mess."

"What do you mean?"

"Because we don't have any money. If you recall, Mrs short-term-memory-failure, you said I had to get a job, gave me an advert with strict instructions that I should take up the post. They're not my Hambletons, they're yours."

"That's right—blame me. Mum was right about you . . ."

Kate stopped talking and started scrubbing hard at something in the washing-up bowl.

"What did she say about me?"

There was no answer.

Bob pulled back the hair from around Kate's forehead so that he could see her face more clearly. She was crying.

"Oh Kate!" He pulled her towards him and kissed her cheek, tenderly squeezing her. "It'll all be alright. You'll see."

"But how? What if this guy's done a moonlight flit and disappeared completely."

"The Hambletons must know who he is. You heard what Thierry said—they'll inform Maureen and ask her all about James' movements . . ." Bob froze in realisation.

"What?" Kate sensed his sudden tension. "What?"

The second question was sterner. Bob let go of her.

"It's impossible."

"What is?"

"He can't be dead."

"Who can't be dead? For God's sake Bob what are you going on about? I'm as nervous as a kitten and you're babbling on . . ."

"James Hambleton couldn't be in the cottage when he was murdered—he was in New York."

"Don't be stupid. How can he have been in New York and at the cottage at the same time?"

"Exactly—it's impossible."

"OK, OK. How do you know he was in New York?"

Kate finished rinsing the bowl out and turned it upside-down in the sink.

"Because I was speaking with him on the phone earlier the same day. It must have been around lunchtime. He'd only just arrived at the airport. I could hear all the tannoy announcements and everything." There was still something about that conversation that niggled away at Bob's mind. "You know what this means Kate?"

"That you flew to New York, stabbed him to death and then dragged the body back to France?"

"No! It means that James Hambleton couldn't have been murdered where or when the police say he was. Someone has made a big mistake somewhere. Either way we're off the hook. There's no way either of us could have gone to New York and we've got an alibi for the rest of the time."

"How's that?"

"We didn't have a car!" Bob started hopping around the kitchen. "How could we have got to the cottage to kill James without transport? We're off the hook!"

"Thank heavens for that," Kate sighed, grabbing hold of Bob as he bounced up and down. "I really thought we were going to end up in a French prison for the rest of lives."

"Yes," Bob pulled her close to him. "The great escape. I suppose I'd better let Thierry know."

"Make sure you do. I don't want any more interrogations from him."

"I take it you didn't get on."

"Hmmph. I wouldn't like to say that he hates women but he's the sort of man that gives feminism a good name. And the sorts of things he asked me."

Kate blushed. Bob felt an overwhelming sense of protectiveness towards her and pulled her closer. He could smell Kate's perfume as she snuggled against him; it was a delicate scent of lavender. He breathed in deeply.

"I suppose I'd better see him now."

"But it's late," Kate protested, hugging him closer.

"Precisely. That means I know exactly where to find him."

CHAPTER TWELVE

"Y OU'RE BOTH IN trouble. Serious trouble." Thierry thumped the *cave* table to underline his point. "And don't think that just because we're drinking buddies I'll go easy on you. I won't. Blood is thicker than rosé." He raised a tumbler-full of wine towards Bob and then gulped the contents down in one go.

"Oh, don't mind him," Gautier was fussing around one of the giant metal vats. "His bark is worse than his . . ."

"No it isn't," Poussin chipped in. "He's done me four times for driving down the road with my seatbelt undone. Bloody cheek if you ask me; I was only going to the chateau."

"Anyway, Thierry knows very well that you can't have done it. He's just being hard on you because you're a foreigner."

A long hiss of air escaped from the vat until Gautier hit it with a spanner, at which point it gurgled, spat and subsided into silence. He waved the spanner at the gendarme.

"You should leave them both alone and get on with the job of protecting the commune. There's obviously some sort of deranged lunatic on the loose and you're persecuting a sober, law-abiding, tax-paying English couple."

"Sober English? Two words I've never heard in the same sentence before," Thierry muttered. 'As for law-abiding; we'll have to wait and see. But I'm telling you Bob, it doesn't look good. There's talk of them appointing a Parisian commander to oversee the case."

This observation prompted a round of communal spitting, the traditional greeting that all French countryfolk gave to the name of their capital city. Paris was considered to be hostile foreign territory to all right-thinking patriots.

"If they do—it means I won't be around to protect you."

"With protection like you," Bob offered, "Who needs the police?"

"You'll laugh on the other side of your face when the boys from the capital get hold of you. They make the Inquisition look like a tea party. And you English know all about that."

"I hate to say it, Bob, but he's right." Poussin was swirling the dregs of his wine around in the bottom of his tumbler. "They treat us all like *ploucs*." He threw the contents of the glass into a corner of the *cave*. "I'll have another one Gautier. All this talk of Parisians makes my mouth feel dirty."

"Of course."

"*Ploucs*?" Bob's French vocabulary had made great progress since they retired to St-Sébastien but this was a new word to him.

"Village idiots. That's what the Parisians call us," Thierry said. "A sophisticated dress sense and they think they know it all. I say death to sophistication."

"But why would someone from Paris take charge of the investigation?" Bob was more concerned about his own future than the end of civilised couture. "Surely the body was found here, so it's your case?"

Thierry leaned back in his chair, ignoring the obligatory creak, and addressed the cobweb-infested rafters that stretched high into the gloomy upper reaches of the *cave*.

"For your information the inter-department policing rules state that the jurisdiction of a crime shall be determined in the first instance by the location of the misdemeanour, where this can be established with certainty. Otherwise, where no locus of criminality can be established, the case is divested by the offices of the Justice department and its officers to an appropriate enquiring authority. It all depends in this case who is appointed as investigating judge. I have made a recommendation, of course, but it will ultimately be determined by a higher authority."

This soliloquy had tested Bob's French. He'd failed.

"Which means what exactly?"

"That the Parisian's will get it." Poussin grunted. He fired a volley of expectorant into the wall beside him.

"But there's no doubt where the crime was committed. James was murdered here in the Vendée."

"You confessing?" Thierry looked dangerously serious.

"No, but he was stabbed wasn't he?" The police chief raised an eyebrow at Bob. "Surely no-one's suggesting that the murderer would drag a dead body all the way from Paris to a cottage in the middle of nowhere."

"It doesn't need to be from Paris. As long as there is uncertainty about where the crime was committed then jurisdiction of the local commander is not automatic. It really does come down to the choice of investigation judge. Let's hope for a bit of luck."

"But I'm the principal witness," Bob argued, less than happy at the prospect of being grilled by a group of Parisian gendarmes out to claim an English scalp. "That surely means that I'll be the centre of any enquiry. As will the cottage."

"You witnessed the murder?" Thierry stared at Bob as he asked the question, imbuing each word with a grave sense of foreboding.

"Yes, of course." Bob replied automatically. Then he realised his error. "No, no, I didn't see the murder being committed but I did find the body. That's got to count for something hasn't it?"

"We're talking about a Napoleonic system here." Thierry sighed again, more resigned this time. "What Paris wants Paris gets. This murder will make a nice little puzzle for a middle-ranking inspector somewhere. Just the sort of case that gets you promoted. If you solve it then you're a hero. If you don't then, *ce n'est pas grave*. Promotion assured either way." He turned to face Poussin. "Instead of which, I just get seatbelt outlaws."

He dropped his head into hands, which appeared to be a signal for Gautier to retrieve the tumbler and fill it from the vat.

"And there's nothing I can do about it?" Bob asked.

"Pray?" Gautier suggested, less than helpfully. "Those Parisian judges really know how to pile the pressure on when they want to."

Thierry slowly lifted his head. "There is one thing you could do."

"Ye-es." Bob was wary now. He had to remember that he was a murder suspect. "As long as it doesn't involve confessing to the crime."

"Ha!" Thierry choked out a laugh across the table. "I know you can't have committed the crime. You English haven't got the balls for it. This is a Frenchman's murder—I can smell it."

Bob grunted and backed away from the table. He felt like admitting to having killed Hambleton just to spite Thierry and his Anglophobia.

"Of course, the Parisians might not see it that way. They might take a lot of persuading that you didn't kill him."

"So, what can I do?"

"You could," Thierry leaned into the table conspiratorially, "persuade the Hambletons to come and stay at the cottage."

"Why would that make any difference?"

"Because the one thing that Paris cops hate more than anything else is being out of Paris. If they think they'll have to spend any length of time down here questioning the family they'll be grateful to hand the case over to me in its entirety."

Thierry gazed meaningfully at Bob.

"Of course I couldn't possibly suggest to the Hambletons that they decamp to the Vendée . . ."

"But I could!" Bob understood. He also understood that if Thierry really didn't think that he was capable of killing then his best chance of escaping from a murder charge was to do exactly what the police chief was suggesting. "I'll get onto it first thing in the morning."

"Another?" Gautier pointed towards Bob's glass.

"Don't mind if I do."

Chapter Thirteen

"I'M SORRY THAT you've been inconvenienced, Mr Hunt. It must have been a great shock for you to have come upon the body." Maureen Hambleton's voice sounded tired.

"It certainly wasn't what I expected to find in the cottage."

Bob wondered how much the police had told her about the location of the corpse and the manner of its revelation. He should really stick to safer topics—subjects that might be less likely to incriminate himself in any subsequent questioning.

"I can't tell you how terribly sorry we are for you, Mrs Hambleton, and for your daughters and the family."

"That's kind of you, but really we must all be very stoic about it. After all, we're English and it wouldn't do at all if we were to start blubbering on like these continentals do. That was one thing that James taught me—how to keep a stiff upper lip in the face of adversity."

"Very wise," Bob replied.

The receiver felt heavy in his hand and he was anxious to get on to the main purpose of his call.

"The girls, of course, are both terribly upset and as for poor little Marc . . . I don't know how I'm going to console them."

Bob saw his opportunity.

"Well, I don't know if it helps but the police have finished their forensic work at the cottage and so Kate and I were planning to go up there and clean it out for you tomorrow morning."

He clasped the phone tightly in his hand. This was going to sound callous but in the circumstances he had little choice.

"If you wanted to come down and stay for a few days then it might give you a break from the office while you come to terms with your bereavement. I can stock up with food and provisions for you."

There was an ominous silence at the other end of the line. Bob held his breath.

"I'm afraid that won't be convenient," she replied brusquely. "Apart from the closeness of the event and the various funeral arrangements that will have to be addressed we do have to think about the business. In James' absence Charles will take control and I imagine that he will need me to look after the office for him. It's a kind thought but I don't really think it's appropriate, do you?"

The last words were said in a tone that gave Bob the distinct impression that he was testing the boundaries of the Hambleton upper lip.

"I'm sorry," he said, furious at himself for having raised the subject with so little grace. "I just thought you might want to get away from Paris for a while. My mistake."

"No, it was thoughtful of you, I suppose. It's just that we are a small family concern and can't really afford to allow an event like this—however tragic for us personally—to get in the way of business. Perhaps that sounds a little mercenary to you?"

"No, not at all."

In fact it sounded very mercenary to Bob, but he understood that grief affected different people in different ways. It looked as though he could expect a visit from the Parisian police and, at the least, face more questioning about the circumstances of the discovery of the body. By then they might have caught up with Timmy Wells.

"We'll clean the cottage up tomorrow anyway, Mrs Hambleton, although I don't think that Mr Wells left anything there."

"Mr Wells?"

"Yes. The guest that Mr Hambleton asked me to prepare the cottage for."

"James spoke to you about a Mr Wells?" Maureen's voice had risen by an octave.

"That's right. Timmy Wells."

"And this Mr Wells," Maureen pronounced the name with a careful bitterness. "He was supposed to be staying at the cottage in Mareuil?"

"Yes. I imagine the police are looking for him now. He does seem to be the most likely suspect in the circumstances. Do you know him?"

"I can't say that the name is familiar to me." Maureen spoke slowly before adding "But then we have so many clients that it's possible he may have escaped my memory. My late husband had a wonderful gift for networking. He managed to get on with almost anyone, regardless of their background or their status."

"I always felt relaxed in his presence."

"My point precisely."

There was a brief pause while Bob decided how to interpret this comment. In the end he thought it best to ignore it. The whole call had been futile. Instead of getting the Paris police off his back he'd simply made a new enemy. And, given that Maureen might have a say in how the enquiry proceeded, things couldn't have gone much worse.

"Well, I am sorry to have troubled you at such a difficult time. Kate and I really do wish you our sincere condolences . . ."

Bob's attempt to make amends was interrupted by an unexpected question.

"Mr Hunt, do you know whether this Mr Wells actually arrived at the cottage?"

"Yes. That is to say, he must have done."

"Why?"

"Because we found a whole load of empty wine and vodka bottles in the kitchen. It was odd really." Bob was beginning to think that none of the situation made any sense. "There was no sign that the bed had been slept in."

"This is all very strange. I have never known my late husband to have made arrangements for people to stay at the cottage. Had he ever approached you like this before?"

Bob thought about it.

"No. I can't say that he has."

"It seems highly improbable to me. As you know I keep a diary for the sole purpose of recording visits to the cottage. There have been no bookings since before Christmas, when Rose went up there for a weekend. I very much doubt whether James would have made such an arrangement with you directly. I feel certain that he would have asked me to do it for him."

"Well, I don't know what to say." Bob sat forward in his chair in the lounge. What he had expected to be a difficult phone conversation was now turning into an impossible one. "He phoned me from the airport to let me know."

"Airport?"

"Yes, at New York."

"What are you blathering about? That can't possibly be true."

"Why not?"

"For the following very simple reason, Mr Hunt; James wasn't due to go to New York until today. As it is I've had to reorganise the schedule and Charles will have to go out there later in the month which is most inconvenient as it may mean we lose some of the potential contracts we were chasing."

"No, no," Bob interjected. "He phoned me from the airport on the Wednesday."

"On Wednesday James set off to visit a couple of our domestic clients in France." Maureen spoke slowly, as if humouring a child. "Rouen on Wednesday, Poitiers on Thursday, Nice on Friday and then back to Paris for the flight on Saturday."

"I'm very sorry Mrs Hambleton, but none of this makes any sense. I definitely spoke to him on Wednesday and he told me to prepare the cottage for Timmy Wells, who was going to stay at the cottage."

"I don't want to call you a liar, Mr Hunt, it's not in my nature, but you are a long way short of the truth. My husband was not in New York on Wednesday. He even phoned me from Rouen to confirm that he'd secured a deal there. It goes without saying that if you are wrong about New York then you could equally be in error about Mr Wells."

"But I am telling the truth Mrs Hambleton, I promise you. There must be some sensible explanation for all this. I know the investigating officer down here—I'll check it all out with him."

"Is that a—hold the line a moment, whilst I refer to my notes . . ." There was a brief pause and Bob could hear paper being rustled at the other end of the connection. "An Inspecteur Thierry Fauconnier?"

"That's right. He's the local police chief here. I imagine he'll want to speak to you at some stage."

"Maybe. I had some local constable visit me immediately after you'd discovered the body. They said someone from the city police would be in touch with me once jurisdiction was determined. I haven't heard a thing from them since then."

"I think they're still waiting to see who's allocated the case. Of course, if you were to want to visit the cottage then that would make things . . ."

Bob immediately regretted trying to get a second bite of the cherry.

"As I said, Mr Hunt, I've no intention of disrupting the business. In fact, if you don't mind, I've got rather pressing matters to attend to as it is."

"I'm really very sorry, Mrs Hambleton. I can't understand how all of this can have happened."

"I'm not certain that I believe any of it did happen. Goodbye."

"Again, our condolences to your . . ."

Maureen had already replaced the receiver and the line was dead.

"That went well." Bob went into the kitchen where Kate was preparing their lunch.

"What's the matter, darling? You look as if you've seen a ghost." Her eyes looked tearful; Bob put it down to the onions.

"It doesn't make any sense. According to Maureen James hadn't gone to New York."

"Oh, she's probably just confused. You have to remember that she's been through a sudden bereavement—it messes about with peoples' heads you know. I've seen it loads of times." Kate took Bob's hands and squeezed them. "Goodness, you're frozen. What's the matter, it's not that cold?"

"I'm worried, Kate." Bob could see from her reaction that he had scared her. "The more I find out about this murder, the less comfortable I become. If I didn't know any better I'd say I was being stitched up."

Kate laughed; an instant release of tension.

"Is that all? Don't be so silly. We both know you couldn't have done it. There's no evidence against you—other than you being in the wrong place at the wrong time—and nobody could convict you on that."

Thump!

It was the front door.

"Who on earth can that be?" Kate spread her hair through her fingers and straightened her collar. "Anyone who knows us comes round to the back."

Thump!

"I'll get it," Bob called. "It's nearly election time—probably just some local party worker who doesn't realise we haven't got a vote."

He opened the front door to find Thierry stood there, mobile phone in hand.

"Ah, Bob." The gendarme quickly scanned the street and then stared Bob directly in the eyes. "Good news and bad news I'm afraid."

"You mean the Parisians have taken the case after all?"

"No. I'll definitely get the case now. That's the good news."

"And the bad news?"

Thierry looked away.

"We've found the murder weapon."

The police chief took a deep breath.

"It's got your fingerprints all over it."

Chapter Fourteen

"OF COURSE THEY'VE got my bloody fingerprints all over them. They're my bloody secateurs."

Bob was angry—and scared. Thierry had insisted on dragging him back to the gendarmerie to answer more questions. The police chief had suggested politely, but firmly, that non-compliance might result in arrest. Bob had agreed, but without good grace. Thierry didn't seem to care about grace.

"And you say that the instrument of death has been lost for some time?"

"Instrument of death! It's a pair of secateurs for God's sake."

"It is also a murder weapon. Used to kill a man that you knew in a place to which you held a key at a time for which you have no clear alibi that doesn't involved your wife."

"I agree, Thierry, it doesn't look good, does it?"

"I should add, Mr Hunt," the police chief emphasised the formality of his address. "That your wife's fingerprints also appear on the weapon."

"Of course they do. She does most of the gardening. She's been nagging at me to get a new pair for ages. Everyone in the neighbourhood has borrowed them at some time. Mainly for wire-cutting, judging by the state they come back in."

"When exactly did they disappear?"

"It must have been over the winter some time. I must admit I didn't think much of it. At the end of the autumn we always just throw the gardening stuff into that big green plastic box that sits in the alleyway between our place and Monsieur Gautier's."

"What sort of stuff?"

"Oh, just gardening equipment. Gloves, trowels, rose spray . . . You know the sort of thing."

"I don't know that sort of thing," Thierry sniffed. "I am a stranger to my garden."

"And every year the secateurs went in there. Until the spring when Kate starts messing around with all the plants again."

"And it would go without saying that all these dangerous items—chemicals, sharp implements and so on—were kept safely under lock and key?"

"Yes." Bob paused. Now probably wasn't a good time for half-truths. "Well sort of." He spread his hands across the police chief's wooden desk. "Under lock yes, but not under key."

"What does that mean?"

"It means that the box was fitted with a padlock but we never actually clicked it into the closed position."

"So it was never actually locked?"

"Not as such, no." Bob felt his face flush. He could see where this was going; straight to a cell if he wasn't careful. "It always seemed like a lot of wasted time, fetching the key just to get to a pair of gardening gloves."

"So anyone could gain access to the box and its contents?"

"I suppose so. But who on earth would want to steal a pair of secateurs?"

"A murderer." Thierry said the words without looking up from his notes. "Who knew what was in the box?"

"Well, anyone who'd seen Kate gardening. So that covers most of the locals; Gautier, Poussin, Madame LaGrange with the white dog . . ."

"Oh, her! That yappy rodent is a damn nuisance. It won't shut up no matter how many stones you throw at it." Thierry looked up and poked his pen at Bob. "I once hit it right on the head. The wretched thing stopped barking and started whining instead. Kept me awake all night."

"You're sure that wasn't your conscience?"

"My conscience is clear, Mr Hunt. It's yours that worries me."

Thierry pulled open one of the drawers in the desk and fished a plastic bag out with his pen. He dropped it down in front of Bob.

"Now then. You're sure that these secateurs are the ones that belong to you?"

"They appear to be the same as ours." Bob took another look and judged that a caveat was required. "Except for all the congealed blood around the cutters and the handle. I think I'd have remembered that."

Thierry gave him a sharp glance. "Blood which we've confirmed belonged to the late James Hambleton. Together with three sets of fingerprints."

"Three?" Bob thought that this sounded promising.

"Yes. Yours, Mrs Hunt's and Madame Poussin's."

"Oh."

Bob slumped back into the stiff plastic bucket seat that seemed to be designed to extract maximum discomfort from the interviewee. Even he couldn't sensibly argue that an eighty-year-old woman had stabbed to death the great bull that had been James Hambleton.

"Aren't you intrigued to know where we found them?" Thierry stroked his greying moustache thoughtfully. "Perhaps you already know?"

"Knowing my luck you found them in the Clio."

"No, not there. Although that does remind me. We will want to search through your car." Thierry gave a small chuckle. "And naturally, we will need to inspect the infamous green box to see what other lethal weapons are in your possession. You'll have no objections to us having a good look round? I'd hate to have to obtain a search warrant. So much paperwork." He spread his arms wide as an indication of the extent of the bureaucracy he had to contend with.

"At least you don't have to worry about the Parisians getting the case," Bob growled.

"Oh, yes. I'm pleased to say that I was able to prevail on that front." Thierry smirked at Bob. "Finding the secateurs ensured that the case would be dealt with locally. The investigating judge has been appointed now. He's a local man; Gaston du Pré."

"Should I be concerned?"

"Very. He's my cousin," Thierry replied calmly. "And on his behalf I will have to ask you some searching questions."

"Be my guest. You might even find my sanity."

"What do you mean?"

"I don't know. Nothing seems to make sense any more. First, there's a mysterious couple in the cottage that I know I saw but no-one seems to be able to trace."

"We've had no corroboration on that." The police chief probed his teeth with the cap of his pen.

"And then there's the phone call from New York made by a man who was actually in Rouen about a guest who may or may not have arrived at the cottage."

Thierry took the pen out of his mouth and waved it at Bob. "We've checked with our colleagues in Paris." He spat into the waste paper basket. "Mrs Hambleton has confirmed that the company has never had a client called Wells."

"All of which makes me wonder whether I just imagined the whole lot," Bob said wistfully.

There was a gentle tap on the wooden door. The young cadet entered. He cast a suspicious glance at Bob before going up to Thierry.

"Can I have a quiet word, capitaine?"

"Is it important?" Thierry threw down his pen. "I'm dealing with a murder here."

"Yes, sir. It's relevant to the case." He looked towards Bob, jerking his index finger at him. "It's about the suspect." He flourished a handful of papers by way of evidence.

"Oh, very well." Thierry hauled himself out of his chair which, Bob noted with envy, was amply upholstered and followed the cadet.

Bob grabbed a notepad and Thierry's half-chewed pencil from the desk and scribbled a new opening sentence for his conference paper.

'King Lear is one of Shakespeare's most complex plays but its central theme is the concept of madness.'

Through the glazed part of the door Bob could see that an animated conversation was taking place. He couldn't hear much except the occasional *"merde"* from Thierry. The cadet seemed to be apologising for something and was backing away from his senior officer down the corridor. Eventually Thierry snatched the papers out of the cadet's hands and marched into the interview room, almost bringing the door down as he slammed it shut.

"Fucking Parisians." He threw the papers onto the table and launched himself back into his plush upholstery. "I have some news for you."

"Good news I hope?"

"Depends on your point of view, I suppose." Thierry chewed on a fingernail before continuing. "It concerns the time of death."

"I thought that you said that it couldn't be determined precisely because of the condition of the body when we found it."

"That was correct." The police chief slapped one of the papers in front of him. It was a computer printout. There was a stain, ominously like blood, on one of the corners. Thierry scraped a piece off and sniffed at it. "Sauce *Provençal*," he declared and licked at it, nodding vigorously. "I'd almost forgotten how hungry I was."

"Time of death?" Bob said hopefully.

"Yes. The point is that the forensic team have done some more work on the blood samples taken from the crime scene. These, together with the autopsy and the photos that we took at the time of the discovery, show that James Hambleton was stabbed at somewhere between twenty-three hundred hours on the Wednesday night and oh-one hundred hours on Thursday morning."

"That was only a couple of hours after I dropped the food and wine off at the cottage."

"But it's a couple of hours that makes all the difference between you being at the scene of the crime and having a perfect alibi."

"I see," said Bob, his brain finally doing some work. "It means that I can't have been at the cottage when James was murdered."

"Not unless you went out again after you'd been with us at the *cave*."

"But I didn't have a car then."

"I've seen your Clio. Strictly speaking you don't have a car now." Thierry pointed at Bob, flicking dried sauce into the air as he did. "That thing's a death-trap. One day I'm going to issue you with a formal warning about it."

"So I'm officially in the clear—at last."

Bob felt the relief sweep through him. He was suddenly very tired.

"Yes. Until I do you for the dangerous use of a mobile death-trap."

"I can go home?"

Thierry appraised Bob, rubbing his pen through his moustache.

"Against my better judgement. And you still can't leave the Vendée until I say so. It all stinks to me."

"Wait till I tell Kate, she'll be thrilled."

"They're damned clever these forensic people." Thierry read from another printout. "Apparently James Hambleton didn't die from his stabbing immediately. He struggled around in the bedroom, too weak to do very much except knock a few things over, for a couple of hours. Typical English—bumbling around in the dark."

"So what killed him then?"

"Loss of blood in the end. Not that there could have been much of that. He'd drunk the equivalent of three bottles of vodka according to the samples."

Bob looked at Thierry, trying to work out what this really meant.

"It's roughly equivalent to eight hours in Gautier's *cave*," the police chief clarified.

Both men sighed in unison.

"It's amazing," Bob said. "They can tell all that from a few samples of blood."

"And the four empty vodka bottles in the bedroom. It looks as though there was quite a party going on."

"We found some bottles in the kitchen as well . . ."

"Yes. Your wretched fingerprints are all over them."

"Oh, sorry." Bob examined his hands carefully. "It's just that James told me that this Timmy Wells was quite a drinker, so I thought I'd stock up for him."

"Stop!" Thierry thumped the table with his fist. "According to Maureen Hambleton there is no Timmy Wells."

"Have you tried to find him?"

Thierry rubbed his hands through his greasy hair.

"Do you know how many Wells there are in France?"

"A few hundred perhaps," Bob guessed.

"Add to which there must be how many in England?"

"I've no idea."

"Nor do I," the gendarme said flatly. "And I've no desire to find out. Do you really think that we've got the time and energy to contact every person that might be called Timmy Wells to check whether they have a cast-iron alibi, simply on the grounds that you claim to have had a phone call from a man who couldn't possibly be where you say he was?"

"But I know I spoke to James. I could hear the airport tannoy announcements in the background."

"Paris have checked the manifest of every flight between Paris and New York in a forty-eight hour period around when you claim to have spoken to him. *Rien!*"

"Perhaps he used an alias," Bob could feel metaphorical straws slip between his fingers.

"Like Timmy Wells?"

"Yes. Why not?"

"No!" The gendarme swept the papers from the table into Bob's face. "No, no, no! It's all too farcical, too improbable, too impossible. The only person who has anything to gain from this story is you—and no-one else can corroborate a single word of it."

"But I know what I heard."

Thierry leant forward and took hold of Bob's shirt collar.

"Listen to me Bob. If it weren't for the new forensic evidence and for the fact that I saw you in the *cave* with my own eyes I would have arrested you by now on a *garde á vue* charge. I suggest you go home and think yourself very lucky. And forget about New York and Timmy Wells and all this other nonsense. Otherwise I'll make up a charge sheet for wasting gendarmerie time. *Comprenez?*"

"*Oui*," Bob said slowly. "And you'll definitely be in charge of the case?"

"Yes, although it would still help if the Hambleton's came down here. It would make questioning them so much easier. Otherwise I'll have to send one of my gormless cadets up to Paris to do it. Are you sure Madame Hambleton can't be persuaded to come down to the Vendée?"

"I'm afraid not." Bob shook his head. "I don't think I'm on her Christmas card list at present."

Thierry looked at him blankly and Bob remembered that it was more normal to exchange cards for the new year than *noël*.

"And you're definitely letting me go? Even though you don't believe me."

"Yes. Go on, before I change my mind." Thierry removed his hand from his ear to gesture towards the door.

"By the way," Bob added, as he reached the threshold.

"You still here?"

"Where did you find those secateurs?"

"Oh those." Thierry had begun to probe the inside of an ear with his little finger. "They were in a drawer in the kitchen of the cottage, wrapped up in a neat little package." He carefully wiped his finger on the bottom of his shirt before continuing. "Addressed to New York."

CHAPTER FIFTEEN

"IT'S SPRING AGAIN," Kate announced joyously.

"I'll sing again," Bob rejoindered, semi-musically.

They were holding hands, looking out of the kitchen doorway at their courtyard garden.

"It was a meteorological observation not an excuse to upset the neighbours."

"But we make such beautiful music together. You're always sharp and I'm always flat. Together it's perfect harmony."

"Either way; spring is definitely here. The sun is shining; the sky is a beautiful Vendée *bleu* and all's well with the world." She beamed at Bob, who couldn't help thinking that it was the first time he'd seen her smile for ages.

"And I'm in the clear," he added for good measure.

"Well almost." She dropped his hand.

"I've got the best alibi in the book; the detective was with me!"

"You and that murder! I wish you'd shut up about it."

Kate turned away from him and started loading the breakfast dishes into the kitchen sink. It had been a week since Bob's interview at the gendarmerie, and he'd seen and heard nothing about it since then. Bob suspected that Thierry was probably keeping the whole thing under wraps for the time being.

"I still can't help thinking it was all very odd . . ."

"I'm beginning to think it could turn into a serial killing and I know who's going to be the next victim. I don't want to be reminded constantly that my husband is a failed murder suspect."

"Doesn't it give me an air of *je ne sais quoi?*"

"No. It just makes me wonder when I'm going to get a replacement set of secateurs."

Kate took the cloth off the kitchen table and shook it out the door. This was a sure sign to Bob that, at least in her mind, the conversation was closed. She replaced the table cloth and stood in the doorway between the lounge and the kitchen, apparently looking for things to do.

"I tell you what, instead of sleuthing around, why don't you make yourself useful and change the temperature control system?"

"Oh, must I?" Bob whined. "There might be another cold spell and you'd regret it."

"There won't be another cold spell. This is the Vendée not Cinderford."

"But it means I've got to go to Poussin's outhouse and lug all the stuff around."

The biannual ritual of, in spring, replacing all the electric heaters with tall free-standing fans and, in autumn, reversing the process was one that Bob hated. He begrudged the amount of energy involved in carrying all the equipment up and down the road, never mind the curious looks he got from the bemused locals. On top of which was the distress of having to see all their old possessions that had been orphaned at the Poussins due to lack of space, with the accompanying recollections of the lifestyle sacrifices that they had made. Most devastating, though, was that the process meant having to tread where no man gladly went—through Madame Poussin's voluminous laundry area, where the garments of four generations met their ablutionary match. It really didn't bear thinking about.

"It's either that or do something about those gates." Kate turned her back on him.

"You and those gates." Any sense of the spring sunshine that might have crept into Bob's life was immediately eclipsed. "Do you think that if you go on about them for long enough that we'll suddenly become rich enough to buy some new ones?"

Kate span round to face Bob and stared at him.

"Don't be so crass. I know damn well that we can't afford new ones. But I thought that you might just care about me enough to want to fix up the old gate so that we're not the complete laughing stock of the village."

"We are not the laughing stock of the village," Bob retorted and then lowered his voice. "Everyone knows that's Madame Poussin."

"Will you stop trying to turn everything into a joke? We're in real trouble financially. My savings have virtually gone and the tax foncière is due next month. Your one contribution to the household income has now dried up and I'm at my wits end to know how to rustle up enough money to pay the water bill. All I get you from you is silly jokes and murder charges."

She approached Bob with her hands stretched towards him imploringly. He thought she might be about to strangle him and took an involuntary step backwards.

"Look! You can't even bear to be near me any more. I get no tenderness or affection from you, just surly one-liners. You spend half your life asleep and the other half trying to guzzle down as much alcohol as your liver can assimilate. I can't remember the last time we had . . ."

"Well, what do you want?" Bob barked. He was starting to feel guilty and that always made him more aggressive.

"I want to be looked after. I want to be cared for. I want to be loved." She started to cry.

Bob went to her and tried to wrap his arms around her waist, but she shrugged him off.

"I'm sorry, Kate, but I've been scared about the murder and what it might mean for us. I've probably lost my sense of perspective."

"Well I've lost my patience with you." She took a handful of kitchen roll and wiped her face. She breathed deeply a couple of times. "I've had enough of all of this. I'm fed up of France. I'm fed up of being a former career girl. Above all, I'm fed up of you!"

Kate spoke in a measured, flat tone which suggested to Bob that she meant it.

"I'm giving you one last chance to prove that we can make a go of it out here in the Vendée, and that you can treat me the way that I deserve. No more broken gates, no more boozy fumblings, no more cheap perfumes." She despatched the kitchen towel into the metal dustbin and slammed the lid down with a clang. "Do I make myself clear?"

"Perfectly, darling," Bob said penitently. "I'm sorry I haven't been more attentive. I will try to be a better husband, but it's just not that easy . . ." Bob trailed off.

He knew that he loved Kate. He had done ever since they first met at the Jazz Festival in Cheltenham. Her, bright and bubbly; him, full of wit and repartée. Or at least that's how he remembered it, but the three pints of lager and a whisky chaser might have clouded his memory. Ever since then he'd tried to live up to her image of the perfect husband and squirreled away all his savings so that they could realise her dream of a retirement to France. Now they were here and she was more dis-satisfied than she had been in Britain. Bob wondered if he could ever give Kate what she really wanted. He wondered if she would recognise it when it came. What more could he say or do?

He was saved from having to say or do anything. The phone rang.

"*Allo.*"

"Is that Mr Hunt?" Bob recognised the professional telephone manner of Maureen Hambleton.

"Yes, Mrs Hambleton. What can I do for you?"

Bob exchanged a glance with Kate, who shook her head sadly and stepped out into the garden.

"Look here, Mr Hunt," Maureen's manner was as efficient as ever. "I think we may have started off on the wrong foot last week and I fear that I may have been rather harsh towards you."

"It was entirely understandable in the circumstances, Mrs Hambleton."

"Do call me Maureen, it reminds me less of James."

"Of course."

"I've taken your advice, Mr Hunt, and we've decamped to the Vendée. We arrived at the cottage yesterday evening."

"If I'd known I would have gone in and cleaned and . . ."

"Don't worry about all that." She lowered her voice. Bob could hardly hear her. "There is, however, one service that you might do for me."

"Yes?" Bob was too taken aback by her change in attitude to demur.

"I would be grateful if you could meet me as soon as possible. Just the two of us, you understand. Is that at all possible?"

Bob was about to refer to a non-existent calendar of engagements when he thought better of it. It was time to be straight with everyone—including himself. And, in any case, his interest was piqued. Why would she want to meet him? He looked at his watch.

"Yes, shall we say in half an hour?"

"That would be suitable," Maureen's voice had descended to almost a whisper.

"I'll come to the cottage."

"No, no! We'll meet somewhere a little more discreet. There is a café just outside of Le Tablier, overlooking the River Yon. Do you know of it?"

"La Roche Grise? Do I need to bring anything?"

"*Non.*" Maureen's voice had risen to its normal volume and, for reasons unclear to Bob, crossed the language barrier. "*Merci, Docteur. Á demain.*" She hung up.

The route to La Roche Grise was as familiar to Bob as the labels of the vineyards that surrounded it; Moutand, Roussell, Harricaux . . . In fact he knew the way so well that he could drive it forwards, backwards, sober and drunk—and had tried all four at various times. He left the Clio at the car park for walkers that faced the café and noted the only other vehicle was a Rover 75. Maureen had obviously got there first.

"Mr Hunt," she practically jumped out of the bushes on him. "Thank you for coming. Perhaps you'd like a walk?"

It struck Bob as more of an instruction than an invitation. The aroma of freshly-brewed Arabica beans drifted from the open air café.

"That would be nice," he replied simply, thinking instead how much better an espresso would suit his mood this morning. He was still reflecting on his row with Kate.

"Right, off we go then." She launched herself down the steep pathway that led between the wild hedgerows at the top of the valley and the craggy route of the river below.

La Roche Grise was appropriately, if unimaginatively, named. The parasols around the tables formed a straggly line of colour around a huge grey outcrop of stone. The rock itself, granite, actually thrust deep under the landscape and was exposed along the course of the river Yon for about three kilometres. The scenery of the valley was completely different to any found elsewhere in the area. The river—a gentle, meandering, unobjectionable trickle along the remainder of its length—suddenly became a raging torrential force as it struggled across rocky dams and over cascades that would force white foam into the air on a breezy day. It was a dramatic place, Bob had always felt. A perfect place for intrigue, excitement and danger. Kate loved walking by the river, saying that it got the adrenalin pumping through her veins. Bob preferred to stay in the café at the top—enjoying the drama as a spectator, with a drink in his hand.

When Maureen reached the pathway that ran beside the river she stopped to let Bob catch up with her. Despite her sixty-plus years she wasn't out of breath at all, which only increased Bob's feelings of inferiority. It really was time that he traded in his six-litre stomach for a smaller model.

"How do you like living in the Vendée?" she asked.

"It's fine." Bob could feel his heart pounding away. He took a couple of deep breaths to steady himself.

"You must have been quite young for retirement?" Maureen had pale grey eyes. They didn't miss much, Bob imagined.

"I suppose so, but Kate has always wanted to come out here to live. Her dream, if you like."

"Yes, but dreams are cheap, aren't they? Reality is a little more expensive, I imagine?"

"Perhaps." Bob was non-committal. He couldn't see where all this was leading.

"To be fair, money was never a problem where James was concerned. He always had an eye for a deal. He'd have been well-off even if he hadn't inherited the business." She stopped and turned to face Bob. She stared at him. "I suppose that's why I've never really understood how people got into trouble financially."

Bob flushed, at first with embarrassment but then with anger. Who did this woman think she was?

"You don't need to worry," she said, calmly picking up a stone from beside the path. "I'm here to help, not gloat."

"How can you help me?" Bob pouted at her. He didn't need her charity.

"Well, for one thing, I can confirm that we'll be keeping the place in the Vendée so your little job with us will be secure."

"But I assumed that you'd sell the cottage. After all it's where he . . ."

"I know. But I'm not a sentimental woman, Mr Hunt. Jasmine and Marc love it out here. They're staying with me now—to make sure I don't throw myself off the cliffs in sorrow, I suspect. Of course that won't happen."

She threw the stone across the river and watched as it bounced and dived into the rapids beyond. Spray skimmed the water where the stone flicked the river, sending starbursts of reflected spring sunshine across the falls. This is a strong woman, Bob thought, financially, emotionally and physically. He wondered whether she could have murdered her own husband. On balance he suspected that she might have been capable of it if she had felt that it was really necessary.

"And so to business." Maureen had started off along the path again. "We currently pay you a monthly retainer of . . . ?"

"About three hundred euros. Something like that." Bob knew it was exactly three hundred euros, but he didn't want to add more fuel to her suspicions about their poverty.

"I really think we ought to double it, Bob. I may call you Bob now—if we're going to trust each other." Her eyes were steely now—calculating.

"That's very kind of you, but what do you want me . . . ?"

"Don't ask that. It's such a sordid question. I don't want you to do anything. I simply want to tell you a rather curious story and see if you can find a happy ending for it."

"I always like a happy ending."

"Good. That's settled then." Maureen stopped and shook Bob's hand. "Thank you for indulging an old widow." She stooped down to indicate a small plant that was growing beside the path. "Mint." She looked back up at Bob. "I have a herb garden you know. This stuff is wiry and stubborn. Just like me!"

"But what about the story?" Bob was mystified. Suddenly he was richer and he couldn't understand why.

"I thought I'd tell you about it all over a cup of tea." She pointed at the parabola of parasols above them.

"If it's all the same to you, Maureen," Bob answered. "I think I could do with a beer."

The café was in its usual state of amiable confusion. Beer was easy; Bob had a glass and a bottle in front of him in seconds. Tea was not.

"We don't have any tea," the young waitress insisted.

Bob hadn't seen her before. She must be new.

"It's on your menu." Maureen poked at the ragged piece of card. Accumulated spots and stains bore witness to its long and productive service.

"That's an old menu." The waitress snatched it out of Maureen's hands. "Wouldn't you prefer to drink coffee instead?"

"*Non, merci*," Maureen insisted. "Tea is all I require."

"And I've already explained that we don't have any." The girl was getting petulant, shaking her brunette bob in vigorous refutation. Never argue with a French waitress was one of Bob's maxims; they invariably have the last laugh.

"It's underneath the sink," he told the girl. "In the tin marked '*sucre*'." He'd had this problem before.

The waitress waved her arm at him in a gesture that indicated that he should have said all this before wasting her valuable time, and stomped off to the kitchen to see if it were true. She returned almost immediately. Apparently it was perfectly accurate to say that there was tea in the kitchen but since she didn't know how to prepare it they couldn't have any. Maureen started to get agitated. The waitress informed them that she'd be left on her own this morning—her second day on the job—because Monday was always quiet and so there weren't supposed to be any problems, and now this English couple had arrived and demanded to drink tea and . . .

She burst into tears.

"Don't worry," Bob said. "I know my way around the kitchen here. I'll make it and you can watch."

And so it was that ten minutes later—and after several patient explanations to the disbelieving waitress as to why milk really was essential for a proper cup of tea—Maureen finally got round to telling Bob her little story.

"It was your insistence that James spun you a story about Timmy Wells that got me worried."

"You didn't sound worried."

"No. But I didn't know that I could trust you then. Did I, Bob?" She emphasised his name conspiratorially. "After all, it's not every day you double someone's salary."

"I suppose not," Bob mumbled. He got the distinct impression that he had been put back in his place again. "Does that mean you really do know someone called Timmy Wells?"

"I have already informed the police that we do not have a client with that name," she snorted.

"Then . . . ?"

"Mr Hunt I wish you to understand that James and I were not exactly a match made in heaven. He certainly wasn't an angel. We met each other through the business. I imagine that from the outside it probably just looked like one of those office romances destined to end up in tears for the junior partner." Maureen sipped her tea thoughtfully, as if weighing up how much to tell him. "The difference between me and other junior partners was that I'm a bit sharper than the average receptionist and so I made sure that James' parents knew exactly what was going on between us. It was one of the advantages of it being a family business, and it meant that my dear late husband couldn't avoid his fate. With me!"

"Didn't he love you then?"

"In his way, yes. But I don't think he ever quite forgave me for trapping him when he was in his prime. There were so many other girls who could have benefited from his attentions. On reflection, there were probably many more who did." She smiled as she watched Bob's surprise. "I always knew that he had a roving eye and that the rest of his body normally followed. He didn't mean any harm. He just appreciated beautiful women." She placed her empty cup on the saucer in front of her. "Take that waitress, for example." They turned to look at the young girl, who was adjusting her *maquillage* in the mirror above the kitchen sink. "By now he'd have been slobbering all over her like a great big St Bernard dog." She shivered.

Bob recalled his meeting with James in Paris. He'd described women as one of life's little pleasures.

"As the business grew so did James' opportunities to widen his *cirque d'amour*." Maureen continued. She didn't sound bitter, Bob thought, just tired. "He travelled away more, stayed in hotels more, changed his appearance more."

"Didn't you challenge him about it? I can just imagine what Kate would say to me if she suspected for a second that I was seeing another woman."

"No. The irony was that I was just as trapped by the morality of the family business as he had been. If I had created a fuss it would have rippled through the Hambletons and destroyed the firm. I was hoist by my own petard. And it served me right."

"But what's all this got to do with me?" Bob was beginning to warm to Maureen as he realised how much of her life must have been a charade. Perhaps that explained her aloofness. Turning a blind eye for so long must breed dispassion in the end.

"I think it is time that I knew." Maureen said firmly. "Now that he's dead. I want to know the whole sordid story. How many women he saw, where he went with them and what they meant to him. I want closure, if you understand me. It probably sounds very macabre to you, but I don't want him to take his secrets to the grave with him. I want to part with James on equal terms."

"I don't understand how I can help?"

"You can make some enquiries on my behalf, Bob. Timmy Wells was probably just a decoy. A *nom de plume* for some girl or other that he planned to entertain in the cottage."

"Oh! I see, I think." Bob wasn't very sure he did see. Why would James risk using a family cottage where he might be discovered, rather than an anonymous hotel somewhere well away from the Hambleton tribe?

"What I'd like you to find out is exactly who his latest conquest was."

"Ah," Bob thought he finally understood. "You think that I know who he was seeing and that I'll tell you if you pay me enough?"

"Something along those lines." The grey eyes scanned his face inquisitively as if searching out any sign of vulnerability. "You see in the last few months before his death he'd taken to calling out in his sleep. One name kept repeating itself. Betty, Betty . . . The more he called it the more it kept me awake. Betty, Betty . . . It bore into the very core of me every night. Into my psyche, into my soul even. I want to find this Betty and repay the compliment." Maureen continued to scan Bob's expression. "Do you think that very harsh of me?"

"I try not to judge," Bob said. "But it does seem like rather a strange way to spend your time and money."

"Money's not an issue. James left me enough—if not everything. I just want to put her through as many sleepless nights as I have had to endure. It's revenge—pure and simple. Not attractive I know, but one of the few pleasures that money can actually buy these days."

"Well, I'm sorry to disappoint you but I really don't know who this Betty could be."

"So he didn't leave any clues when he made the arrangements?"

"No. He phoned me from New York to say that Timmy Wells was coming to stay at the cottage for a couple of weeks and that I wasn't to disturb him."

"Only we both know that he wasn't in New York, don't we?" Her tone was mocking, reminding Bob of yet another fact that he'd got wrong.

"I'm sorry but I really can't tell you anything else." Bob stood up at the table and started to walk past Maureen. "You seem to know at least as much as I do."

Maureen grabbed at his arm. Her grip was strong, Bob noticed. Certainly strong enough to stab a philandering husband with a pair of secateurs.

"Sit down, now!"

Perhaps it was the sharpness of the command or simply that Bob was used to doing as he was told, but he sat back in his seat immediately.

"You listen to me, Mr Hunt, and pay careful attention. I intend to find this woman, whoever she may be, and make an example of her. I've spent my life having to endure the nudging and winking of those who thought I was a fool that couldn't see beyond the end of her well-feathered nest. Now it's time for me to have my bit of fun, Mr Hunt, and you're the man who's going to help me."

"But how?" Bob recalled something that James had said which might be useful. "He did say that Timmy Wells had exotic tastes. I don't know if that helps?"

"Forget about Timmy Wells, forget about New York. They were both inventions so that James could get into bed with his Betty. I want you to focus on finding her."

The mention of a bed reminded Bob of the girl with exquisite legs. Was she Betty? Surely not. Certainly the man with her was too athletic to have been James. On balance he thought it best not to mention this to Maureen at this stage. He'd been wrong about so much already.

"What about this Captain Fauconnier?"

"Thierry?" Bob had forgotten all about the police chief.

"He's in charge of the case isn't he? You told me that you knew him. You can find out what he discovers about the woman that James had at the cottage and then report back to me."

"What if he doesn't find out who she is?" Bob was feeling a bit queasy about using Thierry as a source of information. He didn't feel that he'd made the best of impressions on the police chief during their interviews.

"He will." Maureen was as sure as she was determined. "A gendarme always gets his woman."

CHAPTER SIXTEEN

THE *CAVE* WAS quiet. It had been another sunny day in early March for the Vendée and Bob had spent most of the afternoon culling the cowslips and dandelions that were growing through the gravel in the courtyard garden.

"Vines are full of bugs this year." Poussin broke the silence. It was the Vendée equivalent of small-talk. It required, and received, no response.

"Have you all received your invitations?" Gautier asked after an interval that was punctuated only by a gentle burbling sound that seemed to be emitted by one of his smaller, experimental vats.

"For what?" There was a momentary buzz of interest around the *cave.*

"Dominic's wedding of course." The buzz dissipated immediately. There was a collective groan.

"That's all I've heard about for weeks," Poussin grumbled. "Madame wants a new dress for it. I asked her what was wrong with the one she wore for our Francis' wedding—after all it was only five years ago."

"This girl, what's-her-name . . ." Poussin began.

"Sandrine," Gautier prompted. "She's a travel agent. I think they make a wonderful couple. Don't you, Pierre?"

Poussin shrugged his shoulders.

"My reply is in the post," Thierry chipped in. "It's a no. And I don't have an excuse—I just can't stand weddings."

There was little that could be added to the subject beyond this final judgement and the conversation died again.

Bob started to think about the challenge that Maureen had set for him. How could he engage Thierry in a discussion about the murder without arousing the detective's suspicions? It would require tact and cunning. Thierry presently seemed to be deeply intrigued by something that had lodged itself between his shirt and his armpit. Gently does it, thought Bob, try an oblique reference, something casual.

"How's your murder going, Thierry?" he blurted.

"*Rien,*" he replied, without looking up and farted as if to underline the point.

"I've heard that the Hambletons have returned to the cottage. Is that right?"

Bob could have kissed Gautier as he asked the question. Now it wouldn't look as if he was the one probing the police chief.

"It's never right, is it?" Poussin complained. "For a widow to return to the place where her husband was murdered. *C'est bizarre!*"

A pause. Bob feared his chance was slipping away.

"No. She wants to keep it going for the children." He caught Thierry staring at him suspiciously. "Or at least I imagine that's the case." Bob added quickly. Thierry continued to stare. "That's how women are, isn't it? The maternal instinct?" Bob was relieved to see Thierry resume his armpit investigations.

"Well, it's not how we do things round here," Gautier said. "At least not where a tragic death like that is concerned. She needs someone to set her straight on the matter."

"I'd straighten 'er up," Poussin offered, making it abundantly clear that he wasn't referring to Maureen's haricot-vert.

Another pause. Bob couldn't see how he could keep the conversation going without drawing attention to himself.

"And are you putting her straight, Mr Hunt?" Thierry asked.

"Er, em, no." The question had pole-axed Bob. Did Thierry know that they had met? "What do you mean?"

"Nothing much." Thierry smoothed out his moustache. "It's just that it might be helpful to my investigations if I had someone who could keep an eye on the family for me. You English are such a tight-arsed lot that I could interrogate that lot for years without finding out their Christian names."

"He doesn't mean it personally," Gautier fussed, obviously expecting an outbreak of Anglo-French hostilities. "I'll fill you up," he said and quickly replenished Bob's tumbler.

"Now that Paris have given up on the case it's all down to me. I can't understand these Hambletons at all. On the one hand they seem very proper and above-board, and, on the other," he shook his head slowly. "I don't believe a single word they say to me."

"You don't trust anyone," Bob complained.

"Thank God for that," Poussin interjected. "A policeman that believed everyone would be about as much use as a cow with no udders." At least that was how Bob interpreted the comments.

"If only I could find someone who could gain their confidence and break into their little world for me I'd stand a real chance of making some progress."

The whole *cave* turned towards Bob.

"Are you suggesting that I should pretend to befriend them and then betray their trust so that you can stay updated on all their comings and goings?" Bob's voice rose indignantly.

Thierry shrugged. Bob raised his tumbler towards him.

"*Mon plaisir!*"

After Bob had recovered from the shock of being recruited by two different people to spy on each other he started to think carefully about what he should do next. He couldn't easily go to Thierry and tell him that Maureen wanted a report on the progress of the investigation. And it didn't really make much sense for him to explain to Maureen that the police wanted to use an insider to procure information about her family. Since these were the only two facts that Bob had to trade with at present the prospects for a successfully career in espionage looked weak.

He needed to do something about all of this and the prospect of going up to the gendarmerie to tell Thierry he didn't know anything was too frightening for words. The only answer was to go up to the cottage and see if he could get some more information from Maureen. But what reason could he give for a visit?

Poussin delivered the perfect solution as he passed Bob in the road. Apparently there were going to be wholesale change in the refuse collections for the area. He could go up to the cottage and tell Maureen about the change. Rubbish is a serious business in rural France and the penalties for over-filling, under-filling, mistiming or otherwise transgressing the regulations were punitive beyond the guillotine.

It was with some trepidation that he knocked on the cottage door. What if Maureen wanted to know what progress Thierry had made? Bob would have to stall her. He would tell her that enquiries were still at an early stage or something like that. He wouldn't be able to hold her off for long like that. She was the sort of woman who expected results for her money and wouldn't be too subtle about it.

He was taken aback when the door was opened by a thin bespectacled man wearing a panama hat and holding a ridiculously short cricket bat.

"*Je peux vous aider?*" Bob could tell from the accent that the man was a native French speaker.

"*Je m'appele Bob Hunt.*"

"So you are ze famous Bob Hunt?" The man switched into a slightly stilted form of English. "Or perhaps I could say in-famous?"

Bob gave the man a puzzled look.

"The secateurs!" The man made a cutting motion with two of the fingers on his empty hand.

"I'm sorry, I didn't mean to interrupt you or upset anyone. I was just looking for Mrs Hambleton."

"*Non, non, non.*" The man laughed gently. "Do you play?" He offered the cricket bat to Bob.

"I did learn at school but I generally prefer to watch." Bob didn't add that this was usually from the comfort of a bar, which would have given a more accurate reflection of his commitment to the game.

"*Parfait!* In that case you are not interrupting and will be very welcome to join us here. My name is Alain Deneuve and Madame Hambleton is my—how do you say—*belle-mere?*"

"Mother-in-law."

Alain repeated the phrase, turning Maureen into a "muzzer-on-low" in the process. He ushered Bob through the house and into the garden beyond where Jasmine was kneeling on the grass tossing a tennis ball to a young boy of about eight.

"Of course, you're married to Jasmine."

"That's right, and this is our son Marc." Alain turned to address the boy. "Marc come and say hello to Meester Hunt."

"Can't you see I'm busy?" the boy snapped.

"Hello, Mr Hunt," Jasmine smiled up at Bob. "It's so lovely to see you again." She offered her hand towards Bob who kissed it lightly. He picked out a soft floral fragrance, almost imperceptible and yet extravagantly opulent at the same time.

"My condolences on your loss, Mrs Deneuve."

"Daddy was always so generous to us. But let's not talk of it." She indicated Marc. "He's such a sensitive boy."

Marc continued to pound the grass with his foot while he waited for the pleasantries to finish.

"I really came to see your mother."

"I'm afraid she's gone back to Paris for a couple of days for a medical appointment. She's been having some kind of trouble for a while. She's always visiting different doctors but won't tell us what the problem is." She shrugged at him. "Secrets. Just like a birthday really."

"Mummy, this is boring now. Tell the boring man to go away." Marc pointed at Bob.

"Now zen Marc, you should come and be nice to Mr Hunt." Alain looked mortified and Bob felt himself blush on his behalf.

"I don't want to. I've already told you—I'm busy."

"Jasmine?" The couple exchanged glances and then they both looked at Marc. "We've spoken about this before, *cherie*, he has to learn to be amicable."

"Oh, darling, don't be so stuffy. Marc and I are just practicing his catching. You wouldn't want to be disturbed if you were in the middle of one of your spreadsheets, would you?" She looked back at Bob, her immaculately coiffured auburn hair swaying with the movement. "Did you know, Mr Hunt, that Alain does all the scheduling for the company? He's really the brains of the outfit. He's got everything planned down to the last minute thanks to his spreadsheets."

"Don't change the subject, Jasmine. Marc needs to learn some manners."

"Oh I don't know why? One day he'll be in charge of everything."

"That is even more of a reason for the boy to learn some decorum."

"No, it's just a case of keeping everyone in their place. That was always the way that daddy worked. Isn't that right, Mr Hunt?" She looked up at Bob again as if appealing for his support.

"I think your father knew how to get the best of people," he offered in an uncharacteristically diplomatic reply.

He turned to look at Alain. All traces of the earlier bonhomie in his face had been replaced by anger. The way that he looked at Jasmine was close to hatred. Bob decided that he wouldn't like to appear on the wrong side of Alain's spreadsheet.

"I'm bored. You've stopped playing." Marc complained to his mother. "How can I catch the ball if you don't throw it?"

"Mr Hunt is perhaps just the man to help. He can play at ze cricket very well—almost professional, *n'est pas?*"

"Almost," Bob offered. Before he could say anything else, Marc had organised them all into a ring so that he could practice making them run for the ball when he hit it.

After half an hour Marc had had enough.

"You're all useless," he yelled. "How am I supposed to get any better playing against you lot? I'm thirsty now. Time for some tea."

He flounced onto one of the wicker chairs which had been arranged in a semi-circle around the garden table.

"That's a super idea," Jasmine said. "Daddy and Mr Hunt can go and make some drinks and sandwiches for us all and we can have a picnic out here in the garden."

Bob exchanged glances with Alain.

"We have our instructions, Mr Hunt. Let uz go and discharge our responsibilities, eh?"

The two of them traipsed into the kitchen.

"The death must have really upset Jasmine," Bob said when he thought they were safely out of earshot.

"*Pas de tout*. At least not as much as you would think," was the surprising response.

"I thought she was very close to James."

"Close to his wallet, *oui*, but not to the man. The Hambletons are not what we French would describe as a *famille ensemble*."

Bob thought of the Poussins with their extended family of forty-three. The death of the patriarch would shake the entire family to its foundation. No-one connected to the Hambletons actually seemed to be saddened by James' death.

"I'll make the tea," Bob offered. It seemed to have become his ritual role where this family were concerned.

"*Merci*. I never seem to be able to make it *sans* complaint." Alain started buttering some bread. "In fact I never seem to be able to do anything without causing complaint."

It seemed to Bob that the man in the gold rimmed glasses was offering some sort of confessional. He decided to play along.

"Oh? You strike me as a very well-made family. Almost the perfect life."

"You only think that because we have the money. It is a typical English failing." Alain pointed his knife at Bob accusingly. "Yes, we have the money. In fact we have more now that James is dead and he has left a large portion of his estate to Jasmine. In France this would be unthinkable, *incroyable*, with the wife still alive. But money is not everything." He approached Bob, knife outstretched towards him. "Although I am renowned for my efficiency and my *comptables*, although I am a perfectionist in that regard I know deep down that there is something more important than the money and the business. There is love." He flourished the knife at Bob and then returned to buttering the bread.

"Surely Jasmine loves you."

"Yes, she did at first. And I loved her. It was *une affaire passionnee.* She is a very giving woman. Too giving in truth. She gives what she does not have to give, she gives what she should not give and she gives without judgement or concern for the consequences."

Alain began to construct sandwiches from enormous wedges of cheese. The French really didn't get the idea behind tea, Bob concluded.

"You've seen how she treats Marc. She believes that by letting him have whatever he wants she can make him content. She thinks that this will make her happy. But I know that she is wrong. She will never be happy because she all she wants to do is give, give, give . . . And when there is nothing left to give, what happens then?" He shrugged his shoulders at Bob and started slicing an onion.

"But you said that she will inherit some of James' estate. Surely that will make her—you—rich enough to give anything she wants."

"*Non!*" Alain plunged the knife into the chopping board and advanced on Bob. "Still you do not understand. Certainly, she can give monetary things to people, but she will not have learnt the judgement to give other—more important things—like discipline, compassion and love. Her father's legacy has ensured that these truths will never be revealed to her."

"But I thought you said that she was very loving . . ."

"I said she gave love. Again there was confusion. She mistook sex—which I admit was part of her attraction to me—for love. The sex was plentiful—*fantastique.*" Alain removed his glasses and wiped his eyes. "Foolishly I thought that a more mature kind of love would follow, but I was wrong. By the time I realised my error I was locked into marriage and into the family enterprise."

"Marriages can be broken," Bob said quietly. He poured the boiling water into the teapot. Alain appeared to be lost in thought.

"*Jamais!* For us it could never be. For all his jovial conviviality James was a wily old fox. He told Jasmine that he would cut her out of his will if we ever separated."

"But that doesn't stop you . . ."

"Hah, your English sense of convenience blinds you again! You think that because I am not happy I do not love Jasmine. *C'est l'opposite*! It is precisely because I love her that I am not happy. I have seen her father ruin her through money and avarice and I watch her do the same thing with our own son. I love her deeply but I know that she will never be able to respond in kind, on the same level. I would do anything for her but I realise that it will never be enough. There will always be some other thing that she will want, that I will never be able to give her."

Bob was reminded of Lear and how he had given the wrong things for love.

"Does Rose get an equal share of James' estate?" Bob thought he'd try to get an alternative perspective on the murder. So far only one person seemed to have a financial motive for killing James, and that was Alain's wife.

"No!" Alain snorted. "James knew that Jasmine wanted to be his favourite, and he played his part right to the end. Rose gets a small legacy. A few thousand euros I think."

"I don't imagine that she's very pleased, then."

"She won't mind." Alain arranged the heaps of food into his own interpretation of a sandwich. "I should probably have fallen in love with her. She doesn't care about money. Justice is her passion. Equality, fairness, integrity." He laughed to himself as he adjusted glasses onto his nose. "She almost killed James when she told him at a Board meeting that he should donate half the annual profits to charity. He practically had a heart attack on the spot. The money won't worry Rose, but she'll be furious that the two of them haven't been treated equally. It'll be James' revenge from the grave. I told you he was a cunning old fox."

"The tea's ready," Bob said, lifting the pot. "It'll stew if we don't take it through soon."

"Stewed tea," Alain crooned mockingly, extending the vowels. "That would never do."

Together they took the picnic out into the garden where they were assailed by Marc.

"You've been ages. I'm starving."

"Thank you Mr Hunt," Jasmine said. "Alain, you've made a real mess of these sandwiches again. Marc likes them cut up in triangles, don't you?"

"Yes, these are worse than school sandwiches—and they're rubbish."

"I can make some fresh ones for you," Bob suggested.

"No, thank you Mr Hunt. We've already taken up more of your time than we should." Alain put his arm around Bob's back and led him towards the gate at the rear of the cottage. "It's been very kind of you to help with the game and the tea and everything."

"That's alright." Bob waved at Jasmine and Marc, neither of whom was watching. "Anything you want doing here just let me know."

"There is actually one more thing you could do for me," Alain said in a hushed tone. "We've found James' car."

"Oh, yes?" In his delight at avoiding arrest for the murder of James Bob hadn't given any consideration as to how the victim might have got to the cottage. "Where was it? Somewhere local I assume."

"No, *pas de tout*. It was all a bit strange really. We expected it to turn up in Rouen or Poitiers where his appointments were." Alain stopped and looked Bob in the eyes. "Yesterday we got a call from the Paris police to say that they had found it at Charles de Gaulle Aeroport."

"At the airport?"

"Yes." Alain didn't take his eyes off Bob. "An odd coincidence, don't you think?"

"Very." Bob looked away. He wondered whether Thierry knew this. Would it make Bob a more likely suspect or would it finally provide some evidence that he'd been telling the truth?

"I wonder whether you would be willing to collect James' car from the Aeroport and return it to the company garage just outside Paris."

"Of course, but wouldn't it be easier for someone in the office to do it?" Bob asked.

"I would prefer to keep it quiet. Some of the people in the firm are very upset by the death and others are—to be honest with you—a bit nosey. Since you already know everything I thought you might be ideal for the job. *Vous comprenez?*"

"Oh, I do," Bob said. "Leave it to me. I'll be a model of discretion."

"I'll get the airport to send the details through to you so that you can collect it and I'll arrange for your costs to be reimbursed through the company."

"You really are organised." Bob looked at Alain; his thin face seemed resigned to perpetual sadness.

"I'm afraid I am. *A bientot*, monsieur."

"*A bientot*," Bob replied.

He walked back to the Clio reflecting on the impassioned way that Alain had explained his unfulfilled love for Jasmine. It was a strange thing to confess to an outsider but Bob had learnt that the French were not as reticent about such matters as the English. One phrase in particular tumbled round in his head. "I would do anything for her," Alain had said. Did that include murder?

CHAPTER SEVENTEEN

THE CLIO WAS running melodiously. The engine couldn't be described as purring along but the vibrato of the clutch rattle and the treble of the exhaust whine were harmoniously offset by the bass rumbling of something deeply metallic beneath the driver's seat. Of the items required immediately by the Hunt household a new car was currently surpassed only by a pair of gates, some secateurs and a laptop. Anyway, Bob reasoned, Alain had promised to reimburse his expenses for the trip to Paris and that really ought to cover the cost of a new vehicle if the old one expired. And that seemed to be a racing certainty.

Actually the costs of the trip were beginning to worry Bob. Alain would certainly pay for fuel to Paris and back but would that extend to the minor deviations that Bob had been forced to make *en route*? In France each motorway junction is signalled twice. The first is about forty kilometres before the junction and the second is thirty metres after the turning. The slip roads are extraordinarily short and traffic uses the same piece of road both to join and leave the carriageway simultaneously. The result was that Bob had already done six hundred kilometres on a journey that should only have been less than five hundred in total. On the plus side he'd enjoyed a detour through the centre of Rouen and been the first Englishman to circumnavigate the Rennes Rocade ring-road. In both directions.

Fortunately, the Aeroport was now signed at regular intervals and Bob was confident, Clio-willing, of reaching his destination before the end of the month. He started to think about the events that had led up to this journey. There were those legs—for some reason he simply couldn't get them out of his mind—eye-candy for the middle-aged. Perhaps they belonged to Betty, in which case was she playing away twice at the same venue? But how did she get in? One of the couple definitely had a key, and that would make sense if she really was James' regular girlfriend. Then there was all this business about New York and the phone call. On the one hand James had never gone to New York but on the other he'd driven the car that Bob was about to collect at Charles de Gaulle. Why would he do that if he was planning on having some fun in the Vendée? And then there was that phone call. There was still something nagging away in his mind about it, if only he could think what.

Bob parked the Clio at the medium stay car-park without having made progress on any of the questions. He made his way to the V-I-P garage that James apparently used on a fairly frequent basis, judging by the reasonably friendly reception that he received, and located the appropriate bay. He wasn't at all surprised to find that the car was a Rover 75 with a personalised number plate and all the trimmings. A walnut dashboard, complete with sat-nav system, digital radio and half-filled ashtray, gave it an air of opulence. Compared to the Clio it handled like a tank.

It was about thirty kilometres from the airport to the Hambleton's depot in a *zone industriel* on the outskirts of Paris. The building was an enormous pre-fabricated shell housing a storage area, a handful of loading bays and a small garage where trucks seemed to be in the process of being disassembled into their component parts. The company must be doing well, though, there was a Porsche parked on the forecourt. Bob wondered if they had enough bits to create a replacement for the Clio, but immediately felt disloyal to the old girl and instead found the depot manager, Michel, to let him know that he'd returned the Rover.

"You've brought the old devil's car back then, eh?"

"Yes, Alain asked me to drive it here."

"That figures. He wouldn't bring it back himself, oh no, he's far too important for that." Michel was a short, dumpy man who wore overalls despite having, as far as Bob could tell, a desk-based job. "I imagine they'll expect me to sell it for them."

"I'm afraid I don't know what their plans are," Bob shrugged.

"They'll make a loss on it, for sure. No-one over here wants this sort of car any more. You can't get the parts for one thing. English collectors. They're the only people who'll touch it, and I'm not wasting any of my men's time sending one of them over the Channel to do a trade. It can go for scrap." From his accent Bob judged that Michel was from Normandy, it was rougher than the soft-voweled tones that he was used to in the Vendée.

"It seems a pity."

"Huh." Michel hooked the keys to the Rover onto a screw plugged into the breezeblock walls of the depot. "You don't understand. They've got us all under their thumbs, one way or another."

"They?"

"The Hambletons. That old devil James was a real bastard. I'm glad to see the back of him."

"What did he do?"

The Frenchman's eyes blazed at Bob.

"What's it to you, anyway? You're just one of them. Another bloody *rosbif*. Probably been sent to spy on us."

"Spy?"

"Yes, with the strike and everything. I wouldn't put anything past that Alain Deneuve. In many ways he's worse than any of them. After all he was one of us once. Now all he does is send us these lists and moan like hell if we don't stick to them." He lifted a piece of paper from the desk and showed it to Bob. It was some sort of spreadsheet, with columns of dates and numbers. Michel screwed it into a ball before tossing it towards the dustbin. It missed.

"Strike?"

"You mean that your paymasters haven't told you?" Michel laughed and squatted down into his seat. "Well, I'm not surprised."

He lit up a cigarette and launched the match towards the dustbin. A collection of match stubs on the floor just short of the bin attested to Michel's consistent if inaccurate aim.

"The men of the depot have decided that our conditions aren't good enough. Our pay rates are amongst the lowest in the sector while the bosses get richer off our backs." He jerked a thumb in the direction of the forecourt. "Go and tell your masters that!"

"Well, thanks anyway," Bob said, conscious that he had to make his own way back to the airport using a rather convoluted public transport system, including railway, buses and the metro. Alain had sent him a very meticulous set of instructions. "By the way I found this in the car." He opened up a plastic bag that contained two bottles of cognac and an expensive-looking case of red wine. "I don't suppose I'll be able to carry these around on the bus."

"The bus?"

"Yes, apparently I have to get the number 18 bus to Chelles-Gournay train station so that I can get back to the airport to pick up my car. If it'll make it back to the Vendée that is. I'm afraid it's a rather clapped-out old Clio."

"A Renault?"

"Yes. It's blue. Like everything else in the Vendée."

"That takes me back." Michel blew an expansive haze of cigarette smoke into the air. "My first car was a Renault *Cinq*. The number of girls I pulled with that old banger. It was more than five I can tell you. It's where I decided to get married." He gestured towards a framed photo on his desk which pictured him in a clinch with a pretty brunette. "Bloody women." He flicked his hand across the top of the frame and sent it skidding across the desk and onto the floor.

"Oh well I'll be off then." Bob had no particular desire to listen to Michel enumerate his Norman conquests for him.

"Hold on." The Frenchman beckoned Bob back, scattering ash all over the office floor. "I tell you what. Since you're a Renault owner and can't be all bad I'll do you a deal. If you let me have one of those bottles of Cognac I'll give you a lift to Chelle-Gournay. How about that?"

"Tell you what if you give me a lift to the airport you can have them both."

Michel weighed it up for a moment.

"*D'accord*. It's a deal." Judging by the smile on the man's face it had been a one-sided deal, but Bob didn't care. It meant he'd be back with Kate all the sooner. "It's on my way home anyway." Michel guffawed and slapped Bob on the back. "My car's just over there."

He pointed at the Porsche.

On the drive to the airport Michel told Bob about the impending strike.

"You take what you can from those Hambletons, mate. They're none of them worth trusting. That Jasmine's a stuck-up bitch and her husband is a traitor. Rose is alright," he said grudgingly. "She's all for the workers and that. Good company too."

"You see much of her?"

"Now and then." Michel peered into the rear view mirror, as if he were trying to spot someone following them. "She's quite a good folk singer and has a small recording studio that she built in a barn just outside Chelle-Gournay. I play the guitar sometimes for her. They probably see her as the black sheep of the family."

"What about James Hambleton? What was he like?"

"He was the worst of the lot of them. Don't get me started on him."

"Why?"

"Because he pinched my wife off me."

"But he was married. To Maureen."

"What does that mean to a man like him? He could have it all. He could have whatever woman he wanted. And he decided he wanted mine."

"I'm sorry to hear that." Bob wondered if this could be the mysterious Betty? "Surely there was a huge age difference between them."

"That didn't seem to matter to James. Old, young, French, English, rich, poor, relations or complete strangers it didn't make any difference to him. But to a girl from a humble background like my wife he was definitely a good catch." Michel lit up a cigarette whilst negotiating a three-lane undertaking manoeuvre at 160 kilometres an hour. "I followed them. I tried to reason with her—told her he would dump her when he got bored—but she wouldn't listen. Bet . . ." He braked sharply in front a speed radar. "Bloody cameras! Something else we got from your side of the Channel."

"You said Bet . . . ?" Bob was suddenly optimistic. It looked like he'd found his girl at the first attempt.

"What? Oh yes." Michel continued his recollection of the conversation. "Bet you'll regret ever having met him, I told her. But would she listen? No. I believe she was seeing him on and off right up to the bitter end." He threw the cigarette butt out of the car window, which seemed to be automatically programmed to react to the situation. "He got what he deserved. Anyway let's change the subject before I get really angry."

Bob didn't have the courage to ask the question that was almost burning the inside of his mouth. If he could only discover Michel's wife's name he would know whether she were the mysterious Betty. Instead they spent the rest of the journey in a debate about the relative merits of the French and English football teams, of which Bob only understood a half and cared about even less.

Michel dropped Bob off at the car-park where he discovered that the payment machine only accepted cards. To pay by cash he would have to go into the terminal. Bob trudged into one of the octopus arms of the terminal building and located the car parking help-desk. Like most help-desks it was a semi-accurate description. Of course Bob could pay by cash, provided that he had exactly the correct money which, by sheer coincidence, he didn't. After some negotiation involving the use of a fifty centime piece and bartering half of the case of red wine left over from the Rover, Bob was given the ticket that would enable the Clio to exit the car-park legally—as long as he got to the other side of the airport in the following five minutes.

As the tannoy announced the departure of a flight to some exotic part of French Polynesia that Bob had never heard of, he realised what had been strange about the phone call from James. Bob had heard the public address system announce the arrival of a flight, but in French first. If James had been in New York then the announcement would have been in English first and in French—never, probably. As Bob bundled himself into the Clio in an attempt to beat the ticket deadline he realised what this meant. Whichever airport James had been at when he phoned Bob it certainly wasn't in New York. In fact he'd almost certainly made that phone call from somewhere in France.

Chapter Eighteen

"Y ou've done well, Bob. We'll make a cadet out of you yet."

Thierry Fauconnier plucked at his moustache and read back through all the notes that he'd taken as Bob had described his meetings with Jasmine, Alain and Michel. The gendarmerie was stuffy, but all the windows were sealed shut and there was an overpowering smell of Gitanes.

"There's some interesting stuff here. This James Hambleton was an *homme des affaires* in more than one way."

"I think I know which affairs he preferred."

Bob felt a slight twinge of guilt at not having revealed to the gendarme his meeting with Maureen at La Roche Grise. Perhaps he'd reserve that for when Thierry promoted him to aspirant.

"Well, I hope that I've given you and your cousin something to work with." Bob wondered how he was going to ask Thierry to investigate the name Betty. "It's just I'd like to think that what I've discovered points towards the involvement of a woman . . . ."

"*Bien sur*. The forensic report leaves open the possibility that the murderer could have been a woman." Thierry swatted his hand at a fly that had been circling round his head. "Think about it Bob. Young girl lures a desperate old man up to the bedroom, gets him as drunk as a British tourist and then stabs him. But you're too weak to kill him outright so you climb down the stepladder, close the room up and let him bleed until he's stone cold dead!" He thumped his fist down on his desk and then lifted it up carefully to reveal the squashed body of a fly beneath.

"I hadn't really thought it through like that."

"Of course you hadn't. I'm the capitaine and you're just a . . ."

"Professor?" Bob suggested.

"I deal in realities not theories. And the reality of this case is . . ." Thierry swept the dead fly from his desk with his arm. "That I really don't have a clue."

"You must have some idea?"

"In my routine experience, Bob, I have a dead body, a weapon covered in enough fingerprints to make a sandwich and some stupid local stood over the corpse saying that he didn't mean to hit him so hard. In this case I have a body that's two continents away from where it should be, a weapon neatly wrapped up in an envelope and half of France having slept with the victim."

"I'm sure you'll crack it," Bob said, seeing a chance to restate his cause. "*Cherchez la femme!*"

"Yes, I'll see what I can find out about James' lovers. And I'll look into this Michel fellow. Sounds like a nasty piece of work from what you said."

Thierry used a pencil to poke at the bits of the fly that had caught in the hairs on his forearm. Bob decided that it was time to leave.

"Thanks." He stood up. "See you at the *cave* later?"

"Perhaps." Thierry slapped the pencil against him arm, loosening dust and skin into the air. He turned to Bob and pointed the pencil at him. "A word of advice. You know this wedding?"

"Poussin's grandson?"

"That's it. Don't spend too much on the present, will you?"

"We haven't got the money to spend on presents. Why?"

"I've just got a feeling that it won't last very long."

CHAPTER NINETEEN

MADAME POUSSIN WAS angry. Even from halfway down the road and with about a litre of *apperitif* in his blood system, Bob could tell that she wasn't happy. He could see her standing outside the Poussin's house, arms folded, left foot sticking out almost onto the road itself. As they approached it looked even worse. Her hair was still in curlers—unheard of at this time in the afternoon—her chin pointed out above her capacious chest and her cheeks were puffed up, reminding Bob of Popeye in one of his spinach-deprived moments. Above all he could tell that she was angry because Poussin, who was walking next to him up the street from the *cave*, was trembling.

"What time do you call this?" she demanded when they were about fifty metres away from her.

Poussin and Bob adopted the same strategy. They pretended to be out of range. At thirty metres this approach was no longer viable. Retreat was possible—desirable even—but ultimately self-defeating. Like Napoleon's forces on the march to Moscow Bob and Poussin braced themselves against their icy reception.

"I told you to be back here by two and it's quarter to three now."

Twenty metres to go and Bob could sense Poussin's spirit fading. The strong liqueur seemed to be taking its toll on their defences.

"We were discussing the wedding," the old man wheezed uncertainly.

As a first salvo in the campaign it was less than convincing but did seem to have the effect of distracting the enemy. Bob saw Madame

Poussin pause in her bombardment of the time-keeping abilities of the masculine gender. He even thought he saw a softening of her features, but it could simply have been a function of his alcohol-induced inability to focus. Ten metres. Bob's tactics were simple. Say nothing. No names, no numbers, no hostages. In any case it wasn't really his war. He was only there as infantry support to accompany Poussin up the road until he reached his own front door, which was rapidly approaching. Pierre would have to battle the last five metres on his own.

And then disaster. Unexpected reinforcements arrived to support Madame in the form of Kate, who emerged from the Poussin's doorway just as Bob thought he was safely home.

"This is ridiculous." She snorted, striding towards them, and wagging an outstretched finger at Bob. "How am I supposed to get lunch ready for us when you think it's acceptable to come home at any time of the afternoon?"

"It was Gautier's fault," Bob whined. "He kept us talking for ages and so we didn't know what time it was." The words fell out of his mouth in more or less the right order. He was impressed with himself and his courage roared.

"That's right," Poussin piped up. "It's Gautier's fault." For a moment he stood tall, almost reaching the giddy heights of five feet.

Bob remembered that Gautier was probably following them down the street to his big house which was at the end of the road. He swung round guiltily to see whether their scapegoat was in earshot. With relief Bob noticed that he was nowhere in sight.

"Couldn't you hear the church bells?" Madame Poussin had caught them up, her red cheeks puffing away. "They're loud enough to wake the dead."

"But they're so confusing," Bob argued. "They ring once at one o'clock but also once at half past each hour. It's very difficult to know the difference between half past twelve and half past two."

"And I imagine it gets more difficult the longer time goes on and the more of that stuff you pour down your throats." Kate retaliated.

"That's a bit unfair, darling," Bob wrapped his arms around her. "You'd say it was very rude to leave midway through a conversation about . . . ," he struggled to think what a woman might have a conversation about. "Womenses things!" he concluded triumphantly. Judging by the smirk on Kate's face he had just proved her point for her.

"Augh! Your breath!" She pushed him away from her. "I think I'll switch the gas off before you enter the house like that. One word from you and you're likely to blow the whole village up."

"And one word from you . . ." Madame had taken Poussin firmly by the wrist and was dragging him the final five metres to meet his Waterloo.

"*A bientot*," was his final salute to Bob before he disappeared from view.

"Perhaps comrade," Bob mumbled as Kate pushed him through the doorway.

Kate fed Bob and let him sleep off the worst excesses of the lunchtime meeting at the *cave*, but the reckoning was soon at hand. He was slumped across the sofa in the *sejour*.

"All this drinking has got to stop, OK?" Kate was sat bolt upright in her armchair, wagging her finger towards him. "Our lives are falling apart. We're running out of money and the place looks like a dump. I meant it when I said I was giving you one last chance."

"I know. I'm sorry." Bob had decided that contrition was the better part of valour. "I won't let it happen again, I promise." He felt that perhaps his last sentence was taking things a bit far but it seemed to play well with his audience.

"We've got to get organised. Getting pissed down the *cave* is not the answer." She shuffled round in her chair and rummaged in her sewing box. "Nor is taking my pinking shears. Where the hell have you put the wretched things?"

"I've never touched your wretched fancy scissors. I wouldn't know how to use them if I did."

"That's never stopped you before." Kate pulled her part-finished tapestry out of the box and slammed down the lid. "I've seen you using them in the garden for pruning."

"Perhaps." Bob pouted. "Why are we always arguing? All you seem to do lately is tell me off."

OK, you're right. Credit where it's due. You did well to get the extra money out of the Hambletons, although I still have no idea how you persuaded them given that we were the main suspects in the murder."

Bob had thought it better not tell Kate about his arrangements with Maureen. He feared that she might go all moral on him and tell him to pay back the money they'd received from the company.

"We seemed to be making a go of things," she continued. "But now you just spend your time running round on errands for them and drinking yourself stupid in the *cave* in between. And that's not what I married you for."

"What did you marry me for?"

"Your wit. Your charm." Bob warmed to his wife's reply. "Your bank balance."

"Now I know you're lying."

"I suppose I just find you easy to be with. Life's usually OK between us."

"I've heard worse compliments."

"But then there are other times when I just want to kill you."

Bob was struck by her vehemence.

"What would it take, do you think, for a woman to kill a man?"

Kate threw him an odd look. "You mean to kill a husband?"

"Possibly. Or perhaps a man that had been having an affair with you?"

"Are you trying to tell me something?" Bob was surprised to see a look of genuine concern pass across her eyes.

"No, no." He was relieved to see her eyes clear. "But I was talking to Thierry and he says that a woman might have murdered James. I was wondering what might motivate a woman to do that."

"It could be anything I suppose. Infidelity certainly." Kate stabbed the needle into her sewing. "Although, if I'm honest I'd probably just leave someone that was cheating on me. After all I wouldn't make my life any better just by ending theirs."

"What about money?"

"OK, perhaps. But it would need to be an awful lot of money. I think sleeping with someone is a preferable option. Less messy." She looked up from her tapestry. "Probably."

"Revenge?"

"They say it's a dish best served cold. By which time I imagine all the passion has gone out of it. Besides, what's the point of getting revenge on someone who's not there to see it unfold?"

"I suppose." Bob was starting to think a bit more lucidly now. The fog of *aperitif* was beginning to clear. "So what would it take?"

Kate carried on sewing for a bit. "For a woman it would have to be something that she really cared about. A real passion, like protecting your child or . . ." She waved her needle in the air while the words came to mind. "Righting a wrong. Striking a blow against prejudice or unfairness." She went back to her sewing.

Bob jumped out of his chair and kissed Kate on the top of her head.

"What was that for?"

"You've just given me an idea." He had recalled something that Alain Deneuve had said about injustice. "I need to speak to Rose Hambleton."

Chapter Twenty

A RRANGING A MEETING with Rose had been easier than Bob expected. A brief telephone conversation with Maureen to explain that his progress with Thierry would be greatly assisted if he could ask Rose a few questions met with little resistance and no challenges. Ten minutes later and the rendezvous was agreed. Rose would meet him for half an hour at La Roche-sur-Yon whilst she waited for a connecting train to Bordeaux where she was due to attend an animal rights demonstration.

Rose was late. Bob had been sitting outside the café in the Place Napoleon where they had agreed to meet. It was a bright April morning and a group of students were sat on the steps of the Eglise Saint-Louis. She arrived in a whirlwind of coat, bags and hat, muttering a brief apology for her lateness and sat in the chair opposite Bob, who ordered an espresso for himself and a fruit tea for Rose. He was surprised to see a guitar case amongst the bags.

"You're on your way to a demo?"

"Yeah. I'm doing a gig there." She looked down at the table and fidgeted with the menu.

"It was kind of you to spare the time to see me."

"Mum told me to." Rose's face was covered by her long black dyed hair so Bob couldn't tell whether her brusqueness was deliberate or whether it was simply due to shyness.

"Well, I'm grateful anyway." There was a long pause, during which their drinks arrived.

"You get to a lot of demos?"

"Yeah. I try to do my bit. You know. Amnesty, Animal Aid, Democracy Now . . ." Her voice trailed off. "But you're not interested in all that stuff." She looked up. Her dark grey eyes were alert and thoughtful, sparkling in the sun.

"In my day it was CND and the students' union," Bob said. "But that was a long time ago."

"We should be as organised and as purposeful in our struggles as he was." Rose pointed up at the huge statue of Napoleon that dominated the square and the town.

"Napoleon seems a strange hero for a . . ." Bob hated labelling people. ". . . Communist?" He knew straight away that he'd made the wrong choice.

"I am not a communist." Rose flicked her hair away from her face. Bob could see she was frowning. "Given my background I could never empathise with the working classes."

"But you support their cause?"

"Yeah. That's because I sympathise with them. You agree that the two emotions are entirely different, Professor Hunt?"

Bob swung round momentarily to see who she was addressing before realising that she meant him. It seemed to have been years since he'd last been called by his academic title. He felt an unexpected twinge of sorrow.

"To empathise with someone you must have a shared experience, a common point of reference. But it's only possible to sympathise if you can approach their situation from outside and overcome the differences that stand between you. To empathise is easy—natural really—to sympathise requires sacrifice." She swept the fringe of her jet black away from her eyes and Bob was startled to recognise the physical resemblance between Rose, Jasmine and Maureen. They all possessed a strong face—a look of determination and defiance. "True sympathy is true love." Her pale face blushed slightly. "I'm sorry. I get quite carried away with ideas sometimes."

"That's fine with me. It's my metier," Bob replied. He was actually enjoying the opportunity to discuss issues that went beyond what he was going to eat, drink or clean next.

"I suppose you must find my views a bit strange, what with me being part of a well-to-do family."

"Not really," Bob said. "Perhaps you feel guilty?"

"Sometimes." She leaned over to her coat and pulled a packet of cigarettes out of one of the pockets. "The thing is my upbringing was very traditional, very patriarchal. My formative years were practically feudal."

"Now that is an unusual view." Bob shook his head as she offered the cigarettes to him.

"Not really. You see Jasmine and I have never had to do anything for ourselves. We had it all dished up on a plate. A private education, access to the best social contacts that money could buy and a guaranteed future were all laid on for us. We never had to think for ourselves at all really." She took a long drag on her cigarette, blowing smoke into blue sky. "We were surrounded by people who would do whatever it took to please us and we never really questioned their motives. If that's not feudal then I don't know what is."

"But as you grew up and saw more of the world you must have realised that life is much more complicated than that for most of us. That your good fortune was the exception rather than the rule."

"Yeah." She sighed. "But I suppose that I've always retained a belief in the ultimate simplicity of the world. Because my life has always been easy to change I like to believe that it can be that way for everyone. All you have to do is organise, have determination and the dream can be yours."

"You sound like your sister, now."

"Of course. The only difference between us is that she wants to change the world to suit her, whereas I want to change the world to suit everyone else. I suppose I feel like a crusader in the original sense of the word. Bringing the truth to the infidels."

Although Bob was enjoying their philosophical discussion he realised that he had actually asked to meet her so that he could ask her about the murder.

"What about your father?"

Rose looked up at Bob, her eyes flashing angrily again.

"I'm sorry," he added. "I don't mean to upset you, but . . ."

"No, I'm not upset," she replied in a calm voice. "In fact I'm relieved that he's dead."

"Relieved?"

"Yeah. The world is a better place now that he's gone."

"Why?"

"As long as he was alive nothing could change or move forward. Now that he's dead Jasmine and I can develop ourselves without being in his shadow. It gives us room to breathe and flourish." She yawned, stretching her arms towards the sun. "And, of course, the business can adopt a more enlightened approach as well."

"You think it will?"

"Oh yes. Uncle Charles has always been more understanding that dad ever was." She gazed into her half-empty tea-cup as if trying to divine the future. "Now that he's Chairman I'll be able to talk him into turning the firm into one of the most sustainable, employee-friendly organisations in Europe."

"What about your mother?"

"As long as she feels involved in the running of the business she'll be happy. I'm sure she won't be devastated by her loss. You must have heard the stories about his affairs and the rest of it. Her only regret will be that someone didn't have the courage to do it earlier." She laughed, a ripple of sound rising above the hub-bub of the café. "In fact I wouldn't put it past her to have done the deed herself." She stopped laughing and gazed at Bob, her face suddenly serious. "But then that could go for any of us, couldn't it?"

"Well, the gendarmes certainly thought it could be me. Fortunately I've got a watertight alibi; I was with the detective at the time." Bob looked carefully at Rose. She seemed to be more relaxed now, so he decided to push his luck. "Where were you when the murder was committed?"

Rose laughed lightly.

"It took me ages to work it out when the police asked me that question. Turns out I was with my boyfriend. He works for the firm, you know."

"He does?"

"Yeah. His name's Michel. Works in the car depot near where I live." She gazed suspiciously at Bob. "He told me you'd been up to the garage—asking questions."

"Yes. Well, Alain asked me to take your father's car back." Bob supressed the desire to say that Michel had downplayed the closeness of their relationship. "He seems like a nice bloke."

"I suppose he is." She took another long drag on her cigarette. "He's been through the mill a bit. Wife trouble, if you know what I mean. But he's a solid enough guy and we get along really well despite the obvious social differences." Grey smoke drifted into the air from her cigarette. Rose giggled to herself. "Or perhaps it's because of them."

"You mentioned your fathers' affairs before. How did you find out about them?" Bob finally felt as though he was making progress. Perhaps Rose knew who James' lover was.

"Shit!" Rose jumped up and stubbed the remainder of her cigarette into the ashtray. "I am sorry, professor, but I was enjoying our conversation so much that I lost track of the time." She slapped a fifty euro note onto the ashtray that contained the bill. "I must go or I'll miss the train. They can keep the change." She slid her duffel bag across her shoulders and pecked Bob on the cheek.

"Sympathy for the workers?" he asked as she grabbed her coat and bag from the chair next to her.

"What?"

Bob pointed at the note. She laughed again.

"No, I just can't be arsed to find the change." She shimmied her way between the café tables, her designer jeans accentuating the slenderness of her thighs.

"One last question," Bob called. He had thought of something that didn't make sense to him.

"What?"

"Did your father smoke?"

Rose stopped halfway across the square and looked back at Bob in puzzlement.

"Never," she called. "It's the main reason why I started. Bye!" She waved, turned her back on him and ran towards the station.

Bob sat down and finished his coffee. At least he wouldn't need to pay for it.

He felt mixed emotions about his meeting with Rose. He had enjoyed their intellectualising, but it had also made him wonder if he hadn't given up his academic career a little prematurely. Bob was also suspicious about her sudden departure. Just as he asked her about her father's womanising she ended the conversation. Rose definitely knew something—she had said "and the rest of it" as though there were a more complex story. She was a bright girl, Bob reasoned, and must have known exactly what she was doing. So what was "the rest of it"?

In the meantime his brain had gone into academic mode. Something about Rose's explanation of her childhood had intrigued him. He mentally constructed a new opening sentence for his conference paper; "King Lear is one of Shakespeare's most complex plays but its central theme is the concept of patrimony."

CHAPTER TWENTY-ONE

"DO COME IN Bob." Maureen gestured through the door of the cottage. "We can have some tea together in the lounge. After all, you make it so well."

Bob walked through to the kitchen with her.

"Or perhaps you would rather sit in the garden with a beer?" She hissed the last word as if it were blasphemous. "Although I should warn you that Jasmine and her merry band are in residence."

The emphasis on "merry" suggested to Bob that all was not well in the Hambleton household. He could hear Alain's raised voice. It sounded as though Marc was being obstinate about something.

"How is the firm managing whilst Alain is here?" Bob asked conversationally.

"Charles is doing everything." She looked surprised as Bob gathered the teapot, cups and saucers from the cupboards. "He knows his way around the business better than anyone. Nearly as well as you seem to know your way around our kitchen."

"Well, I keep the cottage stocked up so I put everything here in the first place," Bob explained. "In fact, that was the only reason why I was here on that fateful night."

"Oh yes. That ridiculous story about the girl with the legs," Maureen said scornfully.

"I actually meant the night that we discovered your husband's body."

"Yes, I'm sorry. I'd forgotten that you . . ." She switched on the electric kettle and shook her head. "You know I really think that Charles is the only one who really misses James. He seems to have thrown himself completely into his work. He's practically running the place single-handed." She produced some Scottish shortbread from a tin in the cupboard, and waved it triumphantly. "I found it in the stock room before we left." She laid the sticks of shortbread onto a plate in neat symmetrical rows. "Actually I'm quite worried about Charles. He's been overdoing it since the murder, as if he has to fill James' place. I've finally managed to persuade him to come down here for the weekend with Louise, but they're only staying for the Saturday night."

"A change is as good as a rest."

"So they say," Maureen muttered, as if she didn't really care for what 'they' said. "Now let's go through to the lounge and you can tell me what you've discovered."

As Bob admitted to her, there wasn't much to tell. Michel's ex-wife seemed favourite to be the mysterious Betty, but Bob hadn't been able to determine her name and Maureen didn't seem to know either.

"I think I remember some tittle-tattle about him a while ago, but I can't for the life of me remember what it was," she said.

Bob also explained that his meeting with Rose hadn't revealed a lot.

"There was something she wouldn't tell me about James. Something beyond just having an affair."

"A baby perhaps?" Bob was surprised at the eagerness in Maureen's voice.

"She wouldn't say. It might have been." Bob thought about James and his two daughters. He supposed that, for a man with a strong libido, a third child must be a possibility. "Why do you ask?"

She chewed her lip for a moment and looked through the windows into the garden where Jasmine, Marc and Alain were still at play.

"Bob." She stared at him intently. "Can I share a secret with you?"

"I hope so. After all, we are partners in crime."

125

"An unfortunate choice of phrase," Maureen reprimanded. "However, I believe that I can trust you and, if you are to get to the truth for me, it is important that I don't spare you any of the gory details. No matter how galling those details may be." She considered her fingernails for a moment. They certainly weren't gardeners' hands; pretty rather than practical. She looked up at him. "I just hope that it's worth the cost to my pride."

"I'm sorry," Bob said simply. He wasn't sure what he was apologizing for but it felt right. Maureen's demeanour had become more sombre.

"The fact is that I have reason to believe that there was an illegitimate child." She threw her hands into her lap. "What am I saying? A perfectly legitimate child—a brother or sister for Jasmine and Rose—but one hidden from me."

"A child of James'?"

"Yes. I imagine that I had always feared the day would arrive when I had to face up to James' infidelities in a more real form than just hurt pride."

"And you think that Betty is the mother?" Bob thought he could finally see why Maureen was so intent on finding the girl.

"Yes. You see I found out about the baby at around the same time as James began to cry out in the night."

"It makes sense," Bob agreed. "When was that?"

"About two or three years ago. James was talking to the solicitor on the phone except that he didn't realize that it was a conference call and I could hear what they were saying. They were talking about wills and the lawyer asked James if he'd given any more thought to the child. James got quite angry and said that he would raise the subject when the time was right. Then he slammed the phone down."

"And you never asked him about it?"

"It probably seems strange to you, Bob, but I did not want to open up such a large rift between us. I felt better for thinking that he didn't know that I knew. Reverse logic really. Anyway, you perhaps understand now why I am so anxious to locate this Betty." Maureen looked as close to tears as Bob had ever seen her.

"Yes and, of course, I'll do whatever . . ."

"You! Again!" Alain stood at the door between the lounge and the kitchen. He pointed at Bob. "What are you doing here? I'm getting tired of finding you at every turn. You English have a phrase, I think, when someone appears too often like the bad penny. Well, Monsieur Hunt, I think I could make a fortune for ze amount bad pennies you bring."

"Bob is here as my guest," Maureen interjected sharply.

"*Mais, bien sur.* He always has a reason to be here, but that doesn't make him any less unwelcome. He seems to have a very unnatural interest in our family."

"That's enough Alain!" Maureen stood up and faced her son-in-law at the door. "I don't know what's got into you." She turned back to Bob, her face flushed with anger or embarrassment. "He isn't normally like this. I'm sorry you had to meet him on a bad day."

"*Non, non, non.*" Alain wagged his finger horizontally and approached Bob. "Monsieur Hunt has already had the pleasure of an introduction. To me, to Jasmine, to Rose." He was so close now that Bob could see the dust in the lenses of his spectacles. "Did you know that he has even been talking to Michel about us?"

Maureen froze.

"Is this true, Mr Hunt?"

Bob could see her dilemma. If she admitted to knowing about his enquiries then it might open up some questions about her own motives. Saying nothing would indicate disinterest beyond belief.

"I'm afraid so, Mrs Hambleton."

"You see!" Alain turned to Maureen in his moment of triumph. "He seems intent on discovering everything about the family. And remember, he was the one that found the body. I call that suspicious."

"And I think you have an over-active imagination, Alain," Maureen replied calmly.

"What's going on?" Jasmine came in to see what the fuss was about. "Oh, hello Mr Hunt."

"Monsieur Hunt was just leaving, *n'est pas?*"

"Of course," Bob replied meekly. He turned to Maureen. "I'm sorry to have disturbed you or to have caused offence." He could see her eyes widen slightly in surprise at his submission. She nodded curtly at him.

The three Hambleton's watched in silence as Bob let himself out of the front door of the cottage. He allowed himself to admit that he was still in a state of shock. Not about Alain's outburst, unprovoked as it was. A man like that—with a family like his—was bound to need to let off steam now and again. What had really shocked Bob was that as he made his way out of the house he had caught sight of something in the hallway that had been completely out of place. There, lying on the top shelf of the dresser, were Kate's pinking shears.

Chapter Twenty-Two

"**G**ET LOST!" BOB was stood at the front window looking out at the sharp shadows of the street.

"Stuff you," was Kate's reply from the kitchen, swiftly followed by an airborne missile in the form of a luminous yellow cup.

Bob caught the projectile low down and embarked on a lap of honour around the lounge as if he'd taken the winning catch in an Ashes cricket series.

"It's good to see that the age of the witty put-down is still alive and well in St-Sébastien."

"As you may have noticed," Kate said, as she strode into the lounge from the kitchen. "I'm not really in the mood for wit. In fact I definitely remember getting up this morning and saying to myself—I think I'll have a wit-free day today and enjoy a lovely picnic on the beach with my wonderfully romantic husband."

"It's just a pity that you didn't share this delightful vision with your husband first." Bob handed the cup back to Kate. "Because if you had, you'd have realised that I planned to spend the day working on my conference paper."

Kate glared at Bob. It took all of his courage to maintain eye contact with her. They were like two cats daring each other to back down over their territorial claim. After three seconds Bob's courage failed. Kate took the advantage and moved into the silence between them.

"But why?" her voice bordering on a whine. "It's the hottest day of the year so far, wall-to-wall sunshine, and you want to sit inside sweating away at that stupid Shakespeare thing . . ." She raised her arms in a gesture of exasperated incomprehension.

"Sweating away at earning us some money." Bob could hear his voice rising. I must not lose my temper, he told himself. I must remember that I love her. It was difficult sometimes with Kate, though. She seemed to miss the obvious. "That stupid Shakespeare thing could earn us enough money to take us through next year."

She swept the hair away from her face, and he saw that her normally sparkling eyes were subdued.

"It might even be enough to buy you a new dress." He felt a butterfly ripple through across his heart as her eyes lightened. "But first I've got to write it."

"Can't you do it tonight?" Kate's voice was imploring. "We can spend the afternoon on the beach and then I promise that I'll let you write all evening."

"But it's all here," Bob tapped his head. "And if I don't let it out now then it could be lost forever." He took her hands in his. "I'd love to spend the day with you darling, but just at this moment Lear is calling to me."

"Hello-o-o!"

Bob and Kate both dropped their hands in surprise at the sound of a girl's voice.

"Anyone at home?"

"In here," Bob answered.

"We're very sorry to disturb you." The visitor was in her late teens with ash-blonde hair and pale brown eyes. Over many years of life in a campus environment Bob had become immured to the physical attractions of young women. He had learnt enough about what went on in his students' heads to inoculate him against their looks. And as for their domestic habits—he preferred not to think about it. However, even Bob was forced to admit that this particular girl was stunningly attractive. He felt Kate stiffen in response.

"How can we help you?" he offered before his wife could scare the girl off.

"We come in peace." Bob recognised Charles Hambleton as he entered the lounge and walked up to shake his hand.

"Hello Charles. This is my wife Kate," he flapped a hand towards her. "And you must be . . ." Bob ground to a halt. "I'm sorry I can never remember names. I think it comes from having dealt with so many students over the years."

"Louise." Her voice reminded Bob of a harp. An angelic sound. He sharply told himself to grow up.

"Yes, of course. Well I'm Professor Robert Hunt, but you can call me Bob." He could feel himself simpering.

"Which is far more polite than anyone who knows him does," Kate interjected. "Can I assume that you are Hambletons?"

"I'm sorry darling," Bob tore his eyes away from Louise to glance at Kate. His wife looked on the thundery side of stormy. Bob winced. "This is Charles Hambleton and his daughter." He turned his eyes back onto the girl and relaxed into the view.

"We're very sorry to intrude, Mrs Hunt," Charles' voice sounded genuinely contrite. "I've really come to 'mend a few fences'." His fingers twitched the air as the apostrophes commenced. "Maureen told me about the way that Alain treated you yesterday and we've come to apologise."

"It really isn't necessary." To Bob it looked as though Charles had aged by about ten years since they had first met in the autumn. "We offer our condolences to you both on your loss. I can understand that feelings are running high in the circumstances."

"That is kind of you, but really Alain's behaviour was unforgivable. I know that Maureen was terribly upset."

"Would you like a drink?" Kate asked.

"Something cool would be marvellous," Louise purred. Bob wasn't sure which was the more heavenly, her face or her voice.

"Let's go into the garden," he suggested. "We can try a bottle of rosé from the chateau."

"Not for Louise," Charles said as they walked through the kitchen and into the sunlight beyond. "I don't like to encourage her to drink.

Someone is sure to 'take advantage' of her one day, if you know what I mean."

"Maybe," Bob said, wondering if he stood any chance of being at the front of the queue. "I'm sure Kate can arrange for a glass of orange juice for Louise."

"Of course." Kate smiled back at him, eyes fierce with anger. "I can't think of a better way to spend the afternoon."

The garden could have been described as a typical Mediterranean courtyard had it not been for the asbestos. The garden was bounded on three sides by the walls of the Poussin and Gautier properties. The fourth side was made up of a low wall, caked in white *crepi* beyond which Gautier's vines sloped down to the valley of the Yon below. Propped against the wall from the other side, and just peeking out above it was a huge sheet of asbestos which formed the improvised lid of the Poussin's *fosse*—a septic tank of such size and grandeur that it wouldn't have looked out of place in a mausoleum. Bob had never been entirely sure which was the more toxic; the asbestos or the rancid mix of chemicals beneath. He was always overcome by clarity on the issue when he got downwind of Madame Poussin. Bob suspected that her diet consisted of rather a lot of home-grown haricot-vert.

"Make yourselves comfortable," he said and gestured to the raised decking area that it had half-killed him to build one summer vacation.

"This is all very nice," Charles said, sitting at one of the pale blue garden chairs. Kate had tried several times to arrange the area with a nautical theme but had never been quite satisfied with any of the designs. Bob had spent more than one sunny afternoon shuffling the surrounding shrubs around to complement the changing furniture plan. Comments about deckchairs and the Titanic had been received with less grace than humour.

"We're lucky really. It gets the sun for most of the day, and pretty well all year round." This was mostly true. Although if you got the chair that lay in the shadow of the Poussin's septic tank—and Bob was almost always volunteered for the job—then there was no need to worry about wearing sun-cream. There were some places that the sun was never going to shine.

"Oh, it's lovely," Louise gushed. "Look! You can see right down to the river. This is a much better view than we get from the cottage."

"Perhaps. But we do have a larger garden. Much more room for Marc to play in."

"How is Marc?" Bob asked.

"He's alright. I know he comes across as the '*enfant terrible*' but he's got a heart of gold really."

"Just like my Kate, then." Bob timed the comment to coincide with his wife's arrival with their drinks. Fence-mending in earnest would have to wait until after the Hambleton's had left but, like the *vide greniers*, it was never too early to start.

"And as solid as your silver tongue, my sweet."

Bob could tell that he really was in trouble.

"Of course, it doesn't help that Jasmine spoils him. The money that she spends on that kid! I've always taught Louise to hope for the best and expect the worse. It makes her appreciate the things that she gets."

"Don't be silly Daddy. You've always given me everything I wanted." Louise giggled—a soft, light laugh that seemed to ripple the hot summer air into a gentle breeze. "But you're right. I have appreciated it all."

"Well, I'm very proud of you. You've become a kind and generous young woman."

Bob uncorked the wine, noticing that Kate had chosen a bottle of the chateau's finest reserve collection—which she knew he had put by to enjoy on his birthday. He glared at her.

"I find that so refreshing," Kate said. "Bob and I always like to share the best we have. It helps to spread the happiness in the world." She fluttered her eyelashes at him. "Do pour the wine, darling."

"With pleasure," he returned her fake simper with a false smile. This was war!

"You've got so many butterflies here," said Louise. "I expect it's because you've got such lovely flowers."

"Yes, I've tried to make the garden as natural as possible," Kate replied. "I love the colour in the summer and the renewal in the spring."

"And I enjoy the work it creates all year round."

"Don't be so unfair, Bob. We share the work."

"Yes, but I like to see the pleasure that it gives you."

"Daddy was like that with mum. Weren't you? He always took such great care of her."

"Now, Louise. We try not to talk about your mother."

"I know. But I think we should. After all she was such a big part of both our lives."

There was a long pause, during which everyone seemed to become engrossed by whatever was in their glass.

"It was such a long illness," Charles said eventually. "In the end she died of acute liver failure."

"What caused it?" Kate asked. Bob flashed her a warning look. He sensed that this would all end in tears. Probably literally.

"Some sort of toxin got into her system. It weakened her whole body. It was just as if she was wasting away. Poor mum suffered for weeks before she went." Louise pulled a handkerchief from the sleeve of her blouse. Bob wanted to put his arms round her.

"But how did the toxin get into her body?" Now he wanted to put his hands around Kate's throat. What an insensitive question.

"'Something she ate'." Charles tore huge apostrophes into the humid air. "We had lunch at a Chinese restaurant near the Maison Blanche and I swear they used some illegal ingredient in it. I had hallucinations and dizzy spells for weeks afterwards. Of course we could never 'pin' anything onto them." The tears in Charles' eyes sparkled in the sunlight. "I still feel guilty because there were some days when Margaret was in so much pain that I just wanted her to give in there and then."

"I'm so sorry for you both," Bob said. "But it must have brought the two of you closer together."

"Oh yes." Charles took a long draught of wine. "We're a 'regular couple' now, aren't we girl?"

"Yes, daddy."

Charles pulled a large white handkerchief out of his pocket and wiped his eyes.

"I'm sorry."

"Please, don't be." Kate appeared to be genuinely touched by the situation.

"Don't cry, daddy. Cheer us up with one of those jokes you used to tell."

"I'm sure Professor Hunt doesn't want to hear some corny old jokes from the past."

"Professor Hunt has quite a few of his own," Kate threw in, Bob thought, unnecessarily.

"Then do a Frank Spencer. That always used to cheer me up. You used to do that catchphrase—what was it?"

"Oh the 'Betty' thing. Yes, I remember."

Louise turned to Bob. Her cheeks had flushed a little in the warmth, making her even more radiant than before.

"Daddy's always been such a good . . ."

Smash!

"Oh Louise! Look what you've done now!" Charles jumped up. There was glass and wine across the table. "You can be so clumsy sometimes." He started dabbing at his trousers with the handkerchief.

"Don't worry," Kate got up from the table and headed for the kitchen. "I'll get a cloth."

"I'm ever so sorry." Louise looked devastated. "I didn't realise I'd touched the glass."

"In this heat, it'll dry in no time," Bob said. "The main thing is to make sure that you haven't cut yourself."

"Oh, that's right! Let me look, daddy. It's so easy to get little splinters of glass onto your skin without ever noticing."

Louise checked her father's hands and arms carefully before pronouncing it safe for him to sit down again. Bob reflected on the odd role reversal that their circumstances had created—it was almost as if the daughter had become the mother. He also noticed a determined and focused look in her eyes, which reminded him of Maureen.

Despite her angelic appearance Bob suspected that Louise could be quite stubborn when she needed to be. It seemed to be a Hambleton characteristic.

"There we are." Kate had mopped the table with her usual domestic efficiency and was about to pour Charles a new glass of wine.

"No, no. It's very kind of you, but we really should get going. Since James died I've been looking after the firm pretty well single-handed. Jasmine seems to have given up, not that I can blame her, and Rose has never really 'pulled her weight'." The fingers tweaked the air and Bob noticed that Charles still wore a ring on his wedding finger. It sparkled in the sunlight.

"I wish you wouldn't work so hard, though." Louise turned to Kate. "Do you know he spent over twelve hours solid yesterday working on the computer?"

"Don't exaggerate, darling."

"He did! I've told him that he'll have a stroke or something if he doesn't get someone in to help soon."

"Who can help me? Other than Alain I'm the only one that understands the way the business operates. It's me or the whole thing goes 'down the pan'."

"Well it was kind of you to drop in," Kate said. "We'd just decided that we were going to the beach for the afternoon, hadn't we?"

"Yes. Thank you for visiting." Bob shook hands with Charles. "Do pop around." He kissed Louise on the cheek. "Anytime you're in the area."

"Oh, I will. You've got such a super garden."

"And thank you for accepting our apology," Charles added. "I am so sorry that Alain was rude to you, but he is under so much pressure at the moment." The group had made its way along the side passage of the house.

"It sounds like you all are," Kate said. "Do take it easy."

"I'll certainly try. Goodbye." Charles pulled at the gate, which shed another wooden bar. "Or should I say 'au revoir'?" The fingers danced for a final time as Bob turned back towards Kate. She already had the car keys in her hand and the broad grin of victory on her face.

CHAPTER TWENTY-THREE

THE RIVER LAY meanders gently through the Vendée, easily distracted from its destiny with the Atlantic Ocean as it slips from *plaine* to *bocage* to *marais*. Nestled amidst one of its tighter loops is the pretty little village of St-Auguste where a small stone bridge carries traffic from one *village perdu* to another. Above the bridge, on a gentle hillock that forms the backbone of the village, is mother church—her Romanesque buttresses puffed out in pride at the wonder of creation. And sandwiched between the two is Monsieur Pasquet's establishment.

Pasquet—Bob suspected that he pre-dated Christianity and probably didn't have a first name—was a grey-haired gnome who owned the only shop in the village. Actually, the word 'shop' didn't do it justice and—in his more philosophical moments—Bob thought of it as the embodiment of the capitalist system and its ultimate triumph over all human endeavour. Pasquet advertised himself as *Coiffure-Floriste-Taxi-Ambulance-Funeraire*; all the essential services for a satisfactory existence in the Vendée outside of the *cave*. It was, as Bob had discovered, an overmodest list of Pasquet's achievements limited solely by the length of the shop frontage. Pasquet was also a driving instructor, plumber, taxidermist, printer, dry-cleaner, mason (approved by the St-Auguste district commercial association), accountant (certified), chiropodist (unlicensed), decorator and chairman of the St-Auguste district commercial association. And a purveyor of canoes.

Once a year—twice if he was really unlucky—Bob would be directed to Monsieur Pasquet's by Kate with the sole intention of raising their collective blood pressures. Or, as Kate preferred to call it, "having a pleasant couple of hours messing about on the river". At the back of Pasquet's shop was a ramshackle hut that gave way to a strip of tarmac forming a slipway down to the Lay. On the hut was a button marked 'press here for canoe rental' together with a list of tariffs for the various types of craft and voyage durations. Many fruitless hours of frustrated waiting had taught Bob that pushing the button was a waste of effort as no-one ever answered it. This was probably unsurprising. After all, Bob reasoned, Pasquet must be too busy accounting, printing, instructing, hair-cutting and decorating to worry about a couple of foreigners trying to drown themselves in the local river.

However, Pasquet had obviously also worked out—somewhere between a burial and a stuffing—that turning good money away was a cardinal sin. And, being overlooked by the church, no sin went unnoticed. So he left the door to the hut unlocked. Inside was all the equipment needed for water-borne torture. Canoes, oars, a set of pristine lifejackets and a sketch map of the River Lay showing points of interest within two hours row of St-Auguste—none of which Bob had ever succeeded in reaching. Payment was made by depositing a roughly appropriate sum of money into an honesty box which had appended to it a severe warning about paying in full for all breakages and losses, together with a few ominous words about the fiery wrath of damnation being loosed upon all those who took advantage of Pasquet's generosity.

Bob hauled a two-person canoe out of the hut and down the slipway to the point where the front end of the boat was just dipped into the river. He ran back up to the hut to grab a paddle and a waterproof plastic container, into which he stuffed his wallet and keys. Bob had devised an ingenious and fool-proof system for safely launching canoes. It involved, in lay terms, synchronized bouncing. The passengers would furious jiggle their buttocks up and down in their respective seats. Provided that sufficient weight was jiggled—and Bob's seventeen stone appeared to fit the equation nicely—the canoe would traverse down the slipway and enter the river. Upright. Usually.

"Are you ready?" he called to Kate once he had installed himself into the rear seat.

"OK!"

"On the count of three. *Un, deux,* . . ."

The boat leapt forward immediately and entered the placid river with a satisfactory 'blosh'.

"I'll row if you like," Bob said unnecessarily.

One of the features of a two person canoe is that it allows you to have one person powering the boat and one person—normally at the front and normally only semi-conscious—navigating.

"OK. We'll get there too quickly if I row as well," Kate replied. "Besides, you'll get bored navigating."

Bob rowed upstream, partly to get the difficult bit over with first, partly because it took them out of town the fastest where people might be able to comment on his lack of technique, but mainly because there was a weir immediately downstream of the Pasquet hut. He quickly developed a rhythm. Paddle-to-the-left-two-three-four, paddle-to-the-right-two-three-four. It didn't look attractive perhaps, the canoe zig-zagged across the river like a set of cartoon crocodile teeth, but it moved them forward and Bob counted that as a success.

"Why aren't we going in a straight line?" Kate complained.

"I'm tacking. It's a well-known technique in sailing to cope with the wind."

"But there isn't any wind."

"I'm sat behind you, remember. And you had bran flakes for breakfast."

This seemed to silence the criticism and Bob settled back into his rhythm.

In any other circumstances Bob would have found the setting to be idyllic. The water was calm, there were herons perched on the branches of the trees that lined the river on either side and there was a gentle breeze to take the burning edge of the heat of the warm late April sun. The problem was that they were only millimetres above the water, which meant that they were also only millimetres from being below the water. Bob had just about earned his school certificate for crossing the width of a swimming pool but had never managed the full length.

They made good progress. He had already sped past the back gardens of the houses on the outskirts of St-Auguste, where elderly gentlemen escaped from their wives through the simple expedience of a rod and line. He'd gone around the fruit farm at the neck of the river where orchards marked their progress through a regimented battalion of trees; peach, pear, apple, cherry. And then into open farmland where small pumps extracted water from the river and discharged it over fields of corn, wheat and oats. The arcs of water spurted high into the air and created tiny rainbows where the breeze snatched the spray into the glare of the sunlight.

Bob could almost sense the power in his strokes surging them through the water. It made perfect sense that Bob should be a natural oarsman given the legacy of British achievement in the sport. His rhythm developed a new pattern—"Pin-sent-Red-grave-Hunt, Pin-sent-Red-grave-Hunt". His reverie was broken by a whoosh of air as another canoe zipped past them apparently from nowhere. The oarsman—a young man with muscles where fat should be—gave Bob a curious look as he passed. It was not a look of disdain, or even of reproach or pity, but of surprise. It was a look that said; 'surely nothing—other than a duck perhaps—could travel that slowly on water'.

The passenger was a girl of about twenty, who faced backwards in the canoe apparently entranced by the Adonis with the paddle.

"You see," Kate said. "Rowing is very good exercise for you. If you did this more often then you could look like him."

"No, darling. It would take a let's-reverse-time-and—two-thirds-of-my-calorific-intake machine for me to look like him."

"But it would be good for you to lose some weight." There was a pause. "And tone up a bit." Bob was about to reply when she added "And try some hair-replacement therapy."

"It might be easier for me to try to some wife-replacement therapy," Bob muttered under his breath.

"What's that dear?"

"I just said that I wouldn't want to disgrace my wife."

"Oh, good. So we can do this more often then?"

"Possibly," Bob said non-committally whilst desperately trying to think of a way to change the subject. "Why do you suppose that Alain was so rude to me?"

"Perhaps he wasn't. You can be quite sensitive about these things."

"He told me to go away."

"Are you sure? Your French can be a bit ropey sometimes. Especially after a few glasses of wine."

"I was perfectly sober," Bob protested. "His exact words were 'Monsieur Hunt is just leaving'. In English." He stopped rowing to emphasise the point.

"It must be a difficult time for them all. A death in the family, a murder investigation, a nosey old Englishman prowling around . . ."

"But Maureen asked me to prowl around." Bob started rowing again. "She wants to find out about her husband's extra-marital activities."

"Ex-husbands," Kate corrected him. "And don't you think that's a bit strange? If you died tomorrow I wouldn't want to know all about the hundreds of women that you'd shacked up with."

"If that's the case then I'm in for one hell of a night tonight."

"In St-Sébastien?"

Bob thought about the women of St-Sébastien. Hard-working, good-natured, solid—in all senses of the word—they were, but as potential material for a night of wanton abandon they lacked . . . ? Their own teeth?

"Fair enough," he conceded and recommenced rowing.

"If you ask me Alain's just protecting his mother-in-law."

"How?"

"He's bound to have known what James got up to. He probably thinks that she found out and got someone to murder him."

"What do you mean 'got someone to murder him'?"

"You know. Took out a contract on her husband's life. Something like that."

Bob sighed. "This is the Vendée not Vegas. You've been reading too many of those American detective stories."

"They're Italian actually."

"Same principle, different accent. Anyway it's not her style. Maureen's too proud to get someone else to kill him—she'd do it herself."

"There you are then. She murdered her husband, and Alain guessed this and is trying to protect her."

"Just one problem with your theory. Why would she ask me to keep an eye on the investigation if she already knows who done it?"

"Smokescreen. And to make sure that she knows exactly how close Thierry is to uncovering her guilt."

Bob stopped rowing. What Kate said made sense he supposed, but where did the girl-with-the-legs fit into it?

"Why murder him here, when she could simply have pushed him under a Paris metro train?"

"And you say I read too many crime novels," Kate retorted.

"No, it doesn't make any sense." Bob started to row again as his thoughts marshalled themselves around a theory. "I think that Michel did it, for political reasons. After all, he has access to the company records and to the vehicles . . ."

"As did Charles—and he might have had a more powerful financial motive."

"He's too much of a wimp," Bob dismissed the suggestion. "But you're right about the money—he gains control of the firm. But Jasmine makes the biggest gain from the will—she's set up for life now—together with her precious Marc."

"Which brings us back to Alain," Kate concluded. "I can't help thinking that he's the key to it."

"Either he knows something about what his mother has done and he's covering for her, or he did it himself," Bob mused. "The only trouble is that I've burnt all my bridges with him, so we may never know."

"Can we turn round now?" Kate asked. "All this talk of murder is making me hungry."

Turning a canoe around in the middle of an empty river sounds like a fairly simple exercise. To Bob, however, it generally involved a three-point-manoeuvre which had to be executed with military precision. First, he paddled furiously on the left side against the current which forced the boat to bank itself into the hedgerow on one side of the river.

"We've hit the bank, you idiot," came Kate's customary supportive comment.

Then Bob rowed forward in huge strokes taking them straight into the hedgerow on the other side of the river.

A "Stop-stop-stop" from Kate indicated that Bob should launch into the final—and most dangerous—element of the operation, which involved stretching out of the canoe and prodding the oar against the bank until the boat swang back into the current of the river, floating in more-or-less the right direction downstream.

Timing is everything in rowing. And so it was with the final push away from the bank. As Bob reached out to farthest extent of his arm's reach and swung the canoe into the middle of the river the Adonis-powered boat raced into their path, scouring a tsunami-like wave in its wake. Bob reacted first by re-aligning his weight from one side of the canoe to the other splashing his arms into the water as the boat tilted over. Kate tried to counterbalance this by jerking upwards into an almost standing position. Bob lurched the other way—counterbalancing her counterbalance—with the inevitable consequence.

Splosh-glob-glob!

The sensation of turning through three-hundred-and-sixty degrees, one-hundred-and eighty of which were sub-aquatic, was one that Bob was unlikely to forget. He felt the slime of a thousand years collective plankton ooze its way into every orifice of his body. He experienced the terror of anticipated drowning and the extraordinary relief of being delivered into the air again, intact. And finally, he felt the complete and utter humiliation of the amateur oarsman who failed to make it for an hour on the river without capsizing his boat, his wife and his pride.

When Bob finally retrieved his sense of direction—including the all-important distinction between air and water—he could see that Kate was going to be alright. She was being helped into the other canoe by Adonis himself who was swimming in the river, towing his boat gently downstream with a broad grin on his face. And Kate was laughing.

"Idiot! *Etes-vous-fou?*" Bob screamed and shook his fist at Adonis, who simply waved back.

"It's OK Bob. I'll be fine," called Kate.

"But he cut us up," Bob yelled, allowing river-rage to get the better of him.

"What?" Kate shouted. "I can't hear you. I'll see you back at Pasquet's." She turned back to the Adonis leaving Bob in no doubt about the young man's various powers of pulling.

By the time he reached the hut Bob's anger had abated somewhat. He felt more embarrassed than embittered. Amongst the welcoming party was Pasquet himself. The old man was passing glasses of wine to Kate, her rescuer and his passenger.

"So, you brought her back in one piece?" Bob could only attempt a rough translation of Pasquet's thick dialect which he supposed might be more Latin than French.

"Well, she is quiet a good swimmer and the kind *jeune homme* did the rest."

"Not the woman. The canoe!"

"Oh, I see. Yes." As if to prove the point Bob tugged the boat out of the water, retrieved his valuables from the casket and pulled the canoe up the slipway.

"It's very wet," Pasquet said suspiciously.

"That is one of the pre-requisites of being in a boat." Bob tried his best to be polite.

"You're very wet."

"I like swimming."

Pasquet turned away, clearly less than satisfied with the explanation. He swung back.

"Next time use a life jacket."

"*Bien sur, monsieur,*" Bob acquiesced as Pasquet went back to his shop, carefully reclaiming the remainder of the bottle of wine as went.

"Hi Bob, come and join us." Kate's French had suddenly developed a breathless tone, bordering on girlishness. "This is Dominic." She indicated the Adonis. "He saved me in the river. He's such a strong swimmer. He's a member of the rowing club here. We should think about joining." Her eyes danced with a light that Bob hadn't seen for years—probably since the day before they got married.

Dominic extended a hand towards Bob who shook it. Any muscular benefit gained from rowing was instantly extinguished by the vigorous joint-bursting action of Dominic's grip.

"Thank you for coming to our aid."

"*Mon plaisir.*"

Bells of recollection rang in Bob's head, but he couldn't immediately explain why.

"Do I know you?" he asked.

"Of course you do, silly," Kate intervened. "Dominic is Monsieur Poussin's grandson." Bob stared blankly at her. "The one that's getting married."

"Oh, yes. Of course. Congratulations." He pumped Dominic's hand for a second time and wished he hadn't.

"Strong isn't he?" Kate giggled. Bob ignored her and shook hands with the girl.

"So you must be Sandrine?"

"It's a pleasure to meet you, Monsieur Hunt. My uncle has told me so much about you."

Dominic's fiancée had a petite frame, pretty blue eyes and perfect English. Her immaculately clean blouse and crisp-pressed trousers were in embarrassingly stark contrast to Kate and Bob's river-stained clothes.

"Uncle?" Kate looked puzzled.

"That's right. Sandrine is Gautier's niece. We're keeping it in the *cave*, so to speak."

"We'd better speak in French," the girl returned to her native language. "Dominic doesn't know much English and he gets so jealous if he thinks I'm flirting. Don't you, sweetheart?"

She squeezed up to her fiancé and they embraced tenderly.

"I know you always give such a warm welcome to people", he replied. Sandrine giggled at him.

"I suppose we should get going, Kate," said Bob. "Get out of these wet clothes."

"Must we? I'd like to find out more about the boat club."

You'd like to find out more about Dominic, Bob thought. "But you're hungry aren't you?"

"Oh yes," she growled, glancing at Dominic. "I'm hungry alright."

They said goodbye to the couple and poured themselves into the Clio.

"They were nice," Kate said as she squeezed the remnants of the river out of her t-shirt.

"Yes," Bob replied slowly. "But I can't help thinking I've met them somewhere else before."

CHAPTER TWENTY-FOUR

BOB HAD GOT as far as writing 'King Lear is one of Shakespeare's most complex plays but its central theme is the concept of regime change.' when the phone rang. May had arrived and the paper had made no progress since the beginning of the year.

"Yes, I'm coming." Bob was working from his armchair in the lounge. "Damn!"

The lid of the lap-top snapped shut onto his thumb as he tried to jump up to answer the call. The lead to the machine was caught around his arm as he picked up the receiver so Bob had to speak into the phone with his head caught between the computer and the coffee-table.

"*Allo!*"

"Bob, is that you?" It was Thierry.

"*Oui.*"

"You still in bed?"

"*Non.*" Bob found it was virtually impossible to speak and breathe in his current position.

"What the hell's up with you? You sound as though you're stuck in a cupboard. You're not hiding under someone's bed again are you? I'm sure I can find a law against that you know."

"No-just-trapped-in-a-wire."

"I can fine you for wire-tapping. But you do realise it's supposed to be someone else's phone that you . . ."

"No. Trapped!"

147

"You're trapped? Why the hell didn't you say so?" Thierry sounded concerned—almost.

Bob pulled at the cable and succeeded in launching the lap-top into a nearby cupboard.

"Is there a fight going on there? Do you need me to send someone round? Bob?"

Finally Bob stood up and shook the receiver away from the cable.

"No, it's fine now. Just got a bit caught up in my work. Sorry, Thierry, what can I do for you?"

"Look Bob, I need you to come to the *gendarmerie*. There's been a serious development in the Hambleton case and I'd rather talk to you about it face-to-face."

"Sounds ominous," Bob said.

"It is," Thierry replied. "On the positive side, though, it looks like we've got our man. I just need to go through some of the finer details."

"I bet it's Alain, isn't it? Kate said it was Alain. Oh, do tell me it's Alain."

"Just get your arse over here right now," Thierry said as he put the phone down.

As Bob drove to the gendarmerie he became increasingly excited at the prospect of unmasking the killer. Certain that it was Alain he began to speculate on what piece of evidence had given him away. Perhaps it was a rogue fingerprint left on the secateurs or a hair found on the dead body? Or maybe he had simply confessed everything. Sometimes people just crumbled under the pressure of having to keep a dark secret.

When he arrived at the police headquarters excitement gave way to puzzlement. Thierry was standing at the entrance to the station flanked by two burly police cadets, who would have looked more at home on the playing fields of Parc du Prince, and a thin man in a grey suit. It wasn't until he got out of the Clio and ascended the steps of the *gendarmerie* that Bob noticed Thierry was holding a pair of handcuffs. Suddenly he had a bad feeling about the situation.

"Thanks for coming, Bob. It makes my job a lot easier. I didn't think you'd fancy a couple of vanloads of armed police turning up outside your house. St-Sébastien would never have recovered from the shock." Thierry turned to the man in the suit. "This is my cousin, Gaston."

"Pleased to meet you, Mr Hunt."

Bob found himself shaking hands with the investigating judge, partly out of habit but mostly due to shock.

Thierry shook open the handcuffs and then closed them back again. "I don't think we'll need these, will we?"

"But . . ." The pit of Bob's stomach was churning. He thought he was going to be sick. Thierry said he'd found the murderer. Surely he hadn't meant Bob? "Is this some sort of joke?"

"Have you ever known me to joke?"

"You think I killed James Hambleton?"

"We know you did." Gaston's clipped accent was a marked contrast to his cousin's guttural drawl.

"How . . . ?" In his professional capacity Bob had made a living out of words. Now, at the most critical situation in his life, they failed him.

"Come inside, and we'll explain." Gaston placed an arm around the Englishman's shoulder and escorted him into the gendarmerie.

Bob was taken into one of the interrogation rooms, a sparse and dimly lit space that smelt of raw tobacco and stale urine. He was told to sit on a small plastic bucket seat on one side of a small wooden table, whilst Thierry and Gaston took their positions on the other side. The young cadet smirked at Bob as he passed a thick file of papers to the captain. Thierry slapped them onto the table with a heavy sigh and rubbed at his moustache. There was a knock at the door and a message was whispered into Thierry's ear.

"Yes, yes, send him in straight away." The gendarme flapped a hand towards the door and the cadet scurried out of the room. He flicked a switch on a tape recorder that emitted a faint whirring noise as the spools turned.

"This interview, which is between myself Thierry Fauconnier, the investigating judge Gaston Homeaux, and," he flicked open the file of papers. "Robert Hunt, principal suspect in the murder of James Hambleton. Mr Hunt has been formally detained under *garde á vue* "

"But I didn't . . ."

"I'd save that for the courtroom, Bob." Gaston flashed an insincere smile. "I've made a career out of proving that people who 'didn't' did. By the way I've taken the liberty of appointing a support—advocate on your behalf. He should be here any moment."

On cue the door opened and a familiar gnarled figure entered the room.

"Monsieur Pasquet!" Bob's jaw dropped open.

"Indeed," Gaston continued. "Thanks for coming in at such short notice Phillipe. There's a chair over in the corner, help yourself."

"I presume it's the usual rate?"

"Yes, of course."

"Only I had to cancel a driving test for someone in order to come over here. The poor lad'll have to wait another three months before I get another chance to examine him. Still, I don't expect it'll stop him using his car." Pasquet looked towards Thierry. "Unless you catch him, of course." The old man emitted a cackle that Bob barely recognised as laughter.

"But Pasquet's not a lawyer, how can he act as my . . . ?"

"Young man." The gnome wagged a bony finger at Bob. "I'll have you know that I am a fully-qualified support-advocate licenced . . ."

". . . by the St-Auguste district commercial association." Bob finished the sentence for him.

"*Precisement.*" Pasquet nodded his head in satisfaction at the recognition of his credentials.

"Gentlemen, can we get on with this?" Thierry interrupted their discussion. "I've lost enough drinking time over this case already without you two squabbling away."

"But Thierry, you know that I'm innocent. I could no more kill a man than . . ."

"Non, non, non!" It was Pasquet that interrupted Bob, his finger wagging at him in annoyance. "First, you should address any comments you may wish to make about the evidence presented through me. Together we'll determine whether it should be challenged before disputing it formally with the authorities. Second, you should address Fauconnier as Capitaine and not stoop to the level of calling him by his first name. It simply isn't appropriate, is it Thierry?"

The capitaine waved a deferential had towards the advocate.

"And finally, young man, I would counsel caution. I have seen Fauconnier in action before—more times than I care to remember—and he always gets his man. Trust me, Monsieur Hunt, the simple fact of your being here confirms your guilt. My advice is to say nothing."

"Say nothing? What kind of advice is that? I did not kill James Hambleton so there's no way that he can prove I did."

"The advocate's code of conduct requires me to give you the best advice I can, and I am simply discharging my duty to you. God preserve your soul."

"But he doesn't have any evidence . . ." Bob protested.

Thierry exploded.

"You want evidence? I've got a whole file full of bloody proof here." He waved the papers at Bob. He pulled them out one at a time to underline his point. "One—you have a key to the cottage where the murder was committed. Two—you owned the murder weapon and your finger prints were found all over it. Three—you lied about James Hambleton phoning you from New York."

Pasquet tutted and shook his head at this revelation.

"Four—you were the first person to find the corpse. Five—you struck up a relationship with me in order to subvert the course of justice."

The support-advocate sucked the air noisily and tutted again.

"Six—you have been pestering the victim's family to find out the petty details of their lives so that you could incriminate them to secure your own freedom."

"But you asked me to . . ."

"Monsieur Hunt, I beg you to consider silence as your greatest friend at this time," Pasquet entreated. "And to pray to the good Lord for forgiveness of your sins."

"Seven—and my most recent discovery, which I think will ensure your incarceration for life—the New York police have confirmed to me today that the post office box address to which the murder weapon was to be sent is registered in the name of Mr Robert Hunt with a forwarding address in St-Sébastien des Vignes." Thierry slapped the final sheet of paper on the table.

"I told you—he always gets his man," Pasquet concluded. "You've got to admit that he's very thorough."

"It's nonsense," Bob argued. "I've never owned a post office box in my life. I've never even been to New York. Why would I send a pair of secateurs to America, for God's sake?"

"Take not the Lord's name in vain, young man, lest he strike you down in anger." Pasquet's advice was becoming more apocalyptic by the minute.

"It's a fair question. And one I asked myself," Gaston interjected. "The way I see it is like this. Your plan was to murder James Hambleton in France and then transport the body to New York. Perhaps you would use some kind of meat storage facility or perhaps you would dissect the cadaver into tiny slivers which could be sent individually to your post office box." The judge's pale blue eyes twinkled at the prospect. "Naturally, you couldn't afford to risk travelling with the murder weapon and so you sent the secateurs to the United States where you would reunite them with the corpse." Gaston beamed at Bob. "Clearly, the date of the murder would place you in France and the crime in New York giving yourself a perfect alibi."

"But I already have a perfect alibi. Him!" Bob pointed at Thierry, who looked down at the desk and scratched disinterestedly at his scalp. "I couldn't have committed the murder because I was at the *cave* with *monsieur le capitaine*."

"Ah! That was a nice touch I must admit." Gaston folded his hands on the table. "A spot of luck on your part and you exploited it beautifully. The trouble is that my over-trusting cousin here," he bobbed his head towards Thierry. "Relied on a projected time of murder determined by the labs in Paris." Pasquet saved the capitaine the need to spit. "On this occasion our 'colleagues' were too busy to do the work themselves and 'outsourced' the work." Gaston used an inflexion in his voice which would have given Charles' apostrophes a run for their money. "To Russia, in fact. It means that all the times in their report were based on Moscow Time. This is, of course, three hours ahead of Central European Time. A small fact that my cousin failed to observe."

Thierry coughed and glared at Gaston. "So you conned me into thinking that the murder was being committed whilst we were drinking in the *cave* together. It had really all happened three hours earlier, giving you more than enough time to commit the murder and be sitting with a glass of rosé as cool as you like."

"Ha, very enterprising," grunted Pasquet with a flicker of admiration.

"This is ridiculous. Even if I had done all of this elaborate nonsense . . ."

"Through me, it's safer," Pasquet advised. Bob ignored him and continued to speak directly to the judge.

"Why on earth would I bother? I mean I don't have slightest reason for wanting to kill James Hambleton. In fact, he was my principal source of income so I had a vested interest in keeping him alive. Where's my motive?"

"The Lord moves in mysterious ways," Pasquet quoted. "Lack of motive is not evidence of innocence, young man."

"Eight—your most recent bank statement." Thierry carefully laid out a photocopy of the movements on the Hunt's account for Bob to read. The gendarme picked up a loose paperclip from the file and began using it to conduct an impromptu manicure. He didn't look at Bob as he delivered the final indictment. "Madame Borneau and I are very good friends, going back many years. We have an understanding, if you know what I mean. She tells me that your financial position has been difficult lately. So when a sum of ten thousand euros was deposited into your account three days ago she took the—er—liberty of informing me. As I said we have an understanding. You'll see it there, between the cheque for having your septic tank cleaned out and the withdrawal of ten euros you made at Champ-St-Pere yesterday." Thierry used the paperclip to indicate a point on the statement before returning it to his index finger.

Pasquet whistled between his teeth. "Is that what the bank charges you for the account? I can negotiate a better deal for you than that."

"But I haven't got ten thousand euros. At the last count I didn't have one thousand."

"You have now," Thierry said. "And it's all quite legitimate. Under the terms of James Hambleton's will there is a small bequeath of ten thousand to you and your wife for kind services rendered."

"Very generous," Pasquet commented.

"I didn't know anything about that," Bob protested. "Surely you don't think I would murder someone for ten thousand euros?"

Gaston sniffed. "It is my view, as presiding judge in this investigation, that in view of your current financial position and its general direction I believe that you could very easily have killed someone for less."

"I knew you were a distrustful fellow, as soon as I met you," Pasquet spat. "And when I saw you with Dominic and his young lady the other day I said to myself . . ."

"Dominic!" Bob practically jumped out of his chair.

"What?" Thierry stopped picking at his nails and regarded Bob suspiciously.

"I've just remembered. I knew that I'd come across him before we met at the river but I couldn't work out when. Now I know why. I've never seen him before but I have heard his voice. Dominic is the man with the girl with the legs. He's the man who used the cottage for sex when I was under the bed."

"Young man!" Pasquet was apoplectic.

"Not that old story again, Bob, please." Thierry had folded one of the documents from the file into a small paper dart and was using it to comb his moustache.

"No, I mean it. You should bring them both in to explain why they were at the cottage that night. I bet they committed the murder, or at least saw who did."

"Spare us the lies, Mr Hunt." Gaston pursed his lips. "Do the honourable thing that you English are supposed to be renowned for. Admit the whole affair and I'll do my best to ensure that you get a speedy trial and a humane sentence."

Bob felt drained. On the face of it he did look guilty. He could understand why a court would convict someone in his position. Based on the evidence he probably would have.

"I don't know what I can say to convince you . . ."

There was a sharp knock at the door and the cadet entered the room. He scowled at Bob.

"What now?" Thierry's voice was full of irritation.

"I'm sorry to interrupt, Capitaine, but there's a woman called Jasmine Deneuve on the phone demanding to speak to you."

"She can demand all she likes. Tell her to piss off."

"But she says it's about the Hambleton murder. Apparently she's fairly sure her husband is the killer."

"I told you," Bob jumped up. "It was Alain the whole time."

"There's something else," the cadet added quickly. "She says her husband has committed suicide."

CHAPTER TWENTY-FIVE

I T TOOK BOB three hours to persuade Thierry to release him from the *garde á vue*. The clinching argument was the time of Alain's suicide; about half an hour before the phone call inviting Bob to the gendarmerie. Gaston had to admit that even the most evil and cunning of Englishmen couldn't possibly have travelled that far that fast without a runway a bit longer than the Hunt's courtyard garden. It was Pasquet who took the most convincing. He prompted Thierry three times to double-check the time zone so that there could be no room for errors, especially as the suicide took place in Paris. Alain had jumped out in front of a train timetabled to pass through a suburban railway station at twelve-fifteen. According to the signalling records it had been thirty seconds early.

"Where the hell have you been?" Kate demanded as Bob trudged into the kitchen. "I've been worried sick about you. No-one seemed to know where you were. I've walked the whole length of St-Sébastien searching for you. I've been into every *cave* in the village to see if you were holed up somewhere.

"I'm sorry, Bob said wearily.

"It's typical of your bloody selfishness. Disappear off for six hours without leaving a note or a message or anything that might give me a clue to where you were. Leaving me cooped up here on my own. What did you expect me to do for six hours? Clean the house?" She flung her hands into the air to emphasize how small the building was. "Twice?"

"It couldn't be helped, darling. It's been a difficult afternoon."

"I even phoned the gendarmerie to see if Thierry knew where you were, but they said he was busy interviewing a suspect and couldn't be interrupted."

"I know." Bob collapsed into an armchair in the lounge and stared into the vacant fireplace. "It was me."

"What?"

"I'm his principal suspect. I was under arrest."

"You?" Kate's hand shot up to her mouth. "Oh Bob, what have you done?"

"I haven't done anything. For reasons best known to themselves Thierry and his cousin had created this fantasy about how I'd killed James Hambleton and planned to post the body to New York."

"You hadn't, had you?" Kate seemed more curious than outraged.

"Of course I damn well hadn't!"

"No, no, I didn't mean that. I just meant . . ." She paused and then dropped to her knees beside Bob and lifted his hand. "I just meant that I'm so glad you're home. I've been so worried." She kissed his cheek, and started to cry. "Why did they let you go?"

"Because I'm not guilty?"

"I suppose that is a good reason. Of course they should never have thought it was you in the first place. I'll give that Thierry a good piece of my mind when I see him again."

"Kate, darling, don't make things worse. He was only doing his job."

"He should do it better then, instead of making stupid mistakes." She stood up and moved towards the kitchen. "I'll get you a nice strong drink and you can tell me all about it." At the door she stopped and turned back to Bob. "Can we sue him for wrongful arrest?"

Bob recounted his experiences at the gendarmerie to Kate who was, by turns, surprised, angry, disbelieving and, finally, horrified.

"Alain killed himself?"

"Apparently. He threw himself under a train from a platform. The driver's having counselling, but it seems to be a fairly regular occurrence on that line."

"But why?" Bob realised that Kate had drunk more than him. She was suffering more from his experiences than he had. They were sharing a bottle of white from the chateau, one of the expensive chardonnays. The sharp, fresh taste had sobered Bob up and made him realise how close he'd come to spending the night in a cell.

"Jasmine thinks that it's because he murdered her father and was wracked with guilt. He'd been behaving strangely lately and wouldn't explain why to her."

"He had a go at you, didn't he? I told you he was the murderer." Kate peered into her empty glass and, after a brief internal debate, decided to have another. "It's a terrible shame for the little lad, er . . ."

"Marc," Bob prompted. "I suppose so. Although it'll probably just give Jasmine another reason to spoil him."

"But surely," Kate had started to slur. "Surely, she was with him when James was killed. I thought she was his alibi."

"Yes, but apparently she'd lied. They had a terrible row that morning and he drove off in a temper. He didn't return home until the next day and, when the murder was discovered, she feared the worse. So she said they were together to cover for him."

"Wasn't she afraid that Marc would give the game away?"

"I don't suppose she thought that far ahead. In any case she spent most of the afternoon and evening looking for Alain, so she shipped the boy off to a babysitter until the next day. Thierry was so anxious to tie everything down he even phoned the babysitter to confirm this."

"Did he apologise to you?"

"Do you think Thierry does 'sorry'?"

"OK. Fair point," Kate conceded.

"There was one thing he did say that he regretted."

"What was that?"

Bob thought carefully about how to phrase the next sentence. Although it didn't matter to him who knew about their financial position he realised that Kate would be mortified that Thierry had seen their bank statements.

"Well, I suppose it's good news really."

"Which means that I'm not going to like it 'really'." She emphasised the final word sarcastically.

"What I meant to say was that we're suddenly richer. Ten thousand euros richer."

"How?"

"James left us ten thousand euros in his will. The lawyers paid the money into our account last week. Isn't that great news?" Kate's face was still on the suspicious side of happy.

"And how does a visit to the gendarmerie tell you this? Or do they have a cash-point machine in there so that you can draw the money to pay a fine on the spot?"

Bob thought that this wasn't such a bad idea. It would save a lot of court time and public cost.

"Actually, he'd been in touch with Madame Borneau."

"What?"

"Thierry has an arrangement with Madame Borneau that allows him to see peoples' bank accounts."

"That's outrageous!" Kate's reaction was pretty much as Bob had feared. "Surely he can't do that? Do we live in a police state or something? Can't we complain to the banking ombudsman?"

"Calm down, darling. He was only doing his job."

"OK, but she wasn't doing hers. She's supposed to keep our records confidential. Now I expect everyone in the Vendée knows we're up a financial creek."

"No, no, just Thierry. And Gaston. And the cadet, I imagine." Bob paused. This was getting worse. "And Monsieur Pasquet."

"Pasquet?"

"Yes. Apparently he's a support-advocate." Kate's face furled into incomprehension. Bob decided to change the focus. "Anyway, aren't you pleased about the money?"

Kate pouted. "I suppose so. I just wished we hadn't had to go through all of this to find out. Didn't the solicitors write to us to let us know?"

Bob felt his face flush. "Yes, they did. But I haven't been opening any post lately that looks official just in case they wanted money from us. Our tax is overdue and I've been dreading the letter offering us 'financial counselling'." Bob smiled at Kate. "Well now we can afford to pay it."

"Hey, I've just thought," Kate seemed to have suddenly brightened. "We can get some new gates now."

"Well . . ." Bob hadn't planned to waste the windfall in quite this way. "Perhaps we should hold onto it for now. Ten thousand won't go very far with inflation the way it is. We should put it aside for essentials. It'll keep us going for a few more months without needing to rob a bank."

"Or murder anyone," Kate added ruefully. "Anyway, I'm glad it wasn't you."

"So am I. Pasquet was ready to string me up on the spot."

"I imagine he's the official hangman, licensed by . . ."

". . . the St-Auguste district commercial association." They said the words together.

Kate drained the last of her wine and shook the empty bottle over her glass as if it might be possible to squeeze another mouthful. She was out of luck.

"Anyway," she said belligerently. "I spent over two hours looking for you this afternoon. Do you know how many *caves* there are in St-Sébastien?"

Bob thought he probably did but Kate answered her own question. "Eighteen. And that's without going beyond the *bourg* into Le Gounnier and beyond. Eighteen! And not one of them offered me a drink."

"It's because you're a woman, I'm afraid. The *cave* is the domain of the man and the *cuisine* is the domain of the woman. I'm sure they'd have given you a cup of sugar if you'd asked."

"Bloody chauvinists," Kate grumbled.

"*Bien sur*. The word derives from one of Napoleon's admirers."

"That figures," Kate said. "That man's got a lot to answer for."

"Anyway, I'm exhausted. I could do with an early night. Time for bed."

"Said Zebedee." Kate sprang up from her chair and tugged Bob by the hand, escorting him up the spiral staircase to the bedroom above.

Bob, meanwhile, made a mental note to find out where the other three *caves* were in St-Sébastien.

CHAPTER TWENTY-SIX

THERE WAS STILL one loose end that Bob wanted to tidy up from his interview at the gendarmerie. In the midst of his questioning and the subsequent news of Alain's suicide Bob had almost forgotten his recollection about Dominic. In his mind there was no doubt. Dominic had been in the cottage with a woman, presumably his fiancée Sandrine, but how did they get the keys. He still couldn't get those legs—their perfect line and length—out of his head. So he started to make some enquiries.

From Poussin he learned that Dominic had never had any other girlfriend than '*la belle* Sandrine'—and why would he, after all she was '*delicieux*'.

"He's a good lad—and a lucky one," Poussin had concluded. "Even though he does work for that damn Rogier on a casual basis during the harvest."

Gautier was no help in Bob's attempt to discover more about Sandrine.

"She's pretty I suppose," he had offered. "But she's a quiet one. *Profond*."

There was, Bob decided, only one way that he was going to solve the mystery. He needed to see Sandrine's legs. At the riverside she had been wearing trousers, which had given nothing away. But you couldn't just go up to someone and demand them to see their legs—at least not in the circles that Bob was used to. He needed to find a way of seeing them without arousing suspicion.

"I need to go shopping," Kate demanded. It was a clear May morning with a gentle breeze that sent the tall grasses swaying in the courtyard garden. Temperatures were rising and all the talk in the village was of a hot summer and a bumper harvest. Normally Bob would have argued that it was a perfect day for a barbeque in the garden but on this occasion he simply said "Why don't we go to Talmont for a change?" He remembered that Sandrine worked in the travel agent in the town so perhaps he could do a bit of leg-spotting.

Kate was visibly stunned.

"Are you feeling alright?"

"Yes, fine."

Surprise turned to suspicion.

"Why do you want to go to Talmont? Is there some sort of wine festival going on there?"

"No. I just thought that it would be nice to go there for a change. I can't remember the last time we went out that way."

"And I can't remember the last time that you agreed to go shopping without raising three kinds of hell," Kate said uncharitably, and went upstairs to get ready.

Talmont-Saint-Hilaire is a small market town that is loved and loathed by tourists in equal measure. Loved for its imposing, if ruined, medieval castle which was the alleged home of the infamous Bluebeard and a favourite haunt of Richard the Lionheart. Loved for its chic port at Bourgenay and the pine-clad cliffs that overlook the sweeping Atlantic coastline. Loved for its bustling town centre with a cinema, souvenir shop and no less than three *boulangeries*. But loathed for its traffic congestion. In the height of summer it could take Bob over an hour to crawl through the two kilometres of town. As a consequence it wasn't a place he would visit without good cause. On this occasion he felt that 'those legs' gave him cause enough. He parked the Clio at the foot of the castle mound, which was thronging with early summer tourists.

"Tell you what," he said to Kate as casually as he dared. "Why don't I go and see if there's anything interesting on offer at the travel agents?"

"What for?"

"A holiday of course."

"But you never want to go on holiday. You said that when we moved to France life would be one long holiday."

"Well, there's no harm in looking is there?"

"Besides," Kate dropped her voice to a whisper. "We can't afford to go on holiday, remember."

"We just received ten thousand euros, remember," Bob whispered back. "See you back here in . . ." He looked at his watch. "Half an hour?"

Kate's glare suggested that this wasn't long enough.

"All right then, an hour." The glare continued. "And a half?"

"Back here," Kate said and hurried off towards the main street.

It took Bob ten minutes to find the travel agents. Unlike England, where travel and holidays have become a high street, high income, high profile business French travel agencies are modest, discreet affairs as if the whole notion of 'going somewhere else' was an illicit activity involving unnecessary greed and lust.

A bell tinkled as he went through the door, which was obscured by advertisements for alcohol to deflect attention away from its more deviant purpose. The agency consisted of an office with two desks, one ancient computer monitor and enough glossy brochures to reforest half of the Amazon basin. There wasn't a soul to be seen.

Bob wondered what it would take for someone to notice him. He went back to the door and opened and closed it quickly causing the bell to tinkle again. No-one came. He called out "Hallo" up a set of stairs that ran up one side of the agency, but still no-one came. He sat on a chair at one of the desks and started typing furiously on the computer keyboard, probably creating havoc on the international money markets as a result. No-one came.

He had just started drumming out the rhythm to the can-can using two rolled up brochures on the back of the chair when an elderly man appeared. His reproving stare suggested that Bob hadn't made a gracious first impression.

"Monsieur, how can I help you?"

"Well, I was actually looking for a girl."

The man's eyebrows shot up.

"I mean a holiday. Well, a girl to help me find a holiday."

"I think you must be mistaken, monsieur. Perhaps you have mistranslated somewhere. This is a travel agency, not a . . ." He sniffed reproachfully. "Not a dating agency."

"Do you know where.?" Bob was going to ask if the agent knew how he could find Sandrine.

"I don't believe that such a place exists in Talmont-St-Hilaire." The man sniffed again, more disdainfully. "Of course, it's not the sort of thing I would know about."

"No, no. *Excusez-moi.* I'm looking for Mademoiselle Sandrine. I believe that she works here."

"Oh her." There was a double sniff this time. "I think that you'll find that she's no longer on the market."

"She doesn't work here any more?"

"No. I mean that she is about to get married." The man looked Bob up and down before adding. "And he's a big strong lad, so I'd watch my step if I were you." He glared at Bob and sniffed for a final time before disappearing through a door at the back of the bureau.

Moments later Sandrine appeared through the same door, breathless and, to Bob's intense disappointment, shrouded in a long gypsy-style skirt that fell to her calves. Her bare ankles told Bob nothing.

"*Bonjour monsieur.* My colleague said that you were asking for me."

"Yes, we met about a week ago at the river. I'd fallen in."

"Oh, I remember." Her thin lips pouted. "Your wife seemed very interested in what Dominic does."

I bet she did, thought Bob. "Yes, he works for Monsieur Rogier doesn't he?"

"He did. I don't expect he will this year. Rogier accused him of trespassing on his land." She picked up one of the brochures and flicked through it absently. "Nonsense, of course." She looked up at

Bob, her blue eyes sharp with curiosity. "Anyway, what brings you here?"

"Well, Monsieur Gautier, your uncle, suggested that you might be able to recommend a holiday destination to me."

"*Bien sur.* What did you have in mind?"

There then followed one of the most mind-numbing half-hours that Bob could ever recall having spent alone with a single woman. Sandrine suggested every country under the sun in French alphabetical order and he, in order to keep the conversation going, methodically rejected every one of them according to a range of excuses in English alphabetical order.

"*Australie?*"

"I have an allergy to most of their insects, I'm afraid."

"*Benidorm?*"

"There are far too many Brits there."

"*Chine?*"

"Too claustrophobic, I imagine."

"*Dalmatia?*"

"Isn't that a dangerous dog?"

"*Etates Unis?*"

"Everything!"

Eventually they reached an impasse. Sandrine had built up a huge tower, nearly four foot high; from all the brochures they'd discarded. And Bob ran out of alphabet; everyone knows there aren't enough zoos in Zambia. An idea crossed his mind.

"You haven't got anything upstairs, have you?" He calculated that if he positioned himself in just the right place as she ascended he would get the perfect view of her legs. He didn't feel comfortable about doing it, but he felt even less comfortable being called a liar. This might just solve the riddle for good.

"I don't think so, but I could take a look for you."

"That's very kind of you." Bob moved himself into position as deftly as he could and smiled pleasantly at her as she climbed the staircase. Bob was just leaning his head back so that he would get the perfect view up her skirt when he was interrupted by a sniff.

"*Monsieur!*" The elderly gentleman clearly regarded Bob's viewing position as entirely inappropriate. Bob immediately pretended to have an insect in his eye and mimed temporary blindness and general panic. He'd missed his opportunity.

The sniffer sat down in front of his computer and looked at the screen. Bob muffled a snigger as the man's face froze in horror. He cleared his throat nervously as he pumped the keyboard. He coughed and then sniffed as if outraged by the computer's behaviour.

"Sandrine," he called.

"Yes, Monsieur Dinard?" she shouted down to him.

"I think we have been the victims of a cyber-attack." He gave a double-sniff and stared at Bob suspiciously. "Can you assist me please?"

"Of course." Sandrine practically ran down the stairs, denying Bob any leg-gazing opportunities on the way.

She punched a few of the keys and shook her head.

"*C'est finis!*" she concluded sadly, revealing to Bob the true meaning of the phrase 'computer terminal'.

"Can I make a suggestion?" Bob asked.

"*S'il vous plait.*" She moved away from the keyboard so that Bob could take control. He leaned over the computer and pressed the buttons marked 'Ctrl' 'Alt' and 'Delete' simultaneously. The screen cleared and launched itself into the start-up routine. There was a collective sigh of relief. And a sniff.

"Thank you, *monsieur*. I'm sorry I wasn't able to help you find a holiday."

"Never mind," Bob said. He pointed at the pile of brochures. "I'm sorry you'll have to put all those back."

"Oh, I'm used to it," Sandrine replied, and leant against the top of the pile. "It's part of working here."

Dinard sniffed again.

"I'd get something for that cold if I were you," Bob advised as he opened the door to leave.

As he turned back to close the door from outside he watched the tower of brochures collapse beneath Sandrine, sending her toppling over the top, legs sprawling in the air. They were nice legs, Bob decided, the sort that might enliven a dull day on the beach. But they weren't the legs that he was looking for. About that he was certain. Whoever had been with Dominic at the cottage on the night of the murder, it wasn't Sandrine.

CHAPTER TWENTY-SEVEN

B OB WAS RUNNING late. He'd agreed to give the cottage a thorough clean and restock the kitchen in preparation for the arrival of some of the Hambletons. It had been a fortnight since Alain's suicide and the family felt that it would do Jasmine good to get away from Paris. The advance party, Rose and Maureen, were due to arrive at any moment and Bob had hoped to be gone before they got to the cottage. He had failed.

"Hi Bob," Rose called as she entered the hallway. She was dressed in dark blue jeans and a pale green T-shirt which implored the reader to 'Make the world a better place. Shoot a banker.' She was carrying two large suitcases and started to shunt them up the staircase on their sides.

"Hello Rose. I'm nearly finished here," Bob replied. "Do you want me to take those up for you?"

She glared at him as if he'd suggested something treasonable.

"No," Bob changed tack quickly. "I'm sure you can manage those on your own. I'll go and help your mother."

Maureen was stood outside by the car and seemed smaller than Bob recalled. The late spring blossom floated on the stiff westerly breeze and despite the warmth of the sunshine she shivered in her tweed jacket. Bob shook hands with her and noticed that her face was streaked with tears. She took a large breath of air.

"It's got to stop, Bob."

"Yes, of course." He paused to think. "What has?"

"The killing." Although her face looked sad and tired, Maureen's eyes blazed with anger and energy.

"Surely they will now, what with Alain's suicide and the . . ."

"You don't believe any of that nonsense, do you?" she snapped. "I thought you were a more intelligent man than that."

"But Captain Faucconier told me . . ."

"Gendarmes! They're useless." She moved in close to him. Her breath smelt of peppermint. "That was never suicide. Alain was too much of a coward for that. He may well have killed my husband but he could never have killed himself." She took a step backwards and flung her arms out in a gesture of hopelessness. "And anyway, who leaves a suicide note in an email account?"

"But it doesn't make sense. Why would someone murder Alain rather than let the courts deal with him?"

"To keep it in the family." Maureen wiped a bead of sweat away from her forehead. "You will have noticed, Bob, that we are a very close family. This is partly because of the business and partly because we are still outsiders in a foreign country. None of us would relish the secrets of our family being dragged up in court for public entertainment. That sort of exposure could kill the business."

"Well, what makes you so sure that Alain killed your husband?" Bob asked. "I thought you were convinced that it was all connected to someone called Betty."

"Yes. I'm still sure that James was having an affair and perhaps that was the reason why Alain stabbed him. Jealousy or outrage or . . ." She swatted a fly away with her hands. "Who knows what? He was French and highly strung."

"But there must have been some evidence?"

"Oh, there was plenty of that. On his computer system. We should have thought to look there first, probably. He seemed to love that machine more than he loved Marc. The Paris police found emails from him arranging to have James' body transported to New York using the company's haulage contractors. Of course they denied any knowledge of it. There's even an email setting up a post office box in your name. After his death they checked his computer account and found everything they would have needed to prove he was the killer. I don't understand these things but apparently he hadn't even bothered to secure it with a password or code . . ."

"You mean encrypt?"

"Whatever. It's like a foreign language to me. The police were quite surprised that it was so unsophisticated given Alain's expertise."

Bob pulled the remaining pair of suitcases from the back seat of the Rover.

"So who do you think killed Alain? If it wasn't suicide, I mean."

"Of course it wasn't suicide. Anyone can push someone off a railway station platform. But I'm fairly sure it's another member of the family. That's one of the reasons why I'm so keen to get them all together now. I want whoever it is to understand that things have gone far enough."

"There can't be that many of the family who could have arranged to be at the station. You must be able to trace their whereabouts at the time."

They started walking towards the cottage, Bob sagging under the weight of the cases. Had Maureen brought the family fortune with them in case Alain's killer would accept it as payment to stop?

"Before James' death that would have been true. We had a very well-organised routine. I kept a record of everyone's diary and the whole thing operated like clockwork. But since then I'm afraid I've let things slip. People turn up for work when they feel like it. It's as if the heart has gone out of the place. Thank goodness for Charles. He's kept going like a real trooper—worked all the hours God sends."

"So, who do you suspect?"

Maureen stopped, allowing Bob to drop the cases and have a brief rest.

"I do have one theory," she dropped her voice to a whisper. "It involves Rose. I'm sure that you know she's seeing this Michel fellow, from the garage."

Bob nodded.

"A most unsavoury character," Maureen continued. "But she'll find that out soon enough. It turns out that he and Alain had disagreed about the transport schedules. Michel had complained that the vans were being worked too hard, but Alain showed him how the schedules worked. Again, it's not my sort of thing and it was quite common for there to be disputes. But this time it seemed to be more personal. Michel even came into the office in Paris to argue it out with Alain. I could hear them shouting. He told Alain to get off his . . ." She paused and blushed slightly. "Backside," she emphasized the word carefully. "And see what he was doing to the vehicles and the men that had to drive them. Then he stormed off out. But on the way I noticed he said a few words to Rose. I couldn't hear what they were but she was angry—I could tell that much. And then later on I saw her go into Alain's office for a few minutes. And later that day he's dead."

"It doesn't follow that she killed him."

"No, but I do wonder what she said to him. Not long afterwards he went home complaining of a headache."

"Have you asked Rose about it?"

"I've tried but without success. She just changes the subject when you mention Michel, as if she's never heard of him." Maureen reached out and clasped Bob's hand. "Perhaps you could ask her?" Bob started to shake his head—he'd come as close to murder investigations as he wanted. "I'd be very grateful," she pleaded.

Bob looked at Maureen in a different light now. She was manipulative, certainly, but she was also vulnerable. An elderly widow who feared that her family was in self-destruct mode. Either that or she was a good actress with a very strong motive to incriminate someone else.

"Very well," Bob said eventually. "I'll see if I can get anything out of her, but you'll need to leave us alone for a while."

"That I can manage," she said with a smile of satisfaction, and made her way into the cottage with Bob puffing along behind her.

After the obligatory cup of tea, which Bob insisted on preparing for them after their long journey, Maureen excused herself and went upstairs for a lie-down.

"When you get to my age you find that you can't manage a full day without a nap. Rose, please persuade Mr Hunt to come to our *soirée*. It's a week next Saturday—I'm sure he's available."

"Oh, so that's what it's all about," Rose murmured as Maureen disappeared up the staircase. "I knew she was up to something. She's never needed a nap in her life."

"She's certainly a formidable woman," Bob commented. "But then you're a formidable family."

"Yeah," Rose mused. "That's a funny thing about this whole business—dad and then Alain's suicide—it just seems to have brought us closer."

"So you think Alain did commit suicide?"

"I suppose so." Rose looked at him with a puzzled expression and then laughed. "I see. Mum's been stringing you that cock-and-bull story about Alain being pushed under a metro train."

"You don't believe it then?"

"No. It was suicide. Poor Alain was close to the edge. He and Jasmine hadn't been getting on recently and it must have been so hard trying to keep it secret that you'd murdered your own father-in-law." Rose pulled a cushion from the sofa, threw it on the floor and sat on it. "That's better. It's a more natural seating position for the back to rest in. Why don't you join me down here?"

Bob took another of the large down-filled cushions and squatted on it. Natural it may have been but then so was toothache and sitting on the cushion was about as uncomfortable.

"But why would Alain want to kill James?"

"That's easy," Rose said quickly. "Money. Alain liked to give the impression of being a clever computer geek with no other thought than tomorrow's scheduling but he was as mercenary as the rest of them. He wanted to make sure that Jasmine had everything she wanted. He started getting desperate when they began to argue."

"They had a row when they were here once," Bob recalled.

"Things weren't good between them. Jasmine told me all about it." Rose looked up at Bob and brushed her black fringe across her forehead. "That's what I meant when I said that these deaths have brought us closer together. Jasmine and I have talked more in the last week than in the previous ten years." She smiled at Bob. "It's how families should be."

"Maureen said that Alain was too much of a coward to kill himself."

Rose shook her head emphatically.

"No, he was a real mess. I spoke to him on the morning before he died."

"Oh yes?" It looked as though Bob's luck was in.

"He had a terrible headache—you could see the pain in his eyes. He'd been taking a pile of medicines—aspirin, paracetamol, god-knows-what. I told him to take himself home, have some camomile tea and get some sleep. He said he couldn't go because some fool had been messing around with the schedules and mixed up the computer files. I said that Michel could cope with it and he should just get to bed. That didn't go down well."

"He and Michel didn't get on, then?"

Rose grinned. "You could say that. They fought like cat and dog most of the time. Unsurprising really. The representatives of capitalism and socialism meeting at the sharp end. Industrial relations in the raw. Fascinating." She rubbed her hands together.

"And where do you fit in?"

"On the side of the workers, of course."

"I didn't quite mean that. I thought you and Michel were lovers."

Bob could see Rose's body stiffen.

"What's it to you?" She darted him a look of suspicion.

"I'm sorry," Bob backed off straight away. "I just thought that you must be in a difficult position, being a board member and having a relationship with a union negotiator."

"I balance things up," Rose said sharply and rolled herself forward into a standing position. "Now, I think I'd better unpack and you'd best be on your way Mr Hunt."

"Yes, of course." Bob rolled himself forward and collapsed in a heap on the carpet. "I'm sorry," he said as he finally stood up. "I didn't mean to pry." He opened the door to leave.

"Don't worry. I'm not offended." Rose smiled at Bob and wagged a finger at him. "And you can tell mum that I'm old enough to make mistakes for myself now. Michel is an honest hardworking bloke and I like him. I'm sure he'd do anything for me as long as he kept his principles intact. So she needn't worry on that score."

Bob watched as a momentary flicker of concern passed across Rose's face before she smiled at him again. "And I'll tell her that you and your wife will be delighted to come to dinner a week on Saturday. Seven o'clock prompt!"

CHAPTER TWENTY-EIGHT

"I'LL NEED A new dress," was Kate's immediate reaction to the invitation.

"You can't afford one," Bob retorted.

"But we can afford to go on holiday?"

"Ah, well. That's different."

"Different? Why? Does it require a special type of money? I thought that the whole idea of a single currency was that you could buy anything with it." Kate placed her hands on her hips and gave Bob one of her best uncompromising stares.

"It doesn't matter anyway. I've changed my mind about a holiday. It was a silly idea in the first place."

If Bob thought that this concession was going to win him the argument he should have known better.

"I know what it is with you." Kate pointed at him. It was early evening and the sun was descending gracefully behind the goat-house across the road. "You just don't want to go shopping."

Bob tried to deny the accusation, but failed. Lying wasn't one of his stronger points.

"As it says in the good book," Kate pressed home her advantage. "It is easier to walk a camel through the eye of a needle than to get an Englishman through the entrance of a shopping mall."

"And as I always teach my students," Bob hit back straight away. "The conjugation of the verb 'to shop' is; 'I shop, you browse, she sets up camp for a week' . . ."

"Ha, ha. Very funny." Kate moved across the lounge to Bob and kissed the top of his head. "Can I? Please?"

He frowned at her and shook his head gently. She fluttered her eyelashes at him in mock supplication.

"I promise to be out of your way for at least four hours."

Bob reflected on the complex web of paradoxes that governed human nature. He had spent two angst-ridden years and half a fortune trying to persuade Kate to be his companion for life. He had driven an extra two hours a day for an entire summer just to be with her so that they wouldn't spend longer than a day apart. And now, twenty years later, he had no hesitation in giving her money that they didn't have simply to have four hours of peace. He was reminded of another Biblical saying; as you sow, so shall you reap.

"Alright, then. I could do with some serious thinking time. The deadline for the conference paper is less than a month away and I still haven't really got a proper opening yet."

Kate jumped in the air and did a victory dance around the room. Bob watched her weave between the armchairs with a lithe action that belied her age. Four hours of peace was one thing but he knew that he could never live without her. He had sown well.

"Your budget is fifty Euros . . ."

"But I won't even get a belt for that! Do you want me to turn up at your posh friends" house just wearing a belt?"

"Could make it interesting," Bob replied and pulled her towards him suggestively.

Kate pulled back. "That'll cost you two hundred euros, Mr Hunt. Every girl has her price."

"One hundred is my best offer. I'm a bargain-hunter don't forget." He squeezed her tightly, wondering if what she had said was true. Did every girl have her price? Was James Hambleton being blackmailed by his lover?

"One-fifty and I'll throw in some singing on top."

"One-fifty for you not to sing." He tugged her onto his lap. "What was that you were saying about 'on top'?"

Kate giggled and buried her head into his chest.

The phone rang.

"Leave it," said Bob as Kate reached for the receiver.

Too late.

"*Allo!* Kate Hunt."

She listened for a few moments.

"I'll see if he's available," she said in her primmest French, and then covered the mouthpiece with her hand. "It's Thierry. I think he wants to apologise."

She passed the phone to Bob and mouthed "make him beg".

"*Bonsoir* Thierry. How can I help you?"

"You can help me by making this a short call. *Merde!*" There was a pause. "I'm sorry Bob. I was doing my job and I got it wrong." Another pause. "What do you want—fucking blood?"

"No, no," Bob said quickly. "I think I'm just shocked to hear you use the 's' word, Thierry. Shocked and grateful."

"We're OK then?"

"Of course."

"It's just that with this bloody wedding coming up I didn't want any bad feeling between us spoiling anything."

"But you're not even going to the wedding."

"No, but Gautier's doing this thing at the *salle Lamicque* on Friday night and I wanted to make sure you'd be there."

"Am I invited?" Bob asked.

"Don't you read anything?" Thierry sounded frustrated. "Gautier sent everyone a letter two weeks ago."

Kate had obviously got bored listening to one end of the conversation and started to undress.

"Well, to be fair, I haven't emptied my letterbox recently."

"Why not? What if you got a fine or a summons or something?"

Bob's mind had been summoned elsewhere as Kate paraded around the lounge in her underwear.

"I don't know." He made something up. "It's too far to walk."

"Too far? Where the hell is it? La Roche-sur-Yon?"

"No, no. It's just over the road, near the goat-house."

"And that's too far?" Thierry whistled down the phone, making Bob wince. "And I thought I was a slob. I'm impressed."

So was Bob. Kate was wagging a bare backside in the air and heading up the spiral staircase. Stairway to heaven indeed, he thought.

"Well, count me in Thierry. Everything's fine between us. We all make mistakes."

"I'm glad you said that Bob because those morons in Paris have made another one."

"Oh?"

"Alain's suicide note . . ."

"It was an email wasn't it?"

"How did you know that?"

"I still have my sources . . ."

"The Hambletons?"

"I'm glad to see your powers of deduction are as sharp as ever. Yes, of course it was the Hambletons. Who else would it be?"

"Good, because I need you to come to Paris with me tomorrow."

"Why?"

"You don't need to know that. I'll pick you up at seven in the morning."

Kate was on the landing at the top of the staircase, her legs dangling down into the lounge, blowing kisses at Bob.

"Oh, Thierry." A thought had re-entered Bob's mind.

"What? I thought I'd said sorry."

Bob waved up at Kate.

"Do you think that every woman has her price?"

CHAPTER TWENTY-NINE

T HIERRY ARRIVED ON the dot of seven the following morning, reminding Bob just how easily he had got out of the habit of rising early for work. In England he and Kate had generally been up, breakfasted and out by six-thirty. In St-Sébastien, however, seven o'clock felt like the quiet bit before the middle of the night.

The gendarme's car had raced across the Vendée countryside, streaking up the narrow departmental back-roads with an alarming disregard for bends, junctions and other potential obstructions such as red traffic lights.

"No-one takes any notice of motoring offences," Thierry explained in answer to Bob's casual question about their progress. "Anyway, who's watching us? If they can keep up with my driving then either they're a villain, in which case I'll catch them, or they're another gendarme, in which case I'll give them a warning."

"But is it safe to go this fast?" Bob asked, less casually this time.

"Pah! This isn't fast," Thierry replied. From somewhere—and Bob couldn't immediately identify where—he found a further burst of speed. The car became airborne for a moment as it jumped across a triangular junction and sheared past a tractor which was joining the road from a field. "This is fast." Thierry revved the vehicle beyond a mechanical sound into something close to an operatic high note and looked at his watch. "It'll be a close run thing, though."

"Oh, I thought we had plenty of time?"

"We do. I have a cousin who operates the TGV line at La Roche. He'll keep the train in the station until we're on it."

And he did. The second that Thierry and Bob slammed the train door shut was the moment that the express to Paris departed from La-Roche-sur-Yon.

Two minutes later Bob was installed into his reserved *duo côte a côte* first class seat on the TGV with Thierry leant up against his shoulder snoring like a *couchon*.

About forty kilometres from Paris Thierry woke up and demanded a coffee, which Bob procured from the restaurant car.

"I suppose I'd better explain what we're doing today." Thierry said grudgingly.

"It might help." Bob had feared asking the capitaine directly in case the answer involved some form of imprisonment.

"Put very simply, I'm not happy."

"What's your personality got to do with this case?"

"The English sense of humour," Thierry reprimanded Bob. "It is distinctly over-rated." He slurped into his cup. "Except for Benny Hill, of course."

"Of course," Bob demurred. "So tell me what it is that's making you unhappy on this particular occasion."

"The suicide note."

"I thought it was essential in this sort of case. A suicide without a note is like a . . ." Bob groped for a suitable metaphor. "Sentence without a verb."

"*Non, non, non.* It is more like sex without passion; feasible but unsatisfactory."

"So you should be satisfied. Alain left a suicide note on his computer, didn't he?"

"Yes, but it doesn't feel right." Thierry dipped his finger into the coffee and smoothed it across his moustache. "I can't believe that anyone of the point of taking their own life calmly sits down at a desk and types out an email."

"He was a computer boffin so surely it was entirely in character."

"No!" Thierry banged a fist on the table in front of him; the metal hinges squeaked a protest. "Suicide is an act of passion, a desperate moment. You don't sit around thinking I'll write an email and then go down to the railway station and throw myself in front of the one-fifteen, making sure I'm wearing clean underpants and all my affairs are in order." He glared at Bob. "At least not in this country."

Bob ignored the lightly-veiled insult and considered the implications.

"So you don't believe that Alain killed himself?"

"No, I don't." Thierry took another slurp of coffee.

"You believe that someone killed James and Alain and fabricated a suicide note?"

"I knew I'd make a detective out of you one day! *Mon dieu*, this coffee is disgusting." The gendarme shook his head violently and dug into the pockets of his overcoat. He turned the contents out onto the table; a handful of sweet-wrappers, a pair of tweezers and a miniature bottle of cognac. He poured half of the bottle into his cup and slurped again at the coffee.

"That would limit the suspects down to a very few people. They would need to have access to Alain's computer system and they would need to have been able to have been on the station platform to push him under the train."

Thierry nodded and slurped again. He recoiled suddenly.

"Sod this." The police captain pushed the cup away from him, slopping coffee onto the table. He unscrewed the cap on the miniature and swigged the remainder of the bottle down in one.

"It should be very easy for you to narrow it down then."

"That is where you are wrong, *mon ami*."

"Surely you just need to ask the remaining suspects to provide alibis for the time of the suicide and then check them out." Bob pulled a paper napkin from the metal dispenser beside the table and mopped up the slops from Thierry's cup.

"That's all very well in theory, but I have one practical problem to overcome."

"What's that?"

"I can't ask them anything."

Bob stared at Thierry.

"Why not?"

"Because, my little scrag-end of roast beef, as soon as the suicide took place the case passed into the hands of the bloody Parisians." The morning sunlight sparkled across the trajectory of spit as Thierry vented his disgust in the normal manner. Apart from Bob no-one else in the plush railway carriage even raised an eyebrow.

"So all you need to do is ask them to check out the alibis and solve the case."

"And give them the satisfaction of solving a double-murder!" Thierry was incandescent. "I'd rather make love to Madam Poussin!"

There was a brief silence as the two men tried to picture this scene. The gendarme seemed to be sufficiently perturbed by the possibility that he returned to slurping at his half-finished coffee.

"Why the hell don't they allow smoking on these trains?" he complained. "Besides those Parisians are quite happy to close the case now. Alain committed the murder of James and then killed himself. Two deaths solved and with no effort on their part. Some Parisian pansy gets a promotion and I'm in trouble for not having arrested Alain earlier."

"But if there's nothing you can do then what's the point of coming to Paris?" Bob tried to read the name of a suburban station as the train swept past a platform full of commuters. The TGV averaged 200 kilometres an hour on most of its route and showed no sign of slowing down as it approached its destination.

"There are some loose ends to tie up. I have an appointment to go through the paperwork with one of my Parisian colleagues." A ball of phlegm quickly planted itself on the lush pile of the SNCF carpet. "But that still leaves so many questions unanswered."

"Such as?"

"Is there proof that the suicide email was a fake? Who could have been at the station where Alain was killed? Apparently the CCTV system was switched off for maintenance so we'll get no help from that direction. Did James really have an illegitimate child? Who is Betty?" Thierry counted the issues on his fingers.

"I suppose we'll never know now," Bob said simply.

"*Peut-etre.*" Thierry smiled slyly.

"You're going to ask them." It finally dawned on Bob. "You're going to visit the Hambleton's first and then tell the Parisians that you've found some new evidence."

"What, and break the rules of my profession by usurping their jurisdiction? What sort of man do you take me for?" Thierry seemed to be genuinely upset by the inference of what Bob had suggested.

"I'm sorry. I just thought you might have time to ask some questions while you were in Paris."

"Has living in France taught you nothing? There's enough paperwork to be completed to decorate the Elysée Palace. I'll be lucky if I have time to take a piss. And because it concerns two deaths, it's all in duplicate. I won't be able to ask any-bloody-one any-bloody-thing." Thierry looked thunderous.

"That's a shame."

"But you will," Thierry pointed at Bob, and checked his watch. He grinned broadly at his English companion, and Bob suddenly understood why he was on the train. "You've got an appointment with Charles Hambleton in fifty minutes."

CHAPTER THIRTY

CHARLES WELCOMED BOB into his office with a warm handshake. "I'm afraid that you'll be disappointed." He indicated that Bob should sit down. The standard issue plastic chairs were in marked contrast to the plush furnishings that he had seen in James' office.

"I will?"

"Yes, I said to the gendarme—what's his name?"

"You mean Thierry Fauconnier?"

"That's right. I told him that the suicide message was only three sentences long and I even read it out to him over the phone. But he seemed insistent that someone should come and see it 'in situ'." Charles' fingers twitched the air, and he relaxed into his seat as if relieved at having got his fix of air-apostrophisation. He leaned forward to Bob. "To be honest, I'm glad that he suggested you. If he'd sent another gendarme over here I think it might have been enough to send some of the staff here 'over the edge'. What with the murder and then the suicide, it's made a lot of people very uncomfortable."

"That's perfectly natural," Bob replied soothingly, beginning to see what he was supposed to do. "I was happy to be of help."

"Yes, Captain Fauconnier thought it would be better if someone known to the family came here to collect the evidence. He said that now the case was over he didn't want things to be too formal. But I imagine it's disrupted your arrangements with the cottage?"

"Not really. Your mother and Rose arrived yesterday and they seem to be well on the way to having things organised for the party."

"Oh that!" Charles flopped back in his chair and folded his arms. "Frankly, I wish they weren't."

"Why not?"

"It doesn't seem right somehow. I know that they want to try and cheer Jasmine up and bring the family together. 'Put a line under things', if you know what I mean." His fingers flicked the air angrily, making Bob recoil in his chair. "But I think it's far too soon. I mean the poor man's hardly cold. It could just re-open a whole can of worms for us." Charles sighed heavily. "But Maureen was insistent."

"I am sorry about Alain." Bob looked down into his lap. He had never felt comfortable dealing with grief but he'd come across enough students who had lost their parents while they were at University to have developed a defence mechanism; a series of words that filled the gap between remembrance and reflection. "I know he didn't like me but he must have lived in terrible torment after he killed James."

"I suppose so. The one good thing to come out of it is that it's brought back some of the trust between us. As long as the murder of James remained unsolved I think we all suspected one another. Apart from anything else it made running the business very difficult."

"Who did you suspect?" Bob hadn't meant the question to be quite so blunt, but it had been an automatic response. Perhaps Thierry was right and Bob was turning into a detective.

Charles stood up and went to the office window that overlooked the streets of Paris, filled with tourists and the sharp-lined shadows that come with metropolitan summers. After a few moments he turned back to Bob, who noticed that tears had appeared in his eyes. Charles brushed them away quickly.

"I always knew it was Alain," he said simply and returned to his chair.

"How?" Bob tried to hide his surprise but knew he'd failed from Charles' reaction.

"Oh, a whole bunch of things really. His marriage was on the rocks—we could all see that. But he knew that if he and Jasmine split up James would be devastated and, much as it pains me to say so, my brother could be a vindictive man if he chose. I guess that Alain knew his career would be over if he left Jasmine and so he made 'alternative arrangements'." The apostrophes were made at half mast, as if in respect to the dead man. "And then, of course, there was all that business about trying to 'frame' you. He had access to the logistics chain to the States and could easily have set up the false post office box. Even the use of your secateurs was characteristic of the man."

"It does seem quite compelling," Bob demurred.

Charles returned to the window. "That. And the fact that he told Jasmine he had killed James."

"He confessed to her?"

"Yes." Charles looked at Bob and immediately looked down to the floor. "At least I think he did." He looked up again. "That's what she told me." He moved back to his desk and sat down, clearly flustered. "I probably shouldn't have said anything to you. I don't know whether she told the gendarmes or not. Please don't mention it to the captain; it's really just family gossip."

"But if he admitted to Jasmine that he killed her father then why didn't she go to the police herself?"

Charles cradled his hands together on the desk in front of him and gazed at them. "I think she wanted to protect him." He looked into Bob's eyes. "For all that their marriage was in trouble you have to understand that Jasmine still loved Alain tremendously. All their problems were to do with Marc and the amount of time that Alain spent working. Apart from the practical aspects of life they were perfectly suited to one another."

Bob thought about his relationship with Kate. Charles' comment could as easily apply to their situation.

"She must be very upset by his death."

"Oh yes, she's devastated. But she's being very brave for Marc's sake. I think that's one reason why Maureen is so keen to arrange this party. It'll take some of the pressure off Jasmine and allow her to get some out of the city for a while. So far she's just stayed indoors the whole time. The police here wanted her to identify the body but she wouldn't go, so I had to do it. Fortunately I was down that way at the time."

"Where was it?"

"Oh, Gare du Nord. The odd thing was that he was on a commuter train platform. The one that takes the RER to Chelle-Gournay. We've no idea why. We all thought he was going home because of his headache. The only suggestion that I can come up with was that he knew the CCTV wasn't working on the line. It's possible to tell from the light on the camera, you know. Or in this case the lack of a light. Alain probably didn't want his plan to be interrupted and chose a platform where privacy was guaranteed. With his technical knowledge it wouldn't have surprised me if he hadn't broken the camera himself—it had been out of action for days before the suicide."

"And there isn't any question that someone might have pushed him off the platform?"

"None at all." Charles' tone was stern. "It was suicide, pure and simple." He looked up at Bob. "Which reminds me. You came here for a copy of the suicide note didn't you?"

"Oh that. Yes." Thierry must have asked Charles to hand it over.

"I've arranged for my secretary to make a copy for you. I don't know why but Captain Fauconnier was insistent on having a paper version. I said that I could simply have forwarded the email to him, but he wasn't having any of it."

"Bureaucracy I imagine," Bob said, his face as straight as he could manage.

"Probably. 'The French disease', as I like to call it." The fingers tweaked again. Charles rose from the desk and gestured Bob towards the door. "I'll get Sally-Anne to sort it all out for you now."

They went out of Charles' office and creaked their way along the corridor to another office, which contained two women typing away at computers.

"This is Sally-Anne," Charles indicated a middle-aged woman with pale brown eyes and short brown hair. Bob thought he recognised her. "She'll get a copy for you. I'm afraid I'd better get back to work." He offered his hand to Bob who shook it. "And I'll see you again a week on Saturday at the cottage."

"Of course," Bob said and watched as Charles left the room and returned to his own office.

Sally-Anne stood up and picked a sheet of paper from her printer tray.

"*Maintenant* Monsieur Hunt, you wanted a copy of the . . . ," she paused as if waiting for Bob to suggest an appropriate euphemism.

"The email?"

"Yes, the email." She spoke in French, her delicate voice carefully delineating every consonant. Bob was sure that he'd seen her before, presumably from his last visit to the Hambleton offices, and wondered what she made of the very English culture in which she worked. "I have printed it straight from our internal mail system." She handed the sheet of paper to Bob. "You can see here that it was written at six-fifteen on the morning of the day that he . . ." Again there was a nervous pause. Her brown eyes scanned Bob's face anxiously.

"The day that he went to the station." Bob said. Her face relaxed into a small smile.

"Indeed."

"What a fucking day that was." Bob and Sally-Anne swung round to the other typist. "First he goes and kills himself, which brought the metro system to a standstill. That meant I was late getting in from lunch, and so I had to stay late to make up for it. Then everyone was going around like it was a fucking morgue in here. You had to be so careful what you said. And then, just as I was about to leave, the bloody system crashed."

"This is Paulette," said Sally-Anne. "She doesn't like working here."

"Too bloody right, I don't. Too many fucking English people here for my liking." Paulette stared at Bob and then started typing frantically.

"She doesn't mean it personally," Sally-Anne said and Bob was reminded of Thierry. Perhaps he could fix the two of them up and they could while away their time together finding people to hate. "She's right about the system though."

"Had to redo everything the next day. Letters, invoices, cheques—the fucking lot."

"Why?"

"After the system crashed everything had the wrong date on, it must have reset itself."

"Of course, if that moron Deneuve hadn't fucking killed himself we'd have been alright. He knew how to reboot the system. That fuckwit in there," Paulette waved towards Charles' office. "He thinks he knows it all, but he just managed to make the whole thing worse."

"You're too hard on him." Sally-Anne's gentle voice had hardened in defence of her boss. "He did his best. Got it all sorted in the end, didn't he?"

"Suppose so," Paulette growled. "But if he'd got his act together they would have discovered the suicide note earlier. Might have saved us all a lot of trouble. And got the trains back to normal quicker."

"They didn't find the 'email' until later?" Bob caught himself air-apostrophising; it really must be contagious he decided.

"The next afternoon when the system was back up and running," Sally-Anne said. "They found it in his electronic mailbox as a draft. They don't think he ever actually sent it. He probably just wanted Charles or someone else to find it there when they went through his account after his death."

"Fucking creepy if you ask me. Like a ghost coming back from the dead to confess to murder." Paulette gave a little shiver and returned to hammering away at the keyboard.

Bob read the printout. He was surprised to find that it had been written in English.

"To all my loved ones—sorry. I had to kill James because he was hurting too many of us. My sacrifice should bring things to an end. Alain."

"A man of few words," Bob said.

"You'd have thought it would have been quicker to write it on a piece of paper than log-in, type it and then log-out."

"Not him. That moron was in love with computers. I bet he never switched the bloody thing off. Probably kept it in bed with him. No wonder Jasmine got fed up of him. I'm surprised she didn't give him the heave-ho years ago. But then that's the fucking English for you. Sang-bloody-froid."

"Well, thanks for this anyway." Bob shook hands with Sally-Anne and gazed at her face. He was sure he remembered it from somewhere.

"That's all right. I just hope it puts an end to everything and that we can all get back to normal. Poor Charles is at his wits end. Was there anything else you needed?"

Bob looked at his watch. It was only half past eleven. He wasn't due to meet Thierry on the train back to the Vendée until four. How could he kill the next few hours?

"There is one last thing," he said, a plan forming in his mind. "The captain said he'd also like the addresses of all the family members so that he could complete the paperwork without having to ask them all individually."

"That's easy enough. I'll just copy the Directors list for you. It gives you all their full names, addresses, shareholdings and so on. We have to keep a copy here by law."

"Bureaucracy," Bob grunted as she went to the photocopier.

"Yes," Sally-Anne agreed. "But then most of us would be out of work without it." She gave him the copy. "It was nice to meet you Mr Hunt."

"Likewise," he said. "I'll see myself out."

As he went down the stairs of the old Parisian tenement Bob smiled to himself. It was a big, gloating grin of a smile—the sort he used to reserve for payday. He remembered where he'd seen Sally-Anne before. It had been her face on the photo in the office at the truck depot. Sally-Anne was Michel's wife.

CHAPTER THIRTY-ONE

BOB LOCATED THE address in a quiet street in the fashionable Opera district of the city, almost within the gaze of ubiquitous Napoleon atop the Colonne Vendôme. According to the list that Sally-Anne had provided this was the home of Jasmine Deneuve. There were black iron railings at street level which curved upwards, accompanying a quartet of steps to an impressive wooden door with a brass knocker styled into a lion's head. Bob lifted the knocker and paused. What he was doing was risky. If he got the tone wrong he could upset a lot of people. But he still had three hours to kill and what was the worst that could happen? He decided not to think about it and brought the knocker down with a resounding thump.

It took Jasmine about two minutes to answer the door. Bob knew she was there because he could hear Marc giving a running commentary of her movements.

"*Oui?*" She was out of breath as she poked her head round the door. "Oh, it's you Mr Hunt." She sounded surprised but, to Bob's relief, not angry.

"I'm sorry to disturb you. I've been at the office this morning and I thought it would be rude not to offer my condolences to you." Bob noticed that Jasmine's face was unmade, revealing black wheals beneath her eyes. She looked fragile. He wanted to hug her.

"That's kind of you. Please, do come in." She opened the door to reveal that she was wearing an oversize towelling dressing gown and fluffy pink slippers.

"Oh no." Bob could feel himself blushing. He had expected to get a cool reception from Jasmine and hadn't prepared himself for the possibility that she would welcome an uninvited visitor. Her vulnerable state of undress just made him want to comfort her more.

"Who is it?" Marc screamed down from a floor higher up in the house. Bob decided that it was probably true that children were the most effective form of contraception.

"Oh, it's just Mr Hunt. He's come to see how we are. Isn't that kind of him?" Jasmine closed the front door and gestured that Bob should go into a large reception room, which looked out onto the boulevard. There were three armchairs grouped around a marble fireplace. Everything looked meticulously tidy.

"Mr Hunt? Isn't he that boring English man that you said had murdered Grandpa?"

It was Jasmine's turn to blush.

"I'm sorry." She faced Bob and shrugged her shoulders. "It was what the police told us. They said that you'd been arrested."

"That's more or less true, but fortunately I had a good alibi."

"Oh yes?" Jasmine seemed interested.

"I was with the police inspector when the murder took place." Bob shrugged his shoulders. "As it turned out they were wrong and I didn't have an alibi after all."

Jasmine looked puzzled and was about to ask a question when there was a sudden scampering of bare feet on wooden floorboards and Marc ran in through the open doorway. He glared at Bob.

"Oh, it is you. Come to gloat over Daddy's death have you?"

"Marc! Do try to be nice to Mr Hunt."

"I've come to say that I'm sorry," said Bob. It would be difficult to ask Jasmine the questions about Alain's suicide with the boy present.

"Well you don't need to." Marc crossed the room to his mother and wrapped his arm around her waist, hugging her. "We're going to be much happier now. Aren't we mummy?" He put his thumb in his mouth and buried his head in the folds of Jasmine's dressing gown.

"Don't be silly Marc." She took hold of his arm and guided him out of the door to the bottom of the staircase. "If you go back up to your room and play nicely with your toys then I'll buy you something really special when we go out later."

"I want that new 'Assassin' game for my Playstation."

Jasmine said something quietly. Bob couldn't make out what it was but it obviously pleased Marc.

"You promise?"

"I promise. Now go upstairs and play quietly. There's something I need to talk to Mr Hunt about."

"Well hurry up," the boy called as he thudded up the stairs. "My new 'Assassin' won't wait for some boring old git to get lost."

"Be nice," Jasmine reminded him. Bob doubted whether it would have much effect.

"I'm sorry. He's been especially sensitive since Alain's death, poor lamb." Jasmine threw herself into one of the armchairs and indicated that Bob should make himself comfortable.

"You said that you wanted to discuss something with me."

"Did I?" Her eyes were cast down. She seemed to be lost in thought.

"To Marc just now."

"Oh yes. It's nothing really." Jasmine sat up and gazed at Bob. "Just that . . . It seems silly really . . ."

"What does?"

"I wondered whether I should feel guilty."

"Guilty?" For a moment Bob wondered whether she was about to confess to a double murder.

"For not having loved him more when he was alive."

"But you were very much in love. It was clear to me just to watch you both together. You cared for each other deeply."

"Cared, yes. But not loved." She looked away from Bob. "Or at least I think we loved each other in different ways."

"I don't understand."

Jasmine sighed. "I'm not sure that I do either." She looked back up at him. "The fact is that I just wanted Marc, and I think that Alain just wanted his job. He was always very sweet but maybe it was just a marriage of convenience."

"You married simply to have children?" To Bob the idea seemed unlikely—incredible almost.

"Yes. I love Marc, but I never loved Alain." Her eyes welled up with tears. "At least not until now. And now I miss him so much, and it's all too late!"

Bob groped around in his pockets for a handkerchief but the only thing that came to hand was the paper serviette that he'd used to mop up Thierry's coffee on the train. He got up from the chair and offered it to Jasmine, embarrassed more by his sense of inadequacy in the situation than by her weeping.

"I'm sorry, Mr Hunt."

"Please call me Bob."

"You're very kind," she looked at the serviette with a puzzled expression and then dabbed her eyes with it. "You see, as soon as we had Marc together I didn't need Alain. There were days when he was useful, of course. He did all the shopping and sorted out all the money. He kept everything going. I suppose I can see that now. But most of the time after Marc was born I just wanted Alain to get lost. He was in the way. He came between us."

"It must have been hard for you both," Bob said, although he could now understand why Alain had been so tense all the time.

"Maybe. We drifted apart gradually. Not like mum and daddy of course but the effects were just as . . ." She waved the serviette limply at Bob as if her mind had given up.

"Corrosive?" he offered.

"Yes. That's a good way of putting it. We were rusting away together and one of us was bound to fall apart sooner or later." She leaned her head back and breathed in deeply. Suddenly she sat forward again and screwed the serviette into her balled fist. "And I could have stopped it."

"Stopped what?"

"Stopped poor Alain from killing himself." Her face had regained some colour and her eyes flashed a deep blue, reminding Bob of Rose. Jasmine turned to face him her strong gaze demanding his attention.

"I'm so angry with myself. He told me what he had done and I was so wrapped up in myself that I never even noticed."

"He told you that he had murdered James?" Bob recalled that Charles had said something of the kind earlier that morning.

"Oh yes. Well, sort of. Alain never said anything directly unless he was squiffy. He was always so quiet; it's one of the things that irritated me about him. I should have read the signs better."

"What do you mean?"

Jasmine faced Bob and looked at him, as if deciding whether or not to confide what she knew. She let the crumpled serviette fall onto the floor and wiped her mouth with the back of her hand.

"One night, about a month ago, when we'd both had a bit to drink he said to me that he'd done something stupid and that he hoped I'd forgive him. When I asked him what it was, he clammed up. He said that he just hoped that Maureen would forgive him eventually."

"What did he mean by that?"

"At the time I had no idea but now it all seems so obvious. If I'd taken the time to understand what he was going through I could have protected him and stopped him from . . ." She started crying again and curled herself into a ball in the chair, knees up against her face, the dressing gown pulled tightly against her body. Bob wanted to go up and embrace her, but as a father, not a lover.

"I'm sorry," he said, and stood up to leave. "I didn't mean to make things worse."

Jasmine uncurled herself from the chair.

"No, please don't go. I'm afraid that I'm very emotional at the moment."

Bob looked at his watch; he still had over an hour to go before he needed to return to the station. He reflected on his meetings with the Hambletons. They all seemed to end up the same way. "I'll make us both a cup of tea," he said.

"That would be lovely."

The kitchen was a very modern affair; all stainless steel and automated gadgets.

"I've no idea what half these things do," Jasmine said, passing Bob a small sphere with an electronic readout. "I mean this could be an egg-timer or a thermometer. Alain loved anything new like that."

Bob could see that she was close to breaking down again and decided to change the subject.

"Earlier you said something about your mum and daddy. You said their marriage wasn't the same as yours. What did you mean?"

"Oh, nothing really." She put the unidentified gadget down on the work surface next to the glass teapot. "It's just that me and Alain drifted apart but their relationship was constantly up and down."

"I thought they were the traditional happy couple," Bob lied.

"Oh heavens no. I loved Daddy—he gave me everything I wanted—but he was a devil to mum." She looked up at Bob and gave him a small smile. "I don't suppose it matters if I tell you now, but please don't let mum know that I said anything." She gave a nervous giggle. "Although it seemed to be common knowledge in the office."

"What was?" Bob poured the tea into two porcelain cups—the only obvious concession to traditional cuisine.

"That daddy was having an affair."

Bon feigned surprise.

"Was he? He didn't seem the type."

"Oh he was the type all right. Apparently he was very good at it. Every couple of months he seemed to have a new girl."

"Didn't your mum find out?"

"Of course. Sometimes he would go out for a meal in the evening with his latest floosie and ask mum to make the dinner arrangements for him."

Bob thought about how Maureen must have reacted to this.

"Why didn't she just divorce him? She'd have had a good settlement from him, surely?"

"Yes, but money was never a problem for her. Mum doesn't have extravagant tastes. Her only interest outside of work was the garden, and she even let Uncle Charles do most of that for her." Jasmine leaned forward towards Bob confidentially. "No, she could never have split up with him because of us."

"You?"

"Yes, daddy said that if any of the family ever split up with their husband or wife then that would be the end of the business. He would close Hambleton's down and we'd be cut off from the rest of the family."

"But he could never have made that stick."

"He could. What you don't seem to understand Bob is that the family is the business. Without the business we would be nothing. Alain and I couldn't have afforded for the business to disappear, nor could Rose or Uncle Charles and Louise for that matter. Mum knew that if she ever left daddy it would tear the family apart and that she would risk never seeing any of us again. It would have broken her heart."

"So she put up with it all these years?"

"Yes." Jasmine sipped at her tea, leaning against the worktop. "Of course she made a fuss every now and then, but daddy knew he would always win in the end."

"Cruel, really. Well, I would never have guessed. It just goes to show that you never can tell what happens behind closed doors."

"It drove Alain mad." Jasmine arched her back and stretched her arms upwards as if she were just waking up. "He was always going on at me about how someone should confront daddy about how much he was hurting mum. I told him that if he felt that strongly he should do it himself. He said he would if he ever found any evidence."

"And did he?"

"No. He knew as well as the rest of us that we all depended on mum and daddy staying together for our livelihoods. He once said that he'd heard something about Charles' secretary, not that I ever believed a word of it."

"Where did he get that story from?"

"I think it was one of the mechanics at the truck depot. It was all gossip though, if you ask me. Alain never did anything about it." She finished her tea. "And now he never will." She sighed heavily.

"Well, I'm sorry for disturbing you." Bob could sense that Jasmine's mood had taken a turn for the worse and decided it was time to go. He looked at his watch. "I'd better get going if I'm going to catch the train back to the Vendée."

"It was kind of you to come." Jasmine walked up to him and curled herself around him, enveloping them both in the dressing gown. She kissed him on the lips. Bob pulled her closer, feeling simultaneous guilt and passion. After several seconds he let her go and drew away.

"It's my pleasure," he said honestly. "And I'll see you again soon."

"Oh yes, the dinner next Saturday. I'd almost forgotten all about that."

"I'll see you then," Bob said as he scurried clumsily along the corridor towards the front door.

"I'll look forward to it," Jasmine said and pulled her hair away from her face. "Perhaps we can meet up together while I'm down there?" There was a pause. "Alone."

"Perhaps," Bob replied, and opened the door to leave. He looked at Jasmine, her lips slightly parted, one bare leg poking between the folds of the gown. She was, he decided, both gorgeous and dangerous.

"Mum! This game is so crap."

And a mother.

"*Au revoir*," he said as he stepped out of the door and onto the steps to the boulevard.

"*A bientot*," she called softly as he closed the door behind him.

CHAPTER THIRTY-TWO

B OB HAD BEEN standing on the platform for over ten minutes hoping to spot Thierry before he boarded the train. He looked down again at his watch. Three minutes to go before the TGV would launch itself southward at a stomach-testing 220 kilometres-per-hour. Where on earth was Thierry?

Bob watched with concern as the controleur moved along the platform, ushering assorted waifs and strays into their carriages. The TGV was famed for its determination to run to schedule and the controleurs were notorious for straining every sinew against the innate French imperviance to timeliness. Already, with two minutes still left before departure the SNCF official was becoming distinctly Napoleonic, his firm requests to passengers to *"donnez vos places"* echoing across the marble colonnades of the Gare Montparnasse.

"Board the train, *monsieur*." He approached Bob, chest puffed out and pointed the antenna of his radio towards an open door.

"But my friend has not yet arrived and he and I are due to travel together."

"That cannot be helped." The controleur consulted an oversized pocket watch. "This train will leave in precisely ninety seconds. With or without your friend."

"But I can't leave without him." A practical thought had struck Bob. "He's giving me a lift home when we get to La Roche-sur-Yon."

"Eighty seconds," the petty official replied. "With or without you." He strode towards the nearest open door and slammed it firmly shut as if to prove his point.

"But I'm sure he won't be long. The train can easily make the time up . . ."

Bob realised instantly that this was a mistake.

"Stand aside, *monsieur*. This train is about to depart." A whistle was produced from a pocket by one hand whilst Bob was pushed aside with the other.

"I've got to catch that train," Bob said, making a sudden bolt for the one door that remained open.

"Too late," the controleur cried gleefully as he grabbed Bob's arm, stuffed the whistle into his mouth and puffed up his cheeks ready to blow.

At which point his radio bleeped into life.

"*Oui?*"

Bob tried to move towards the train as a conversation ensued over the walky-talky, but the controleur was determined not to let go of him. After a few seconds the radio went silent.

"You will not be permitted to board the train. You are too late."

"But the train is still in the platform. Surely I can just get on it."

"The train is regrettably delayed, this is true. However, it is only for a few moments whilst an important official embarks. He is on business of the state and I have been instructed to hold the train for him." He looked disdainfully at Bob. "The TGV schedule has not been disrupted so that itinerant Englishmen can board. You are best to present yourself at the ticket kiosk so that you can rebook your journey, *monsieur*. You will not be travelling on this train."

Bob thought about arguing, but decided against it. Haranguing a railway employee was probably a capital offence in France and he'd spent enough time in custody lately. He started to trudge towards the station concourse when a familiar figure came into view.

"Ah, my distinguished traveller arrives," the controleur said, running up behind Bob. "I told you he wouldn't be long. Apparently he is investigating a very complex murder case. National security is at stake. Not that a foreigner like you would understand."

Thierry scurried along the platform like a maimed squirrel. His unkempt hair billowed around his head and somehow he had managed to get his coat tangled so that one arm was correctly inserted by the other was on inside out. Two plastic bags of documents and papers were strapped to his back with his belt and he was using one hand to hold his trousers up, whilst the other desperately clutched at a packet of Gauloise.

"Capitaine Faucconnier?"

"Yes, yes."

"This way sir." The controleur pushed a metal panel on the side of the train and a door swished open. "It's a pleasure to be of service to the state. The TGV is honoured to be of assistance at such a time." Bob caught Thierry's eye and the policeman indicated that he should follow him onto the train.

"*Merci, monsieur.*" Thierry smiled at the controleur. "And many thanks for your assistance to my colleague."

The controleur looked puzzled. Thierry indicated Bob, who stepped through the open door and onto the train.

"Him?"

"Yes, *monsieur* Hunt is my most trusted assistant. I'm sure that you will have rendered him the customary warmth of the TGV."

The controleur's face flashed through the colours of a traffic light; paling suddenly and then rising through an unhealthy orange pallor to a flushing red, crimson with anger and embarrassment.

Bob turned to Thierry and began to say "Well, actually . . ." but the rest of his remarks were lost behind the screeching pitch of a train whistle being blown with the strength of about gale force nine.

"So how did you persuade them to hold the train for you?" Bob asked after they had been installed into their seats.

"Former colleague of mine at the Justice Department. He and I go way back. We were still finishing lunch when I realised that I would be late for the train. He knows the direct number of the station master, who owed him a favour over an unpaid parking fine or something like that, and here we are."

"Lunch? At four in the afternoon?"

"We had a lot to catch up on." Thierry gave Bob a reproving glance.

"Fair enough."

"He was very helpful."

"Oh, yes?"

"Hmm." Thierry began to rummage in one of the plastic bags, tossing out sheaves of paper onto the vacant seat next to him. "Ah, I wondered where I'd put that." He lifted a crumpled polystyrene cup out of the cup and placed it carefully on the table between them. Several handfuls of documents later he seized a sheet of paper and held it aloft. "Here she is! This could solve our little mystery for us." He passed the sheet to Bob. "See!"

It was a list of shareholders of Hambleton's of Paris, identical to the one that Sally-Anne had given to Bob.

"Snap!" Bob said, producing his copy for the gendarme to see.

"Great minds," the detective said, obviously disappointed to have been matched in this way. "I'm surprised you aren't crowing with delight, *mon ami*."

"Why?"

"Because the mystery becomes deeper!"

"I don't understand. I haven't had a chance to read the list."

"Then you must. Out loud, please. I want to see your face when you get to the key part."

Bob straightened out the piece of paper. There didn't seem to be anything exceptional about it. It was just a list of the ownership stakes in the business together with a list of directors and their addresses. The main shareholders were James and Charles with smaller holdings for a large number of family members.

"Read it," Thierry urged.

"James Reginald Philip Hambleton, forty percent. Charles Andrew Michael Hambleton, forty percent. Maureen Lucinda Hambleton, eight percent . . ."

"No, lower down, you fool."

"Err, what about Xavier Michel Montablon, two percent. Louise Elizabeth Hambleton, two percent." Bob stopped as he read the next name. He could hardly believe his eyes. "Timothy Charles Wells, one and a half percent."

"Interesting *n'est pas?*"

"But Timmy Wells doesn't exist." Bob thought back to his conversation when James Hambleton was at the airport. "Maureen told me that James had made the name up to cover for his affair. It was a red herring and I fell for it hook, line and sinker."

"A very wealthy red herring. And one we should fish out I think." Thierry stretched his arm forward to take the sheet of paper from Bob.

"Hold on."

"What now? *C'est tres facile.* Find Timmy Wells and we've caught ourselves a murderer."

Bob was poring over a name right at the bottom of the list with an ownership stake of just half of one percent. Didier Patrice Rogier. Wasn't that the same surname as the farmer at Longchamp? Bob shook his head. Rogier was a common enough name in France. Anyway, he reasoned, how could a farmer in the Vendée own shares in a Parisian import-export business?

"I suppose you're right." Bob handed the paper to Thierry who folded it carefully and placed it in his trouser pocket. "But I can't think why an imaginary person would kill a business partner. It doesn't make sense."

"I have a friend in the business ministry who's trying to find out."

"You've got a friend?" Bob's incredulity was only half in jest.

"Alright then, perhaps not a friend. More an acquaintance."

"Let me guess. He owes you one because you let him off a speeding fine?"

Thierry pursed his lips and blew out his cheeks. He stared at Bob narrowly.

"It was a petty theft case actually. And it was his niece, so it wasn't a direct relative."

"A friend should bear his friend's infirmities." Bob was delighted to have remembered the Shakespearean quote, even if he couldn't recall which play it was from.

"Anyway if he can't trace our mysterious Mr Wells then no-one can."

Bob began to sink back into the soft upholstery of the TGV. It had been a long day and instead of things become clearer, they had simply uncovered more bits of the puzzle that didn't fit together. Alain had confessed his crime to Jasmine, and Timmy Wells really did exist. As Bob felt himself slip into the warm embrace of slumber he realised that Maureen must have lied to him. She had said that she had never heard of Wells but if he was a shareholder in the company then she must have. He made a tired mental note to ask her about this when they next met. There wasn't long to wait; the dinner party was only five days away.

As the warmth of the train carriage enveloped him, Bob started to think about what it must be like to be wealthy and own large houses and host grand dinner parties. He found himself sliding into a comfortable dream state filled with happy families and genteel conversation. It was all very seductive.

"Wake up." Thierry slapped Bob firmly on the face. "Who owns your house?"

"What?" Bob had just entered that peaceful state between waking and sleeping where you are aware enough to know that you are at your most vulnerable but sufficiently unconscious not to care.

Thierry's tone was insistent. "Come on. It's not a tough question. Who owns your house?"

"I do, of course. Now let me go back to sleep."

Thierry slapped him again.

"Don't be stupid. Of course you don't. Listen to me carefully. Who owns your house?"

"I do," Bob insisted. And then he fell back into consciousness. "Oh no, of course I don't. Kate and I own it jointly." With consciousness came a pervasive sense of vulnerability. "Why?"

"*Precisement*! Why do you own it jointly?"

"Well, because that's only fair. After all Kate's money paid for the house as much as I did. More probably."

"Exactly! And I assume you have some form of *tontine* clause in your house purchase so that if Kate dies then you will be able to claim at least a half-ownership in the property."

"That's what I like about you Thierry; you're such a cheery fellow."

"But it's important. If you didn't organise it that way then under French law some distant relative of Kate's might be able to claim the house for themselves. And you'd be out on your ear."

"Is this what you do for entertainment?" Bob mimicked the voice of a TV host. "At Thierry's tonight, you too can enjoy the prospect of your wife's death and house repossession."

"*Non, non, non*! This is serious Bob." Thierry was waving a document at the Englishman. It was clipped at the corner top with a cardboard triangle, in the style much used by French legal firms. Bob could see a large red wax seal on the front page. "This is the will of James Hambleton. In his case he had two daughters and each of them is entitled to one third of his estate as the *reserve legale*. His wife is entitled to nothing by law."

"So you're saying that Maureen is homeless?"

"No, not at all. James has used the *Quotit Disponible*, that is the remaining portion of his estate, to ensure that Maureen is well provided for and has a roof over her head. In any case she is entitled to live in the matrimonial home as a life tenant should she wish. The will takes care of all of that very neatly."

"Good for her," Bob was genuinely relieved. Despite the fact that it now appeared that she had lied to him, Bob knew that Maureen had worked tirelessly for the firm and it would have felt wrong to him had she been left with nothing. "And I suppose it means that she doesn't have a motive for committing the murder."

"Not a financial one, at any rate," Thierry agreed. "But that still leaves jealousy, anger at being cheated on and general marital disharmony as possible motives."

"General marital disharmony?"

"Don't underestimate that." The policeman wagged his index finger. "In my experience some of the most brutal killings have been caused by the grinding pointlessness of domestic bliss. The longer the marriage the more vicious the crime usually." He looked up from the will to stare at Bob. "How long have you and Kate . . . ?"

"Oh ho, very funny. What about James' will?"

"It seems that out of the *quotit disponible* he also made a small legacy to Louise and left some paintings and jewellery to members of staff."

"Perhaps to a woman called Sally-Anne? She's Charles' secretary." Bob thought back to his meeting at the office.

"I can't remember but it's possible. Why?"

"Just that she was probably one of his lovers. Was there anything else?"

"Just a letter to his brother."

"Oh, yes. What does it say?"

"I've no idea. The solicitor said that the envelope was sealed and marked 'strictly confidential'. He refused absolutely to open it. He'll give it to Charles when he next sees him. James was very insistent that it should be delivered by hand."

"At least it's nice and clean. No great cause for disputes. No ancient family skeletons strutting their way out of closets."

"Clean, my arse!" Thierry snorted. "The whole thing stinks."

Bob thought about how these new pieces of information fitted into the murder of James Hambleton.

"So it was probably Alain who murdered him after all," he concluded.

"Impossible! Now, shut up. I need to think."

Before Bob could argue Thierry cleared his throat of phlegm, closed his eyes and began to snore.

CHAPTER THIRTY-THREE

"W E'LL BE LATE."

Bob looked at his watch again. The engagement party was being held at the *salle l'amique* just three doors down the road from them but they were definitely going to be the last ones there. It should have started about half an hour ago.

"The French are always late," Kate shouted down at him from the bathroom. "We've got ages still."

Bob knew she was probably right but despite the amount of time they had spent in France he still couldn't quite get over his English compulsion to be on time.

"What are you up to, anyway? You've been in that bathroom for the last two hours. You do know that you're not the one getting married, don't you?"

Bob could hear Kate stomping around above him. The wooden boards that formed both the ceiling of the lounge and the floor of the bathroom bowed slightly where she walked.

"Yes—and it's not fair. She's marrying a hunk of French loveliness and I'm stuck with you."

"But I'm a classic piece of British beefcake."

"Beefburger more like."

Bob felt quite hurt. He'd tried—mostly unsuccessfully—to keep himself fit since they'd moved to France in spite of the temptations on offer. It wasn't his fault if their lifestyle brought them into contact with wine, cheese and crème brulée. There was a loud gurgling of water, followed by a splash. Some drops fell onto Bob's head from between the cracks in the bathroom floorboards.

"And don't get everything wet up there. We can't afford to replace it."

"It's about bloody time I replaced you."

Bob reflected that things had gone from bad to worse between them. He wasn't sure if it was the money situation or simply that their close and constant proximity caused them to rub each other up the wrong way. In England they had both been at work during the day and so they had valued the relatively little time that they had spent together. Now they seemed to live in one another's pockets and there was never enough space for them both. Bob worried that perhaps it just meant that they were incompatible.

He thrust his hands into his pockets and fiddled with the house keys.

"I can hear you. Jingling the keys won't make me go any faster." What felt like half a bucket of water drenched Bob's head. "If you're in such a rush why don't you go down there on your own? With a bit of luck I might be able to pull someone decent without you around."

"The French have got more sense," Bob shouted, more upset than angry, but his retort was lost in the blast as Kate fired up the hairdryer.

Bob sighed. This meant that there was at least another forty minutes to go before she would be ready, by which time all the best wine would be gone and most of the guests would be drunk to the point that his usually adequate grasp of French dialect would be tested beyond its limit. Perhaps he should take Kate's advice and go down to the party now. He wandered into the kitchen and looked at himself in the small mirror that Kate hid behind the pasta jar—just in case someone dropped in unexpectedly. He wasn't that bad looking, if you didn't mind a man who'd been around for a few years and lost most of his hair. He thought he looked distinguished in a shabby chic sort of way. A sort of rugged book-keeper style; just what French women of 'a certain age' went for he'd read somewhere. At least that's how he thought it translated.

He would show Kate. He'd go out and find himself a local girl at the party. That would teach her not to take him for granted. He smoothed the garland of hair around his bald head and nodded to himself in the mirror. He threw the keys onto the kitchen table and headed out of the back door full of confidence. He could get himself another woman if he wanted, he told himself as he strode around the side of the house and into the main street of St-Sébastien. He just hoped that 'a certain age' was less than seventy.

"*Mon dieu*, you're early," Gautier muttered to Bob as he entered the *salle l'amique*.

"Oh, I thought it was supposed to start at eight."

"Yes, and it's only quarter to nine. There'll be hardly anyone else here until ten."

"Sorry," Bob said miserably.

"Don't worry," Gautier slapped him on the back gently. "You can give me a hand setting everything up. I've done the hard bit—organising the wines by region so that no-one gets an unpleasant surprise."

Bob looked at the line of wooden trestle tables that spanned the length of the room, each marked in Gautier's neat handwriting; 'Borgougne', 'Bordeaux', 'Val de la Loire' and so on right up to two entire tables dedicated to 'Fiefs Vendéen'.

"The trouble is that now there's the food to arrange." He gestured towards five large crates stuffed full of plastic cartons. "Francoise has been at it for days. I think she's even slept in the kitchen. God knows what's in all those boxes but somehow we've got to fit it onto there."

Bob turned to where Gautier was looking. A solitary trestle table covered in a floral plastic tablecloth stood beside the window. "I put it there because it's likely to be less smoky."

"I didn't think you were supposed to smoke in here.

"You're not."

"Oh?"

"But we will." Gautier said this matter-of-factly and Bob suddenly remembered that he was in France where rules were enforceable in inverse proportion to their likely impact. Not maintaining the number plate on the front of your house was unlikely to ever cause a problem to anyone and was, therefore, a matter of great importance whilst killing yourself by smoke inhalation represented the exercise of personal liberty and, consequently, was of no concern to the authorities.

"Let's just put them in rows," Gautier concluded. "After all, it is just food."

Half an hour later Bob and Gautier had managed to squeeze all the cartons onto the table. In some cases it had meant stacking them into a tower in which all the foods were more or less the same and in other cases it had required the contents of cartons to be pooled. Bob wasn't sure that Francoise Gautier would be overjoyed that her tart tatin now sported a rhubarb roulade topping but she was busy getting ready and, hopefully, wouldn't notice.

"*Bonsoir messieurs.*" Poussin shuffled into the hall dressed in what looked like an old military uniform. He would have looked tremendously distinguished had it not been for the fact that the jacket and the trousers appeared to come from different regiments and were both about three sizes too big. "I bring sustenance."

He carefully handed a bottle of dark purple liquid to Gautier. Despite the absence of a label it became clear that both men knew exactly what the bottle contained.

"Are you certain?" Gautier's voice was reverential.

"Of course. He's a good lad is our Dominic. He deserves the best."

"But this is . . ." Gautier glanced around conspiratorially. ". . . your special brew."

"As I said—the best."

"It's very generous of you." Gautier pulled Poussin towards him and the two embraced. As they pulled away from each other Bob was surprised to notice that even Poussin had tears in his eyes. This was going to be a truly unique occasion.

"What is it?" Bob was intrigued.

Gautier glanced around nervously and lowered his voice. "This is Monsieur Poussin's trouspinnette. It is his own secret recipe and very few people have ever had the pleasure of tasting it."

"But you have quite a few vines Monsieur Poussin. Or does this come from a particular location?"

"No, no. The vines are all the same and I produce one hundred and forty two bottles every year."

"Then why is it so rare for a bottle to make it out of your house?"

"How do you suppose I cope with Madame Poussin?"

The three of them fell into fits of laughter.

"Anyway," Gautier said, wiping tears from his eyes. "I'll pop it behind the sound system, out of harm's way and make sure that Dominic gets it later on."

The sound system, which Bob and Kate could sometimes hear from the house on a warm Saturday night when the windows were open, turned out to be an oversized ghetto blaster, circa-1985. Judging from the music that they had heard, it had one CD welded into it which was of a similar vintage. Gautier placed the bottle carefully behind it and turned the music on. Oh yes, Bob thought, this was the one, as Tina Turner declared that we don't need another hero. A music-loving dog barked in the distance.

It was a call to arms. By the time Tina's voice faded out—or as close as was possible—at the end of the track the *salle l'amique* was almost full. Bob couldn't work out where everyone had come from. Perhaps they'd been sitting in their cars, hidden in the vineyards, since eight o'clock just waiting for a sign that the party was on. There seemed to be hundreds of them and certainly more than the entire population of St-Sébastien des Vignes put together.

Gautier was, as might have been expected, an exemplary host. He ensured that everyone knew exactly where they favourite wine was and revealed a crate full of beer for the infidels. In fact everything was going well and Bob was beginning to relax when Francoise Gautier arrived with Sandrine. The bride-to-be looked radiant in a powder-blue silk mini-dress with a cream ribbon bow tied off at the waist with very little of the skirt below. Bob recalled the incident at the travel agency. The dress meant that no subterfuge was required to get a full view of her legs on this occasion.

His reverie was interrupted by a squeal from Madame Gautier. She had spotted the food table.

"Who has done this?" she demanded, her normally quiet voice raised in a tone of genuine anger. "Who has desecrated my gift to the happy couple?"

"Ah, *ma cherie*," Gautier emerged from the startled crowd. "I think it looks tremendous. You've put so much effort into providing something for everyone. We're all looking forward so much to eating it."

"But it's a mess. An utter devastation!" She pulled the celery out of the crème caramel and gasped as she saw that the smoked salmon had been folded over a line of saucisson in what Bob had thought was one of his cleverer space-saving ideas.

"I'm sorry my love. I can see now what you mean. It is a bit of a mess." Gautier was starting to stammer in his anxiety. "I'm afraid that I was too busy setting up the music to notice." He licked his lips and his eyes darted around nervously before settling on Bob. "I left it all to my good friend here." His voice became more confident. "Didn't I Bob?"

Bob felt the whole room turn towards him, as the CD player pounded out the first few bars of 'Walking on Sunshine'. His mouth went dry and he felt a hundred pairs of eyes burn into his back as he faced Madame Gautier.

"I'm sorry," he said quietly as he quickly invented a suitable excuse. "But I'm afraid that *haute cuisine* is not my *metier*. After all I am an Englishman."

The *salle l'amique* erupted into laughter and the tension disappeared in a moment. Francoise pulled Bob to her crimpled bosom and kissed both his cheeks in forgiveness before going back to the table to rescue what she could of her party menu.

Bob exhaled a long sigh of relief. It was, he decided, a good moment at which to get a drink. He had always prided himself on having an organised mind. If you were going to get drunk, he reasoned, you might as well do it methodically. After all he was a professor and so he ought to approach the task scientifically, as if it were a research project. Tonight, he decided, it would be a geographical enquiry. He would start in the north-east of France, with a glass of Champagne and then work his way south and west until he reached the Pyrenees or oblivion—whichever came first. The way Bob felt tonight, he didn't really care which it was.

About an hour later as he approached the Bordeaux table, looking to see if there was a decent Graves to be had, he felt a rough hand pull at his wrist. Bob turned back unsteadily, eight-hundred kilometres of wine-crawling was starting to make an impact, and he recognised the face of the man tugging at his arm but couldn't place him.

"*Monsieur?*"

"Ah, you don't recognise me?"

"I'm sorry . . ."

"But you are an Englishman?" The man shook his head gently. "I think that excuse can be used only once."

"I know! The car. You're Monsieur Rogier." Recognition came suddenly to Bob.

"That's right." The old farmer pumped his arm as if they were long lost schoolfriends. "Didier Rogier."

"Not Didier Patrice Rogier, by any chance?" Bob asked as another sliver of memory flickered across his alcohol-softened synapses.

"Yes."

"So you must have known James Hambleton?"

Rogier's bushy eyebrows narrowed.

"Ambleton? I don't think so . . ."

"You own shares in a company that he used to run. Hambleton's of Paris. They're an import-export company."

"Shares?" Rogier laughed. "Me? Afford shares." He slapped Bob on the shoulder. "You're a real joker."

Bob's head was reeling. He had enough trouble standing up as it was, without trying to cope with hearty gestures. Perhaps he should have stopped the wine trail just north of St Emilion.

"It's just that he was murdered." Another memory passed through his mind. "It was the night that I met you on the road. You were driving . . ." Bob suddenly felt very sober. Rogier was glaring at him as the words ran out.

"I don't know anyone called 'Ambleton." Rogier separated each word carefully before turning to a young woman standing next to him. "This is my daughter, Betrice." He added proudly, "She's an estate agent."

"I'm very pleased to meet you, er . . ." Bob was sufficiently sober to recognise that he was slurring—and sufficiently drunk to have already forgotten the girl's name.

"Betrice." She kissed him on both cheeks and he could smell lilies and lavender infused with alcohol. He suspected that the latter scent was his.

"The pleasure's mine," Bob said. She had small lips and glassy brown eyes, both of which had been carefully made-up. She looked at him curiously, as though he were an exhibit in a freak-show, and her white neck twisted away as she appraised him.

"I'll leave you two together then," Rogier said. "I'm sure I can trust you with her. You are, as you say, an Englishman." The farmer shook Bob's hand again and kissed his daughter before moving towards the hall door. Bob couldn't be sure, but he thought that the two exchanged brief words as they embraced. Betrice pushed her dark hair behind her ears and flashed Bob a brief but suggestive smile. He didn't know if he liked the idea of being set-up by a girl's father. There was only one way to find out.

"Would you like a glass of wine?" he slurred.

"*Non merci*. I can't stand the stuff."

"Then you probably chose the wrong place to be born." Bob giggled at his own joke.

Betrice didn't.

He looked at her more carefully. She was probably in her late twenties but had dressed in the sort of polka-dot summer dress that was usually worn by someone twice that age. Her face was pretty, certainly, but it was almost too carefully made-up as if she had been determined to put on a show for someone. Underneath it all Bob could see that she was scowling. Whatever she had arranged for the evening was clearly not going to plan.

"You don't mind if I do?" he said shaking his empty glass towards her.

"It doesn't look as if anyone has minded yet," she grumbled. She shook her head and muttered something towards the roof of the hall. "For Christ's sake get me a glass of whatever's strongest." Bob raised an eyebrow at her. "Before I change my mind," she hissed back.

Bob was back to her in a trice with a glass of white Bordeaux. He clinked glasses with her and took a sip. He saw Betrice wince at the first mouthful, and then close her eyes as she drained the glass in one gulp. She pushed it out towards him for a refill.

"I hate this place," she said, her chin jutting forward. "Are you the man to take me away from it?"

Bob's jaw slackened and he could feel the warmth of the room on his tongue. The sound system was cranking up to full party mood as Mel and Kim were unleashed onto the assembled throng.

"Erm," Bob had always been reticent with women, unable to read their motives. "I suppose I could be," he said eventually.

"Isn't that your wife?" She draped one arm over Bob's shoulder and twisted his head to face up the hall.

"Oh, yes."

"She looks like she's having fun."

This was true. Kate had her arm around a man wearing tight jeans, whose back was turned towards them.

"Who is it?"

"That would be our guest of honour," Betrice replied casually. "Dominic Poussin." She looked Bob in the eyes. "They call him the heartbreaker."

"Oh yes, he's my neighbour's grandson. I've met him once." He recalled their canoe expedition and Kate's sudden interest in boating. "He was with his fiancée." Bob scanned the crowds nervously. "I presume she must be here somewhere."

"He's not in love with her," Betrice said quietly, still staring towards Kate.

"I suppose I should be relieved at that."

"Not with your wife, stupid. He's not in love with Sandrine."

"Oh, I think he is. They make such a lovely couple together. She's obviously devoted to him."

"Not quite as much as your wife is, it would seem."

Bob watched in horror as Kate wrapped her arms around Dominic and kissed him full on the lips. He could feel the anger rising in his chest and his hands started to tremble. Betrice flashed him a demure little smile and folded her arms. Bob felt hot. How dare Kate flaunt herself in such a manner? He was her husband and she seemed determined to embarrass him in front of the entire village.

"Get fresh for the week-end," urged the sound system.

Two could play at that game.

"I'll take you wherever you want, my darling Betrice," he declared loudly.

He pulled the young woman's head and sucked at her face as though it were a slice of over-ripe melon. After a few seconds he could dimly sense her pummelling his stomach with her fists. He released her and she heaved air into her lungs as though she had been about to asphyxiate.

"All in good time, handsome." Betrice retrieved a paper tissue from her sleeve and mopped her face. "At the moment where I really need to go is the loo."

Bob looked around. He knew that there was only one toilet in the building—reserved for women. Most Saturday nights when there were events on at the *salle l'amique* the unwary visitor to St-Sébastien might encounter a straggling line of men, backs to the road, returning the goodness of the vine back to the soil from whence it came. It was recycling in the raw Bob had always felt.

"Look at the queue for Christ's sake."

"Oh yes." There were about six or seven women lined up outside the toilet door. Either they were all desperate or their dancing wasn't very good, Bob decided, as they seemed to be shuffling from foot to foot almost—but not quite—synchronised with each other.

"But I'm bursting," Betrice urged. "Oh my God, what a sodding awful night."

"I know!" Bob found a glimmer of inspiration. "Come round to our place. We only live three doors down the road. You can use the loo there."

"Take me," Betrice said urgently. It wasn't a phrase that Bob had heard very often.

When they reached the house Betrice raced up the wrought iron spiral staircase before Bob could explain where the bathroom was. He heard her try the bedroom door first, then swear in anger, before she opened the bathroom door and swear in relief. She was not light on her feet. The wooden boards pounded up and down as she ran across them and it brought on a burst of thumping in Bob's head. What he really needed to do was lie down for a few moments. He could collect his thoughts, recharge his energy levels and then he would be able to give Betrice the attention that she deserved. He stretched himself out on the couch, his head nearest the staircase. No, he corrected himself; it was the attention that he deserved. Kate thought she could flirt the night away with any old bit of French trouser but he would show her. He could still pull the young girls when he wanted to, and the classy ones at that.

"Shit!"

"What's the matter?"

"I got here too late," Betrice sighed.

This was followed by two minutes of gurgling water, rounded off by a sigh that lasted nearly as long.

"Are you alright up there?" Bob called.

"Yes, but I'll have to go home."

"Oh?" Bob felt a mixture of disappointment and relief. He closed his eyes.

"I've wet my knickers. Sorry."

"Oh."

"Have you got a bag?"

"What for?"

"To put them in." Her voice was tetchy now. "I can't very well walk down the street with them tucked up my sleeve, can I?"

"Oh. No. I imagine we've got one somewhere down here." Bob didn't really care any more. His head was pounding and he really just wanted Kate to come back and look after him. All this flirting business was just a bit too much like hard work. He heard Betrice slam the toilet lid down and trudge her way across the bathroom floor onto the landing.

"I'll bring them down then?"

"Yes, you do that."

He could hear her stepping onto the staircase. Thud, thud, thud . . .

He opened his eyes.

The view was a revelation. Betrice was stood on a step directly above his head holding the banister with one hand and her knickers in the other. He could see straight up her skirt and felt his face crimson as he realised where he was looking.

He jumped up on the couch, just as the front door opened. Betrice's dress billowed up as the warm breeze floated into the lounge and rose over Bob's head.

"What the hell is?" It appeared that Kate was home, although Bob couldn't see her because he was entangled beneath Betrice's dress. And he had seen something quite astonishing.

"It's her legs!"

"You disgusting little man." Betrice starting beating Bob around the head.

"I can't believe you would do this to me." Kate grabbed Bob's hands and pulled him away from Betrice before slapping his face.

The pounding in his head grew dimmer as the two women took it turns to assault him.

"Bloody English pervert. My dad was right."

"I should have known better than to marry you. You womanising lazy good-for-nothing scumbag."

"It's her legs!" Bob cried out to them, as if it explained everything. "She's the one that had sex in the cottage."

"You had sex with her in the cottage?" Kate had clearly misunderstood.

"No, no. I watched her having . . ." Bob started and realised his error almost immediately.

"You were watching?" Betrice was scandalised. "You really are twisted. I'm getting out of here."

"You watched her . . . ? In the cottage?"

"It was only her legs. I didn't know who she was."

"Well, you can bloody well sling your hook. Get out the pair of you."

Kate started slapping Bob's face and he backed out of the front door.

"Don't you come near me, you disgusting man," Betrice backed away from him, down the road, still holding her knickers. Bob had a dim awareness that a crowd was beginning to form. He could see Madame Poussin, hands on hips, glaring at him.

"Go away. All of you, just go away!" Kate was half-shouting, half-crying.

"But I love you," Bob called back and tried to walk towards the house.

Then he felt his legs give way as he crumpled onto the pavement and into oblivion.

CHAPTER THIRTY-FOUR

BOB'S HEAD SCREAMED into waking. He was aware of brightness; intense white-as-a-dentist's-teeth light. Bob wasn't sure which was worse. The unremitting pounding in his head recalled the time when he had smashed open one of the local cantaloupe melons with a mallet in order to get at the juice inside. The light, even with his eyes screwed shut, was cruelly fierce, chasing his consciousness into tiny corners of his mind where it might hide. Underpinning everything was the insidious stench of stale tobacco. Breathing seemed to bring the fumes into his soul. Not breathing simply brought on a craving for more.

"Go on. Throw up. You know you want to."

"Thierry is that you?"

"Who else would be stupid enough to take you in?"

Bob blinked open his eyes. Since when had light been that bright? He quickly shut them again.

"You fucking idiot."

Bob thought of a hundred insults to hurl back at the gendarme but they all came out at once in the form of a gargling noise.

"Use the bowl!"

Thierry brought Bob's head into contact with something plastic. There was a brief scent of coffee and toast. Bob was sick.

"Nothing like a good puke to set you up for the day," Thierry grunted in satisfaction.

Bob opened his eyes fully for the first time. Oddly enough he did feel better. The light seemed to have dimmed a bit and the pounding in his head had become a little less apocalyptic. He tried to haul his body into a sitting position but for some reason he couldn't move his arm.

"Is that a handcuff?"

"Yes," Thierry replied casually.

"Any particular reason . . . . ?"

Thierry turned to Bob and stared at him.

"You don't remember?"

"Remember what?"

"Oh let's see . . ." He began counting on his fingers. "Smashing up your own front door, hurling drunken abuse at innocent bystanders, tearing down the direction sign to the *salle l'amique*, lewd behaviour towards a young woman . . ." Thierry glanced at his thumb and licked something off it. "Not to mention the threats to murder your wife?" He paused a moment. "To be fair I can't recall who made the first threat, but it seemed prudent to keep you apart." He stared at Bob. "After we'd managed to separate you, that is."

"Oh no!" Bob closed his eyes.

The feeling of nausea in the pit of his stomach was quickly turning into one of fear. How could he face Kate or any of their French neighbours? He had ruined Gautier's celebrations, turned Dominic Poussin's party into a riot and made a fool of himself with a girl who was half his age. Above all he'd obviously treated Kate very badly. He could feel the hurt welling up behind his eyelids. He opened them to let the tears roll down across his cheek. On the positive side, Madame Poussin would probably never speak to him again. Not that it would matter. He'd have no option but to move away and live somewhere else. Bob could imagine himself arriving back in Portsmouth with no money, no home and no dignity.

"I've made a list of apologies for you."

"*Pardon?*"

"It'll make a man of you." Thierry wandered off into another part of the house and returned with a couple of sheets of paper.

"What will?"

"Saying sorry." He pulled a small wooden chair next to the couch on which Bob was lying. Cigarette ash rose around the police inspector which the sunlight framed into a glowing aurora.

"You're a saint."

"And you're a bloody stupid sinner." Thierry shook his head. "What on earth possessed you?"

"Oh, I don't know. Jealousy I suppose." Bob looked at the list. It appeared to be quite long. "Or stress. Or both, perhaps."

"I suggest you start with Gautier. He's a soft old sod. You can use that to your advantage."

"But how can I ever face any of them again?"

"Because they're your friends. They know what you're really like." Thierry felt at his pockets and patted down his legs. A cigarette fell out of the bottom of his trousers. He picked it up, blew on it and then placed it in his mouth. "Actually it might do your image a bit of good." He lit the cigarette and inhaled deeply. Light blue smoke, peppered with flecks of grey ash, raced out of his mouth and nostrils on the exhale. "You don't want to be known as 'that boring British git' for the rest of your life, do you?"

"Is that what they think about me?"

Thierry sighed.

"Not now, it isn't. Look my advice is just to be honest about it. You got drunk. You had a fight with Kate. You saw a bit of skirt that you fancied . . ."

"But that's not how it was," Bob protested. "Kate was . . ."

"Oh no." Thierry wagged his index finger. "Don't blame anyone else. Make out it was all your fault. No-one will believe you, but you'll seem all the nobler because you were the one prepared to confess."

"But I didn't fancy that girl . . . What's her name?"

"Betrice? In that case why was she running out of your house waving her knickers in the air?"

"Because she'd . . ." Bob thought about how to express it delicately. "She'd had an accident."

"She says you'd taken her round to your place under false pretences and then been staring up her skirt."

"I didn't!"

"Then why were you going on about her legs?"

"Well, I did see up her dress but it was an accident."

"I know." Thierry blew a thin column of smoke into the air. "The sort of accident that most men only dream about."

"No. But her legs . . ."

"Stop dreaming Bob . . ."

"They were **the** legs. I mean the ones from the cottage. You know, on the day of the murder?"

"God! We're not back onto that, are we?"

"Yes. She must have been the girl with Dominic."

"Are you sure?"

"Certain. Trust me; you don't forget legs like those."

"Well, let me give you a piece of advice."

"Yes?"

"Don't mention it when you go around apologising to people. It mightn't go down very well." He cleared his throat and adopted a fluting tone that was obviously supposed to be an impression of Bob's accent. "I'm ever so sorry I ruined your engagement party but did you know that the bridegroom's having it off with the local farmer's daughter."

"I see what you mean."

"Which reminds me. I think you ought to keep out of Rogier's way for a while. He's err . . . How can I put this?" Thierry rubbed at a patch of stubble under his chin. "He's not a man that I would mess with. Betrice is not exactly his pride and joy—he thinks she should have been married off years ago—but he still takes a dim view of anyone who messes with her. He's proud of what she's achieved for herself. Round here it's quite an achievement to work in an estate agent's office."

"Of course! That's how she got the keys."

"What are you babbling on about?"

"She must have had access to the keys for the cottage from before it was sold. She knew it was rarely used for visitors, so where better to feather a little love nest." Bob's mind was working in overdrive. "I'd left the Clio down the road because it had broken down so she wouldn't have known that there was anyone in the cottage."

"I said leave it." Thierry's voice was a menacing growl—and Bob didn't think it was just because of the Gitanes.

"But she might know who murdered James. She might even have done it herself." Bob was beginning to feel better. "And I'm sure Rogier has shares in the firm. He was very evasive about it when I asked him . . ."

"You asked him about the Hambletons?"

"Yes."

"You idiot! You bloody idiot." Thierry jumped off his chair and stubbed his cigarette on the wall. "Just leave Rogier out of this. I know him and he has nothing to do with the murder . . ."

"But he was driving past the cottage at the right time. He picked me up if you remember?"

"I do remember. It's because Rogier is a straightforward, friendly man. But he's also a very strong man and not the sort of person you want to turn into an enemy."

"I still think it's very suspicious. His daughter is inside the cottage when she shouldn't be and he happens to be driving past about two hours before the murder."

"Just leave it, *mon ami*. Apologise to Betrice when you next see her and move on."

"If you say so . . ." Bob felt ready to sit up and tugged at the handcuff. "Any chance you could get rid of these?"

"Only if you promise me one thing."

"I've just said that I won't upset Rogier."

"It's not that."

"What then?"

"I want you to promise me that you'll make up with Kate."

"Why?"

Thierry bent over Bob on the couch and picked at the lock with the end of a steak knife.

"Haven't you got a key?"

"Lost them all years ago. The gendarmerie is so short of money they won't let me have a new set. Anyway they're dead easy to get off." There was a metallic snap and Thierry pulled Bob's wrist free. "*Voila!*"

Bob sat up on the couch and rubbed his head.

"So, why do you want me to make up with Kate? She was lusting after that Dominic all night."

Thierry sat next to Bob on the couch. Bob could smell the tobacco intensely. Thierry was like a walking, breathing, living nicotine patch.

"Because you're right for each other."

There was a pause.

"Is that it?"

"Yes."

"Because we're right for each other? Even though we have very little in common and hate each other's guts?" Bob felt he was being a bit overdramatic but recently it had seemed like the couple really didn't have anything that was keeping them together.

"Yes." Thierry turned and faced Bob. "What else do you need?"

"You mean apart from affection, respect, shared interests . . . ?"

"They're all irrelevant. The main thing is that you belong to each other. I've seen enough marriages dissolve in violence and hatred over the years to know that yours isn't destined to end that way."

"I wish I had your confidence."

"Be honest Bob. You'd miss her wouldn't you?"

"Like the plague." But as he said the words he knew it wasn't really true. Not hearing her voice was like being deaf, not seeing her was like blindness. He already felt incomplete. "She'll never take me back."

"She will." Thierry stood up and stretched. "Although probably not today. If I were you I'd go and have a good long walk and I'll feed you later. Tomorrow we can go and make your apologies. By then she'll be aching for you to come back."

"Do you think so?"

"Probably. There are no guarantees in this world."

"Alright." Bob stood up and stretched. He coughed as the smoke fumes pulled on the back of his throat. "A decent breath of fresh air and I'll be as good as new."

A puzzle came into his mind.

"What were you doing there anyway? I thought you weren't going to be at the party."

"I wasn't," Thierry replied. "I'd just discovered something to do with the murder and came round to tell you."

"What was it?"

Thierry smiled at Bob. His yellow teeth poked out beneath the greying moustache.

"I've found Timmy Wells."

CHAPTER THIRTY-FIVE

THE AFTERNOON WAS almost gone by the time Bob felt able to walk with any confidence. Thierry had gone out leaving a scrawled note that said 'Called to incident. Don't be stupid. Wash up.' As if to underline the point there was an unsteady arrow at the bottom pointing in the general direction of the kitchen.

Bob's mind had been alive with speculation about the murder after the gendarme's revelation about Timmy Wells. Apparently he was a British financial consultant who had helped convert Hambleton's of Paris into a *bona fide* limited company. Wells himself couldn't have committed the murder according to Thierry because he had been in New York at the time. Apparently three independent witnesses had testified to his location at the time of the murder although Bob could tell that the gendarme still had his doubts.

For Bob suspicion was falling elsewhere. For one thing Maureen had clearly lied to him about the existence of Timmy Wells. Or had she simply forgotten? The conversion to a limited company had taken place twenty years ago so it was feasible that she might not have recollected the name. On the other hand he still appeared in the list of shareholders and Bob didn't think that Maureen was the sort of person to forget that very easily.

And then there was Rogier. His name was also in that list of shareholders. It really didn't seem likely that a farmer in the Vendée, who drove a beaten-up van and couldn't afford to repair his own out-buildings, would own shares in an English company based in

Paris. Rogier had always been relatively friendly to Bob on their previous meetings and certainly wasn't the ogre that Poussin and the rest portrayed him as. But he had said something to Betrice before allowing her to spend the evening with Bob. Perhaps he had instructed her to get him drunk, or to wreck his marriage or to find out how much he knew.

What was Betrice's role in all this? She was definitely the woman that Dominic had been with in the cottage on the night of the murder. Had she done that for her father as well? Possibly, but Bob was sure that she was genuinely attracted to Dominic. The way she had looked enviously at Kate as the two had flirted had been enough to convince him on that score.

Kate! How was he ever going to be able to talk to her again? It was only natural that she had wanted to spend some time with a handsome younger man. Bob realised that he must appear very unattractive to Kate in comparison. When they were in England and too busy with their jobs to think beyond the conventional things were straightforward. But now Kate was free to consider other ways of life and other lovers—and Bob knew he wasn't in contention. And, of course, she obviously thought that he had tried to have sex with Betrice. Yes, she was a pretty girl but she lacked all the maturity and sexual savoir-faire that a real woman like Kate possessed. Besides, how could you have sensible pillow talk with a girl called Bet . . .

That was it! Betrice could easily be Betty! James Hambleton had called out for Betty at night. And Rogier owned shares in Hambleton's company. It all made sense now. Betrice had checked out the cottage under the guise of an affair opening the way for her father to commit the murder later that night. Bob had caught the farmer as he was on his way to the cottage and this explained why Rogier had been so keen to find out how much he knew. There was still the small matter of Deneuve's suicide for Bob to resolve but he was sure he was onto something. Now he needed to prove it. He looked at the sink full of mould-encrusted crockery and shook his head. He would have to go to Rogier's farm and confront him with the truth.

The sun was flirting with the horizon as Bob slammed the door of Thierry's house. It had been a beautifully warm day and the cerise glaze that reflected from the fields around St-Sébastien seemed to promise a similar day tomorrow. Bob couldn't easily take the Clio without arousing unwanted attention and so he began to walk along a path that ran between a field of sunflowers on one side and vineyards on the other. It would take him at least an hour and a half to walk to Longchamp, but that was alright; it gave him the time to work out exactly what he was going to say. He was glad that he'd grabbed one of Thierry's fleeces as he'd left the house. It was going to be a long night.

As he progressed, ambling beside maize taller than himself for most of the journey, Bob became more and more convinced of his case. Betrice had been James' lover and had given Rogier shares in the business to keep him quiet. James had bought the cottage in the Vendée so that the romance could grow, but away from Maureen's prying eyes in Paris. Rogier had tried to blackmail the Hambleton's further but failed and struck back by killing James. Deneuve had somehow found out about the murder, possibly on one of the regular family visits to the cottage, and Rogier had been forced to kill him as well. In Bob's mind it all fitted beautifully. He would present the farmer with the facts and a confession would follow without doubt.

The light had almost entirely faded by the time Bob reached boundary of Longchamp. A large hand-painted sign tied onto the side of a barbed wire fence announced that this was *'propertie privee'* and that trespassers would be dealt with violently. Bob believed they would and it wasn't a risk he was prepared to take. He was determined to survive for long enough to confront the murderer even though that would mean walking all the way around the perimeter of the farm to get to the front gate. He could see the lights from the main farmhouse on the top of a low rise directly in front of him. To his left were the disused barns and outbuildings, silhouetted firmly against the grey-pink smudge of twilight. The fence ran along the bottom of the hillock, maintaining a good distance from the buildings. Bob sighed. It would be a long walk round.

"Shit!"

Bob swore as he caught his foot in a bramble and tripped into narrow ditch that ran alongside the wire fence. His legs were already tired from the walk so far and it felt as though he had wrenched his ankle quite badly. He sat in the ditch and tried turning his foot from side to side.

"Shit! Shit! Shit!"

It hurt.

Things seemed to have gone from bad to worse, Bob reflected. Not only had he fallen out with his wife, lost his home and his dignity but now, it appeared, he was lame as well. He tried standing but it was clear that his left foot wasn't going to be able to take much weight for a while—and weight was about the only thing that Bob hadn't lost in the last twenty-four hours. Somehow he needed to get to the farmhouse so that he could get a lift back to Thierry's place. At least there he would be able to rest up for a while and give the ankle a chance to heal.

Bob dragged himself round a bit more of the barbed wire fence, but it was tough going. Each time he moved a few yards further he had to lift his left leg with his hands to bring it level with his right foot. At this rate it would take hours to get to the front of the farmhouse. If only he could go directly across the farmland, past the old outhouses and in at the back of Longchamp it would be so much quicker. And far less painful.

After a few more yards along the fence Bob sank back down into the ditch, sitting on the low earthy ridge that formed its bank. This was hopeless. It would be as easy for him to spend the night sleeping in the ditch and hope his ankle had recovered by the time he woke up. Sleeping in a ditch—it seemed to sum up Bob's current fortune perfectly. He put his hands into the pockets of the fleece and sighed heavily.

He sat up again just as suddenly. In the right hand pocket was something metallic. Bob pulled it out and stared at it in the moonlight. It was a pair of scissors. No. On closer examination he could see that the blades weren't straight. They were Kate's pinking shears. What the hell was wrong with the wretched things? Couldn't they stay in one place—even if it was the wrong place—for any length of time? They seemed to be following him around like a bad luck charm. Bob swore under his breath and then smiled. Perhaps this was the right place for them after all. He scrambled to his feet and dragged his body across to the fence. Gingerly, and with great difficulty, he started to cut at the wire, pulling it apart with his fingers as he progressed upwards. Eventually he managed to prise a gap in the wire large enough for him to squeeze through. He hauled his body between the thorny stalks of metal and stood up on the other side of the fence. It wouldn't be easy but at least now he could drag himself to the farmhouse by the shortest route, via the old barn and through to the back entrance. What if Rogier caught him trespassing? Bob concluded that things probably couldn't get any worse.

It was slow progress but gradually Bob made his way through the fields of maize towards the outbuildings. The crop was about waist-high at this time of year so Bob could see the direction in which he needed to travel. He had to move in straight lines between the rows of corn and occasionally fight his way through a clump to keep making progress towards his destination. As he approached the outbuildings he heard a dog bark in the distance and began to wonder what Rogier would really do if he caught him out here? He loped towards the nearest barn in a mix of hopping and limping. For a moment he paused. He thought he could see a small chink of light coming from a crack in the barn's roof. That couldn't be right. These buildings had been derelict for years—Poussin had said that.

Bang!

The sound of an explosion just to Bob's left made him recoil, almost falling over onto his bad ankle. It had sounded like a shotgun but Bob couldn't see anyone. The dog in the distance started howling—and sounded much nearer now. Bob shuffled to the right, taking him closer to the second barn but away from the main farmhouse.

Bang!

Another shot, this time to the right. Still Bob couldn't see anyone but he could hear voices approaching from the newer buildings. Time to make an escape, he decided, and started to hobble backwards. Perhaps this hadn't been such a good idea after all.

Bang! Bang!

Two explosions in quick succession, one each side and closer, caused Bob to topple backwards. His fall was broken by one of the statuesque stalks of corn and he tumbled onto the ground onto a carpet of crumpled maize and straw. After a couple of moments the tall plants of corn parted and all that Bob could see, towering as a silhouette above him, was a figure dressed in a dark jacket carrying a rifle.

"You! Are you bloody stalking me?"

It was Betrice.

"No, I was just trying to get to the farmhouse."

"Why don't you go round by the footpath like everyone else does?" Her voice sounded more annoyed than menacing.

"I twisted my ankle, so I decided to come by the most direct route."

As if to prove his point Bob struggled onto his knees. The position seemed appropriate—he felt more in need of prayer than at any time before. Anything less than a miracle probably wasn't going to help.

"*Abruti!*" Betrice pouted at him in disgust and then slowly extended an arm towards Bob. "I don't suppose you can make my weekend much worse."

She pulled him out of the maize and gestured with the rifle towards the farmhouse.

"Dad'll be overjoyed to see you!"

Bob remembered just how hurtful sarcasm was when it came from the mouths of young women.

Bang! Bang!

"Shut up," Betrice shouted into the air.

"What-the-hell-was-that?"

"Oh, just the alarm system. That's how I knew you were up here."

"Alarm system?"

"Yes. Well, bird-scarers really but it has the same effect. There's a whole cordon of them around the barns. It means that if any of those bloody tax people come nosing around then we can stop them before they get to the outbuildings. Usually the stories about ghosts and dead bodies keep people away, but the explosions help to underline the message that no-one's welcome. It keeps the nosier natives away." She looked scornfully at Bob. "Except for the really stupid ones of course."

"But what's so special about the barns?"

Betrice stopped walking and stared at him.

"You don't know what's in the barns?"

Bob shook his head.

"You really are stupid aren't you? Don't you listen to any local gossip?"

"Yes, but I'm English and sometimes it's hard to translate the local *patois* . . ."

"Bloody hell." She started walking again and Bob struggled to catch up with her.

"So what is it?"

"It's a grass farm." She gestured across at the outbuildings. "The barns are full of marijuana."

Bob's jaw fell. So that was why Poussin had tried to warn him off coming up here. A grass farm—it made so much sense now.

"And everyone around here knows what it is?"

"More or less. It's very small scale in the scheme of things but it's helped make dad a few euros over the years. I'm sure he'll be happy to tell you all about it himself. He's having a quiet drink with a mate of yours at the moment."

By the time they reached the main farmhouse Bob's entire left leg was throbbing. Betrice had led him across through the swathes of corn with an efficiency borne from experience, and at a pace that flared through Bob's ankle as if it were a lightning conductor for pain.

"Papa!"

"In here." Rogier's voice sounded gruff. Bob wondered what happened to people who accused French drug barons of murder. It might, he supposed, make a difference if the accusation was made in a remote farmhouse, late at night, over twenty kilometres away from the nearest gendarmerie. He suspected he knew the answer, and then remembered what had happened between him and Betrice the night before. The pain in his ankle seemed suddenly irrelevant.

"Are you alright?" Betrice faced Bob in the doorway to what appeared to be a kitchen. "You look very pale to me."

"It's my leg," he mumbled. "I think I should probably sit down."

"That's OK. You can sit with Papa in the *sejour*. It's just through there." She indicated a source of light down a corridor.

"Who's that?" growled Rogier.

"Just some bloke I picked up," she winked at Bob.

"Another one! I just hope he's a damn sight younger than that drunken idiot you went for last night."

"Funny you should mention him," Betrice said as she entered the *sejour* and waved Bob into the room.

"Fucking hell!"

"Thierry!"

"What in the name of all that's holy are you doing here?" The gendarme's face was flushed red and he sat bolt upright in a thickly upholstered armchair opposite Rogier.

"I could ask you the same?" Bob folded his arms defiantly. Judging from the three empty wine bottles on the coffee table between them Thierry's colour wasn't just down to surprise.

"What's the problem here?" Rogier asked. "Sit down," he gestured towards a sofa. "You're making the place look untidy." He shouted towards his daughter. "Get your man a drink—looks like he needs one."

"Get me one too," Thierry yelled after her, slurring slightly.

Bob sat down carefully. The throbbing in his leg made any sudden movements impossibly painful but he was acutely aware that he needed to be on his mettle in case events took a turn for the violent.

A thought occurred to him.

"I know why you're here, Thierry."

"I bet you don't."

"It's to do with the murder."

The gendarme raised his eyebrows and leant back into his chair.

235

"Lucky guess," he conceded.

"Ah, no. Not a guess. You see I know who did it. You've come here to arrest Monsieur Rogier for a double-murder."

"What?"

"Is this imbecile a friend of yours?" Rogier started to rise and began rolling up his sleeves.

"More of an acquaintance really." Thierry waved Rogier to sit down. "Leave him to me. He's English."

"That old excuse again," Rogier grumbled and sank back.

"He's a murderer," Bob repeated defiantly, pointing at the farmer. He'd come to the conclusion that death was probably less painful than a twisted ankle.

"Nonsense," Thierry said. "Apart from anything else how could he have got into the cottage?"

"Perhaps he has a key. Betrice certainly has."

"And perhaps you have a brain—although it is less likely I admit."

"But he's a drug grower," Bob implored.

"I know that."

"You do?"

"Of course. I'm a gendarme. It's my job to know who's up to what. Monsieur Rogier has been a very considerate member of the local community for many years now."

"Since when has it been considerate to grow marijuana?"

"Its medicinal properties have been known about for centuries." Thierry was beginning to struggle with some of the longer words. "Just like alcohol. Which reminds me—where's that drink Betrice?"

The girl appeared on cue with two large glasses of dark red wine.

"Settle down you boys," she said, handing them each a drink. "It's Sunday—a day of peace. Whatever's got into you?"

"He says your dad's a murderer."

"Papa? A killer?" The slender woman head jerked backwards and she let out the shrillest laugh that Bob had ever heard.

"I don't see what's so funny." Bob sipped at the wine. He recognised the earthy red-berried flavour of one of the local vineyards.

"The idea that papa could kill anyone is ridiculous. He is renowned in these parts for his squeamishness. He can't even bring himself to wring the chicken's neck for dinner." She let out another shriek of laughter.

"That's why he grows marijuana," Thierry explained. "Of course he does sell some of it on the open market for recreational purposes but a lot of it goes to local people who are suffering with arthritis, depression, glaucoma . . . The doctors round here often prescribe a quick detour to Longchamp on the way to the *pharmacie*."

"I'm a bit of a saint really," Rogier added matter-of-factly.

"Even I wouldn't go that far," Betrice said, and sat on the arm of the chair next her father, ruffling his beard with her long fingernails.

"But at least he doesn't look up womens' skirts," Thierry noted.

"So why are you here?"

"You were right to think that it was due to the murder, but for all the wrong reasons. Because I turn a blind eye to Rogier's crop, he keeps me up-to-date with what's happening on the dark side."

"A police spy!" Rogier announced proudly.

"So I was just checking with him whether there's any talk about the murder in the criminal community."

"And . . . ?"

"There isn't. But someone connected to the Hambletons has been up to something."

"Let me guess—it's Michel, the mechanic." Having dismissed Rogier as a suspect Bob's mind was now running in another direction. "I bet he's operating a scam on vehicle mileage and James caught him out . . ."

"Whoa!" Thierry raised his hand to Bob's face. "Stop inventing stories. No, the person involved is Louise Hambleton. Apparently she's been paying quite a lot of cash to a doctor in Le Mans recently, who's been laundering it through some less salubrious channels. We can't tell what she's paying for—although blackmail would seem an obvious conclusion given the amounts involved."

"Perhaps she was pregnant and . . ."

"Shut up and drink your wine," Thierry counselled.

"Are you going to challenge her about it?"

"No. I thought we'd just write it down on a piece of paper and file it somewhere quietly."

"Are you joking?"

"Of course I'm fucking joking. On Tuesday I'll head down to Bordeaux to quiz the doctor involved and see where that leads me." Thierry slurped down the remainder of his wine. "Probably a *cul-de-sac*, but you never know."

Bob sipped at his glass and the warmth of the wine swept through him, easing his leg and quietening his mood.

"I really can't believe that Louise is the killer," he said. "She's so gentle and quiet."

"They're the worse," Thierry snorted.

"Yes, just like poor papa." Betrice let her father's head slip from her hands and he fell back into the chair mouth open, fast asleep. "Look at him. How could he kill anyone?" Another crescendo of laughter burst across the room.

"I'm sorry," Bob said. "It seemed to make sense at the time."

He looked at Betrice who came across the room and bent across him. He felt the coldness of her lips touch against his bald forehead.

"You're forgiven, *cheri*. It's all too comical. Just wait until I tell my brother." She looked Bob in the eyes. "Now he can get violent. He once beat someone almost to a pulp just for looking at me."

Bob felt the well-being drain from his body in an instant.

"I think I'll have another drink," he mumbled.

CHAPTER THIRTY-SIX

"**S**TOP MOPING AROUND. You're driving me mad." The gendarme's patience was running thin.

"It's easy for you." Bob scowled at Thierry. "You haven't lost a wife, a home and a reputation."

"I never had any of those things to start with. It's safer that way."

Bob threw the tea-towel he'd been using to wipe the dishes across the tiny kitchen. He'd been working hard to tidy up Thierry's house—it took his mind off those things which he should really be addressing—and this was all the gratitude he got.

"That's rubbish. You've got this place for one thing."

Thierry picked the tea-towel off the floor and folded it very carefully before jamming it into the space between the bottom of the sink and the unsteady wooden cupboard that passed for a china cabinet.

"This isn't a home. It's a refuge." Gendarme's traditionally lived in free accommodation inside the gendarmerie. Thierry, however, preferred his independence. "More like an asylum actually." Bob suspected that the other gendarmes were probably grateful.

"It's still more than I've got."

Thierry carefully opened the cupboard and selected a saucer from the bottom shelf.

"What are you doing now?" Bob grumbled. "I spent most of this morning disinfecting that lot. There were things growing on those cups that I'm sure are only supposed to survive in deep oceans or places that never see the light. It's amazing that you never caught the norovirus."

"I'm going to consecrate our friendship in the way that lovers do." Thierry carefully weighed the saucer in his hand. "Now, get the hell out of here!"

Without further warning he launched the saucer like a frisbee straight at Bob's head.

"What on earth . . ." Bob ducked as the missile smashed into the kitchen wall behind him.

Thierry had reloaded, and the next piece of crockery—an ancient dinner plate—was already on its way. Bob dived for cover behind a rickety wooden dining chair with a high faux-leather back. The plate hit the top of the chair and crashed into the floor, scattering shards of porcelain across the ground.

"Are you mad?"

"No, I feel fine. Perfectly domesticated," yelled Thierry, as he lobbed a sugar bowl into the air.

The trajectory was hand-grenade perfect and Bob calculated that it would drop on him after clearing the back of the chair. His only escape route was to break cover and use the chair as defensive shield. He deflected the bowl onto the wall and retreated through an archway into the *sejour* under a volley of teacups. Thierry had clearly got the bit between his teeth and was getting through the crockery faster than an English bargain hunter at a *vide grenier*.

"How do I concede?"

There was a pause.

"Do you want to concede?" Bob could no longer see what Thierry was doing but there was an ominous sound of cutlery being prepared.

"Yes, of course. We're friends aren't we?"

A quiverful of teaspoons hailed into the chair. It wasn't quite the answer that Bob had expected.

"You need to go back to Kate. Those are my terms."

"Never!" Bob was surprised at how instinctive his response was. He hadn't thought of himself as a proud man but the idea of returning to Kate would mean all sorts of concessions that he couldn't possibly contemplate. Bob suddenly realised how stubborn Lear must have felt as the forces against him gathered.

"In that case, you die!"

Bob saw the wine glass glide through the air seconds before it skimmed over the top of his head and bounced into the carpet beyond him. He resisted the urge to call 'missed' and instead backed off further from the kitchen. A couple of forks and a spoon fell short of him before a long-handled bread-knife embedded itself into the back of the chair. Shocked, Bob dropped his shield and dived behind the sofa bed just as a crystal decanter shattered into the wall above him.

"You bloody English! Never know when to give in do you? Just you wait!"

There was an ominous silence for several seconds. Eventually, curiosity got the better of Bob and he peered round the side of the sofa. It was all the opening that Thierry needed. Bob got a good view of the missile as it sailed into the air, a well-primed parabola with one destination in mind. It was a large old china teapot that Kate had donated to the *croix-rouge* when they had been in downsizing mode after the move to St-Sébastien. Why on earth Thierry had bought it was a mystery to Bob, but it homed in on its target and Bob could only watch with wonder as it crunched spout-first into the metal frame of the sofa, showering Bob with porcelain debris, and the lid—completely intact—slapped onto Bob's bald pate, sending the world momentarily black.

The next thing that Bob recalled was a strong acidic stench of alcohol. He wondered what was happening and then remembered the crockery fight. His head was throbbing with pain and there seemed to be a light source close to his face. He could tell he was lying down and there were bands of fabric around his neck and thighs holding him in position. He opened his eyes slowly, expecting to find himself in hospital with stitches and bandages around his head—perhaps he'd even broken his shoulder or arm after the teapot had hit him. Instead Bob was disappointed to see that he was in the *cave*, laid out across the seat of the 2CV with the seatbelts restraining him.

"I told you he'd be OK," Thierry said enthusiastically.

"He's still alive—I'll give you that."

Bob started to turn his neck to look at Gautier—and immediately wished he hadn't.

"Aah, my head is falling off."

"Don't be such a baby. It's just a bit of mild concussion. Nothing that a glass of Gautier's finest won't cure." Thierry's voice didn't contain the slightest note of irony.

"Stay still," Poussin's voice came out of the gloom to Bob's left. "If you've broken your skull then any movement might dislodge a bit of your brain. You could be paralysed for life then. I learnt that when I was in the Brigade."

"Were you in the Foreign Legion?" Bob was impressed.

"No," Poussin responded tartly. "In the Farmers Boys' Brigade. When I was about fourteen. Mind you, I would have served in Vietnam if we hadn't run out of money. As it was I did my conscription in the Dordogne. That was before it fell into British hands."

"Ignore him and concentrate on my finger," Gautier said gently. "See if you can follow it around as I move it."

Bob watched the Frenchman's digit carefully as it slowly curved through the air in a figure-of-eight.

"I know a variant of that test," Thierry said brightly. "How many fingers am I holding up?"

Bob made a rapid gesture towards the gendarme with his index and middle finger.

"See. There's nothing wrong with his reactions," Thierry concluded.

"Yes," Gautier sighed sadly. "It does seem that he responds well to the vision test. Let's take these straps off and get you sitting up. I suppose it just goes to prove the truth of the old adage that for the English everything really does stop for tea."

Gradually Bob was eased into an upright position and he found he could move his head through enough of an arc to study the looks of concern on two of the three faces around him.

"Get him a drink, then." Thierry was smiling broadly. "And I'll have one while you're at it. I think this calls for a celebration."

"You mean the fact that you won't have to explain to your colleagues why you half beat a man to death?" Bob found that sitting up just made him angrier.

"No! I'm celebrating the fact that you're going back home to Kate." He raised the glass that Gautier passed to him towards Bob. "Back where you belong."

"You're going back to Kate?" Poussin asked. "That's a shame. I was just about to make my move on her." He cackled until his throat broke into a hacking cough.

"You're welcome to her."

"You don't really mean that, Bob." Gautier's voice was tinged with genuine concern. "She's missed you desperately you know."

"Rubbish. She shacked herself up with that orang-utan, err . . . What's his name? The rowing boy."

"Oh Dominic." Gautier pronounced the name with a disapproving air. "I think you'll find that a few chickens have come home to roost with that one."

"What do you mean?" Bob slurped back half a glass of rosé. The chill liquid hit his tongue in a refreshing burst of sweet fruitiness.

"It seems that Dominic has been seeing another woman during his engagement to Sandrine. He's quite a lad as it turns out. He was seeing at least two other women, sometimes in the same night!"

"It's the Poussin genes," Dominic's grandfather said proudly. "We've got a reputation to maintain you know."

Gautier gave the old man an uncharacteristically harsh look. Poussin carried on drinking without noticing.

"Of course it's embarrassing to have to cancel the wedding but I think it better to have cleared all this up before they took their vows." Gautier had gone back to fussing with the valves on the wine vats. "My understanding is that they've agreed to go their separate ways in a very amicable and mature manner. I think they both knew it wasn't really going to work out and are really rather relieved. And it's all thanks to Bob noticing Betrice's legs. I, for one, am very grateful."

"I doubt whether Kate is," Bob sighed.

"Dominic certainly isn't," Poussin grumbled. "He was looking forward to the wedding night." He face broke into an impish grin. "All those bridesmaids!"

"There was one curious thing," Gautier added. "When I asked Dominic about that evening with Betrice he told me that he went back to the cottage later on."

"Why?" Thierry sat up and leaned forward on the wooden table.

"Oh, he'd left his mobile phone behind."

"It was probably under the bed with Bob," Poussin joked.

"When was this?"

Even in the darkness of the *cave* Bob could tell that Thierry's mood was serious.

"About ten or eleven I imagine. Why does it matter?"

"Because it was the night of the murder," Bob realised why Thierry was suddenly interested.

"Did he see anything?" the gendarme asked quietly.

"That's the odd thing." Gautier approached the table and looked earnestly at the capitaine. "According to Dominic just as he was leaving the cottage a car pulled up and a man and a woman got out."

"Why the fuck didn't he tell us this before? He could have witnessed a murder and he keeps his mouth shut. I'll have him on so many charges he won't know what day of the week it is." Thierry was bouncing up and down in his chair. "Did he describe them?"

"He did. The man was elderly and I would guess that it was your victim, James Hambleton. Dominic said he was fat and jolly in an English way."

"What about the woman?" Thierry boomed out the question and smashed his fist onto the makeshift table.

"That's the interesting part. She was a lot younger, probably only sixteen or seventeen. She must have been pretty because Dominic described her as an angel."

Bob and Thierry looked at each other and spoke together.

"Louise!"

A few soothing rosés later Bob waved goodbye to Gautier, Poussin and Thierry from outside the little stone house that should have been home to his French dream life with Kate. He had decided that, although it was late, it was time to talk to her. He was less anxious than he had expected. Gautier had persuaded him that the worse that could happen was that Bob would discover for certain whether Kate hated him. This, together with enough alcohol to encourage bravery without bravado, had led him to conclude that it was time to resolve the situation one way or another. Gautier and Poussin had accompanied him to the house offering encouragement and support. Bob assumed that Thierry's attendance was merely to ensure that he got there and wouldn't be returning to the gendarme's home any time soon.

As he stood on the pavement, summoning the last nuggets of courage that he needed to knock on the blue wooden door, Bob thought about how his relationship with Kate had come to this point. They had shared a dream about how their lives in France would be different; more time, less stress, better quality. A life rather than an existence. But perhaps their dreams had been different. For Bob more time was about enjoying the moment more, but for Kate more time allowed you to do more things. It had been the same solution but for different problems. As for quality of life—Bob felt he had no idea what that really was for either of them. Perhaps it was for the best if they went their separate ways.

Bob banged the shutter door firmly with his knuckles, noticing that the Vendée blue paint was beginning to peel around the keyhole. He ignored the observation. There were more important reparations to attend to at the moment. He heard the inner door unlock and the shutter sprang towards him revealing light from house. It shone as an aureole around Kate as she leaned out into the street. She was wearing a thick sweater and her hair tumbled carelessly across her shoulders.

"Oh! It's you."

"I come in peace. I thought we should talk."

"You mean Gautier thought we should talk. He's been trying to persuade me to go and see you for the last couple of days." Her eyes glinted coldly in the moonlight. "I held out."

"I didn't," Bob replied. "Or perhaps I should say that I couldn't."

"You always were too soft."

"Not something you've ever been accused of."

This wasn't going well. Bob could hear the unintended harshness in his voice. He had to focus—get back to the script that he'd rehearsed in his mind a thousand times in the last week.

"I'm sorry." He swallowed. "I'm sorry for everything. For drinking too much, for caring too little, for being too soft, for . . ." He shrugged his shoulders. "For being me."

There was a long pause. Enough time for hope to die.

"I miss you," Kate replied.

She looked tired, Bob thought, and more vulnerable than he could ever recall. And more desirable.

"God knows why. I'm a mess." He held back. He wanted to step across the threshold and kiss her but he knew from professional experience that the gap between words and meaning could be fatal. To miss him was one thing, but that didn't automatically extend to wanting him back.

"OK. Perhaps I need a little untidiness in my life."

"Then you should try living with Thierry."

"I'd rather try living with you. Again."

"I don't think I ever stopped living with you," Bob sighed. "All the time we weren't together I just kept imagining what you were doing."

"Am I that predictable?"

"No. Just irreplaceable."

"Like that damned fleece. I thought we'd lost that for good last autumn. Where on earth did you find it?"

"Don't know. I just picked it up at Thierry's. I assumed it was his."

"It's your style," she said, pointing. "Cheap, baggy and a bit rough around the edges. I reckon it is yours."

"I suppose it's like all good things." Bob dared a brief grin at her. "It always comes back home."

"I love you," Kate whispered, gesturing him into the house. As Bob entered the *sejour* she added "I hate you as well."

"We've got the rest of our lives to solve that," Bob said. "Let's focus on the love for now."

The following few hours blurred past Bob—a mixture of rediscovering romance and catching up with an old friend. Kate had seen through Dominic almost as quickly as he had moved onto his next conquest. She had considered going back to England to catch up with old girlfriends and even thought about seeing if she could get her old job back. In the end it had been Madame Poussin who had told her to stay put.

"They always come back in the end," she had said. "Poussin and I have split up at least seven times, but the old dog just can't get enough of me. He'll come home with his tail between his legs, you'll see."

"She was right," Bob said.

"Only just. I really thought we'd had it for a while."

They were cuddled up together on the sofa in the *sejour*. Bob had built up a small fire in the hearth and the gentle warmth suffused them both with a sense of *bien-etre*. The strange thing was that he didn't feel the slightest bit tired. It was just like falling in love; when energy is endless and time is irrelevant.

"We do need to think about what we're doing here," Kate said. "We can't just drift through our lives anymore."

"And we need to get some money in. I hate to be practical but we'll be bankrupt in a few months if we keep on as we are."

"I know. I suppose I just thought that the pressures would be different here. More manageable."

"Oh, we'll manage." Bob wasn't as convinced as he sounded. "Something will turn up, as Micawber said. I can always get a job."

"And there's always the paper."

"Oh that thing. I'm not sure it's really ready for submission, and the deadline's next week."

"It's OK. I read it while you were . . ." Kate chose her word carefully. ". . . away. I think you capture some useful points. But there was one thing that puzzled me about it."

"What's that?"

"I always thought that Lear had three daughters."

"He did."

"But you've only really written about two of them. As if he'd never had a third child."

"To Lear she wasn't his child. After all he disinherited her. She was both the least important and, ultimately, the most important."

"Perhaps you should emphasise that a little more. Less of the sibling rivalry and more about the banishment." Kate hugged him closer. "Anyway, I think it's time for bed." She kissed at his stubble.

"What did you just say?" Bob sat bolt upright.

"It's time for bed."

"No, no. Before that."

"Something about emphasis. What about it?"

Bob knelt down beside Kate, took her head in his hands and kissed her more fiercely than he had done for a long time.

"I think you've just solved a murder."

CHAPTER THIRTY-SEVEN

"I TOLD YOU we'd be late. There's nowhere to park." Bob pointed towards the front of the Hambleton's cottage and shrugged his shoulders at Kate.

"But this is France. It's impossible to be actually late."

"Yes, but this is a very British affair. The Hambletons are sticklers for punctuality. Look," he gestured towards a battered old Fiat which had been blocked in by a variety of newer vehicles. "Even Thierry has managed to get here before us."

"I don't know why they invited us here," Kate complained. "It isn't as if we're family or anything."

"They're having a '*soirée*'." Bob couldn't resist the opportunity to mimic Charles' trademark gesture. "I think they see us a reminder of the poverty stricken country that they've left behind."

"Oh, I'll just park on the verge," Kate decided, reversing the Clio just beyond the gateway.

"Besides, Thierry and I have a little surprise for one of the guests." Bob smiled at Kate. "Actually I think they'll all get a shock."

"You sound far too inscrutable for my liking," Kate said, as they got out of the car. "And why does Thierry keep calling you? If I'd known he was going to be on the phone every ten minutes I'd have told you to stay with him."

"All will be revealed," Bob said in a voice that he hoped sounded enigmatic.

"Welcome, welcome." Charles opened the cottage door and ushered them into the hallway.

"I'm so sorry about the time," Kate said. "But Bob insisted that it was chic to be late."

"Oh, don't worry. Everyone's here now. Come into the 'dining room'."

"Very elegant." Bob had to admit that the re-arrangement of the lounge had been effective. A large trestle table had been erected in the centre of the room and, by the artful use of candles and enough silverware to solve the eurozone debt crisis, an ambiance of genteel grandeur had been created.

"Kate, I don't think you know everyone." Maureen sat at the head of the table and beckoned the late-comers to take the two seats either side of her. "May I present my daughters Jasmine and Rose." Bob was surprised to see Rose wearing a dress. She looked glamorous and sophisticated, unlike her companion. "And this is Rose's partner Michel who works for the firm. Marc I think you already know."

Kate nodded her head. "And of course I know Charles and Louise."

"And Thierry," Bob added, grinning at the gendarme.

"I'm never likely to forget him," Kate muttered.

"The pleasure's all mine," Thierry replied facetiously.

"Can we eat now?" Marc asked his mother "I'm famished!"

"After grandma's said grace," Jasmine said quietly.

"I think we can dispense with that this evening," Maureen said. "I want us all to relax and have some fun."

Bob felt his stomach churn. It wasn't in his nature to spoil a party but what he had to say wasn't likely to lift the atmosphere. The revelation he was about to make would split the family apart and, for all their eccentricities, he had come to feel an attachment to them. But all that unpleasantness could wait until after the meal.

The food was excellent. Maureen had hired someone from the local bistro, a surly-looking elderly chef with a classical handle-bar moustache, to put together an extravagant five course meal. It concluded with a cheese plate that encompassed all that was magnificent about

French cows from Abondance to Valençay. In contrast the conversation had been distinctly English; convivial small talk ranging from the weather to wine. Bob had been careful to keep his alcohol intake low; he would need to have his wits at their sharpest for his after-dinner talk.

Coffee was served at around ten o'clock and Bob was getting looks from Thierry indicating that the time was right to begin proceedings when Maureen pre-empted him. She tentatively tapped a teaspoon against her wine glass to get the attention of the room. She seemed uncharacteristically nervous, and Bob could see a delicate beading of sweat line her upper lip.

"I think it would be appropriate for me to say a few words on this occasion."

Bob felt strangely relieved. It would defer his unpleasant task for a few minutes more.

"As I'm sure you are all only too well aware life has been very difficult for me." Maureen stopped. Her fingers were trembling.

"Dad's death was a great loss to us all." Rose said, filling the awkward silence. "You've coped remarkably well in the circumstances. We're all very proud of you." She leant over and rubbed her mother's forearm.

"Don't patronise me." Maureen pulled her hand away and breathed in deeply. "I know you mean well, my dear, but it's time we all faced some rather difficult facts."

Bob tensed up. He was supposed to doing this.

"When I say life has been difficult for me I don't mean in the recent past. It wasn't long after I married your father that I realised I had made a mistake. Don't misunderstand me; James was a loving man and a devoted father. The problem was that he loved too much. Or perhaps I should say too many. He was unfaithful to me on more occasions than I care to think—probably far more times than I dare to know."

"Oh, I'm sure that's an exaggeration," Jasmine interrupted. "Daddy was always working so hard."

"It always worked the same with you two," Maureen snorted. "Neither of you could see the wrong in each other. I hate to break up your idyllic image of your father but he was a womanising cheat. His so-called business meetings were no more than camouflage for liaisons with his mistresses. Even on the day he died he was meeting another woman. That's why he pretended to Professor Hunt that he was phoning from New York when he was really still in Paris."

"Umm, well . . ." Bob tried to interject. It would probably be better if he took the story from here.

Maureen, however, was not in a mood to be stopped.

"In fact at least one of you here knew he was seeing other women." She looked down for a moment. "Who am I kidding? You probably all knew the truth." The chef began to clear the table of glasses, refilling their cups with coffee as he went.

"No, you're right." Charles spoke from the opposite end of the table. "I was aware that he'd seen other women." He turned to his left. "I'm afraid that one of them was your former wife, Michel."

"So I get his daughter in return." Michel took Rose's hand in his. "A more than fair exchange I think."

"Hardly a 'match made in heaven'."

"You idiot, Charles." Maureen retook control of the conversation. "You always wished you'd had James' courage. He was a leader and you simply followed. You may have known he was seeing other women but I bet that most of the time you wished that it could have been you in bed with them."

"That's very unfair, Auntie Maureen." Louise's usually melodic voice was shrill with anger; her eyes flashed with determination. "Dad's never thought of another woman except poor mother. He misses her so much."

"Unfair is it? Perhaps you'd like to tell your father which *femme fatale* it was that met James on the night he was murdered."

There was silence as all heads turned to face Louise. Her face paled like the most delicate porcelain and then flushed into a bright crimson.

"I think perhaps . . ." Bob really felt that now was a good time to intervene.

"You disgusting little hussy. I'm sure your mother would be proud of you now." Maureen's lip curled in disdain. "Anyway I got my revenge in the end."

"What do you mean?" asked Thierry.

"Haha! Granny killed Grampa." Marc yelled triumphantly. "I bet she killed Daddy too."

"Marc—stop it!" Jasmine turned to her son and pointed at him. Then she turned back to Maureen. "Did you? I know you never liked Alain, but he wouldn't have hurt a fly. He was such a gentle man—most of the time. He was just a bit . . ." She paused to think of the word. "Delicate I suppose. It didn't take much to disturb him. That's why he committed suicide."

"It wasn't suicide," Michel said sharply. "It may be convenient for you as the family and for the business to have it recorded as suicide but he had life far too easy to ever kill himself."

"No, it has to be suicide." Tears were beginning to form in Jasmine's eyes. She turned to Thierry. "Tell them that it's suicide."

"I'm afraid I can't," Thierry said slowly. "It was murder. We now have the proof."

"If I may . . ." Bob took this as his cue to reveal what they knew.

"Hold on." It was Charles. He turned to face Maureen. "If you killed James then you must have . . ."

"I never killed James. I may have hated him but I would never have hurt him. At least not physically."

The sudden silence was punctuated only by the discreet clinking of coffee cups.

"Then what did you mean by revenge?" Thierry pressed.

"There's one person here with whom I've shared a very deep secret."

"And I was very humbled," Bob took this as his cue to begin. "It was actually what started me thinking . . ."

"Not you! I'm talking about Timmy Wells."

"Who the hell is Timmy Wells?" Michel asked.

"I am." The chef put the coffee pot on the table and walked up to Maureen, placing his arm around her shoulders.

"You see, what's sauce for the goose is good for gander," Maureen explained. "Or probably that should be the other way round in this case. Whilst James was seeing other women, including you my dear." She pointed at Louise. "I took the opportunity to have an affair of my own. I met Timmy years ago when he did some work to tie up all the legal and financial aspects of the business after James and Charles inherited the firm." She turned to Bob. "I'm afraid that I lied to you about that. I couldn't risk my relationship with Timmy coming out into the open whilst the murder investigation was fresh. It would cast too much suspicion on him. That was why I was so keen to find out what the investigation had uncovered."

"And I was puzzled to hear that James had arranged to prepare the cottage for me." Timmy Wells has the clipped tones of an old-fashioned sergeant-major. "Certainly he and I had been in touch recently but it was about a business matter. If he had known what Maureen and I were up to he would probably have shot me." He guffawed with laughter.

"I thought that perhaps James had found out," Maureen said. "He would find it terribly amusing to pretend that the cottage was being set up for my lover when actually it was for one of his liaisons."

"What makes it more interesting," Bob started. "Is that Mr Wells has recently been holding some shares in the company . . ."

"On behalf of James. That was the recent deal that we worked on." Timmy's moustache framed an amiable smile. "The shares were to be held in trust for Louise." Louise blushed again. "Of course it was very difficult for me. On the one hand I had to maintain client confidentiality with James and, on the other, I desperately wanted to tell the woman I loved that I had the evidence with which she could commence divorce proceedings and free the way for us to be together."

"And you did the right thing, darling." Maureen wrapped her arm around his waist. "If you had told me that he was sleeping with his niece then I might very well have murdered him."

"I think it's time I confessed to something," Louise said. Her pretty face looked sad and her party dress sagged at the shoulders. "It's not very pleasant but since we're playing unhappy families . . ."

"Speak for yourself," said Michel. "If this is what happens to the rich then I think I'll stay a poor humble mechanic."

"Shut up." Rose slapped him on the arm. "Anyway, you're not a poor humble mechanic . . ."

"More revelations?" Charles asked. "What an evening we're having. 'Skeletons in cupboards' and all that."

Thierry cast Bob a quizzical look. This certainly hadn't been in their plan.

"I was only going to say that Michel is a man rich in integrity and honour. And I, for one, value that more highly than money or ties of blood." Rose squeezed Michel's hand but Bob noticed that the mechanic did not respond.

"And blood is my confession." All eyes swivelled back to Louise. "You see I'm not James' niece."

"Don't be silly, darling." A frown creased Charles' forehead. "What are you talking about?"

"She's his daughter," Bob said quietly.

There was a moment of chaos, followed by absolute silence. Finally Bob had his audience.

"It's all to do with Lear. In the play Lear is a king first and a father second. A bit like James really. Except in the play Lear disinherits one of his daughters whereas in James' case he had to pretend that one of his daughters wasn't his own."

"How did you find out?" Louise asked.

"It was something Kate said to me. She said I'd only written about two daughters when there were really three in the play. It got me thinking; what if James had an illegitimate daughter?" Bob turned to Maureen. "I remember you telling me that you'd heard rumours about the possibility. You also told me that you'd heard him calling out the name Betty in his sleep."

Maureen nodded.

"Well, it wasn't his mistress he was summoning. It was his daughter."

"Betty?" Maureen looked puzzled. "But her name's Louise."

"Louise Elizabeth Hambleton. I found that out from the list of shareholders in the firm." Bob turned to Timmy. "The same list that showed you had a large shareholding in the business. Again, the reverse of Lear. James had put by an inheritance for his third daughter, even though he couldn't acknowledge her."

"I was going to make him." Louise's eyes flashed defiance in the trademark Hambleton manner. It had been a characteristic that had helped to convince him that his suspicions were on the right lines.

"Yes, I believe you would have. You see, Maureen, that's why Louise met James on the night of the murder. Not for an illicit love-nest but to tell him that she had found out the truth."

"And she got the proof from a clinic in Le Mans," Thierry added. "I went there this morning. You supplied them with a DNA sample from a cup that James used and they were able to provide a genetic match fairly quickly."

"He drove me up to the cottage on his way down from Rouen and we had a very stormy meeting. He told me that he cared for me but that he could never acknowledge me as his daughter because it would crush Maureen." Louise gazed down the table. "He loved you more than you realise, I think."

"This morning Thierry managed to identify the taxi driver that picked you up from the cottage later on that evening. It would have helped save at least one life if he had come forward earlier but James gave them a lot of money to maintain discretion. It also explains the cigarette in the car ashtray. Your one little vice I believe?"

"Yes," Louise nodded. "James gave the taxi driver a handful of fifty-euro notes. He even told him to put the ambulance emergency lights on to make sure I was back in Paris before midnight."

"Which was about the time that James was murdered." Bob was confident of his ground now.

"But you said that he'd phoned you from New York," Charles insisted. "He couldn't have been in New York and in the Vendée at the same time. It doesn't make any sense to me."

"That was all part of a stupid plan to put me off the scent," Thierry grumbled. "And I fell for it."

"The phone call was supposed to set me up as the killer," Bob continued. "First I was meant to believe that James was in New York and then it could be proved that I was a liar when the body was found in the Vendée. The killer went to a lot of trouble to frame me. They had an American post office box set up in my name and created a paper trail that suggested I was planning to have the body cut up and sent there. They even went through the green box in my garden and stole some secateurs and pinking shears."

"What on earth are pinking shears?" Timmy asked.

"Fancy scissors to you, darling," Maureen replied, patting him on the hand.

"But how could you hear someone's voice that was already dead?" Rose asked.

"The voice could have been recorded when James was alive," Thierry replied.

"You have access to a recording studio, don't you?" Bob looked straight at Rose.

"I do, but . . ."

"Bloody hell. They're trying to lay your dad's murder on you now." Michel's voice was harsh. "Typical bourgeoisie whitewash. She couldn't have done it—she was with me!"

"That's not quite true, is it?" Bob asked. "You were keeping an eye on your wife that evening."

"How do you know that?"

"Because she saw you," Thierry said. "I checked today with her. She was actually quite flattered. Said that she thought it proved you were jealous and wanted her back. She even suggested that if you wanted a . . ."

"Little slut! I wouldn't give her the time of day."

"Which brings us back to you, Rose." Bob was enumerating the points he had to cover in his head. By his reckoning, he was nearly there. "You don't really have an alibi for the night of James' murder, do you?"

Rose shook her head slowly. Her long black hair swayed across her neck, casting candlelit shadows on the wall behind.

"Fortunately, however, you do have an alibi for the murder of Alain. You had a conversation with him and then told him to go home. You stayed at the office."

"I don't have an alibi, though," said Michel. "I could easily have followed Alain into the Metro and pushed him in front of a train. God knows there were enough times when I felt like doing it."

"Except that the platform he was on was the one for the train to Chelle-Mourtain, where the garage was based. Far from you following him, it was more likely that he was on his way to see you. Anyway, you couldn't have done it."

"How do you know?" Michel's voice was arrogant.

"Because you didn't have the opportunity to commit the first murder."

"What if we worked together and Rose killed her father?"

"I'm not talking about the murder of James," Bob said. "The first murder happened years before that. It was the poisoning of Margaret Hambleton."

"Louise," Thierry leaned forward to whisper. "We're going to have to go through all your mother's medical records."

"Why?" Louise stood up suddenly. The chair behind her crashed to the ground. "Haven't I been through enough already?"

"You have," Bob said. "And you very nearly gave me the final piece of information that I needed."

"What do you mean?"

"Do you remember when you came round to our house with Charles and sat in the garden?"

"Yes."

"You were so sad when you talked about your mother's death that you needed cheering up. You turned to Charles and asked him to tell us a joke and you were about to say what a good . . ."

"Impressionist he is." Louise continued.

"But you didn't get the chance to finish the sentence because he never let you. He blamed you for breaking the glass during the conversation but he meant to stop you from telling me."

Thierry stood up and walked towards Charles.

"Why would you want to hide a skill like that?" Bob asked. "Unless of course, you'd been impersonating the voice of the man you hated most in the world. A man who'd cuckolded you, outshone you in the business and become the acknowledged king of the family. But the real breaking point came when he told you that your daughter—your pride and joy—was really his." Bob could see the fear rising in Charles' eyes and, with it, an unadulterated expression of hatred. "Your brother and your wife; both traitors in your eyes. But you made sure that they paid the ultimate price."

"We've had the company's computer system looked over by our technology team in Paris," Thierry paused briefly, presumably to despatch a virtual spit. "They found the computer files that Charles created to make the link between Bob and New York."

"You went to a lot of trouble to frame me. I think you probably had the whole thing in mind when you first recruited me to look after the cottage. Even Kate's pinking shears were planted in the cottage to throw yet more suspicion on me."

"Oh yes, those." Thierry looked at Charles disdainfully. "You claimed you didn't know what they were when you brought them round to me. Said that you'd found them in the kitchen and thought they might be evidence." The capitaine slammed his hand onto the table. "You knew damn well what they were and who they would incriminate. But by then I'd already worked out that Bob hasn't got the balls to kill anyone so I just put them back where they belonged."

"Perhaps he thought I was a . . ." Bob couldn't resist the temptation and sliced the air with his fingers. ". . . 'sitting duck'".

"But what about my poor Alain?" Jasmine sounded confused. "Surely he wasn't involved in all of this?"

"I think Alain knew about the affair between Margaret and James but because he didn't like to rock the boat he never said anything. This is what he apologised to you for, not the murder. Then he would have discovered the changed computer files and confronted you," Bob continued, turning to Charles. "I think he was on his way to check the details out with Michel when you decided to challenge him at the Gare du Nord. A second post mortem has found two sets of small bruises around the lower back, presumably where he was pushed onto the tracks. It was an ideal opportunity to reframe the murder onto him rather than me. My alibi was working out rather well and you must have been nervous about where suspicion would fall next."

"The Paris boys also found that the computer date was shifted back soon afterwards, enabling a suicide note to appear to have been emailed before Alain's death," Thierry explained.

"And it was this time shift that created so much trouble on the company's system. Only the system manager would be able to make such a change." Bob pointed at Charles. "No wonder you were so busy with work, trying to get all your little lies to line up nicely."

"You bastard!" Charles stood up slowly. As Thierry approached him from behind, Charles sliced his elbow into the gendarme's groin and ducked under his flailing arm. He ran out of the lounge door, through the hallway and out of the front door.

"Stop him," called Bob, somewhat feebly in the circumstances.

"I think I'll need some help." Thierry was having trouble straightening up.

Bob grabbed hold of Kate's sleeve and tugged her towards the door.

"Looks like it's up to us," he said.

She simply nodded and started running.

Chapter Thirty-Eight

O UTSIDE THE COTTAGE Charles had already started his car, a sleek-looking BMW, and was reversing out of the parking area.

"Quick—the Clio," Bob said, using three words that he had never previously thought of as belonging in the same sentence. "I think we're going to lose him."

"Not if I drive," Kate said. She leapt into the car and had the engine running before Bob could shut the passenger door. "Hang on tight!"

The BMW sped off down the country lane away from Marieul-sur-Lay and towards the *bocage*. The road tracked down the hill and then wound along the valley of the river Yon in a series of gentle curves. The BMW quickly outpaced the Clio. In the dark all that Bob could see was tail-light of Charles' car as it intermittently appeared in front of them.

"He's getting away," he said unhelpfully.

"Time for turbo then."

"But we haven't got a turbo, darling. Remember this is the cheap model."

"We have if I do this . . ."

The Clio's interior light was presently broken in the 'on' position and in the dim luminescence Bob could see that Kate was smiling. When he looked more closely he could see that it wasn't a genuine smile; it was more like an inane grin. He suddenly became very afraid.

Kate jammed the clutch into a position somewhere between second and fourth gear and there was a squealing of metal arguing with metal. The Clio jerked across the road coming to an almost complete stop before relaunching itself at almost twice its previous speed. The engine squealed briefly before settling into a gentle humming sound—almost like a purr.

"What on earth . . . ?"

"I discovered it by accident one day. I couldn't the damn thing in gear and suddenly it took off like this. Great, isn't it?"

It was certainly fast. Bob watched with growing incredulity as the speedometer rose smoothly out of the 80 kilometers-per-hour range and past the 100 mark. It quickly took 120 and 140 in its stride before moving past the line at 160.

"We're doing a hundred miles an hour. In the Clio."

"I know. It's great fun!" Kate was enjoying this far too much. "There's the bastard."

The back of the BMW came into view as they entered a long straight stretch of road that Bob knew ran along the back of Longchamp. Both cars sped up and it wasn't long before the needle of the speedometer was resting against the plastic stop at the end of the gauge.

"I hate to say this, darling. You do know there's a roundabout in about half a mile?" They had almost caught the BMW but there was no sign that Kate had any plans to slow down in the near future.

"Bloody back seat driver. I know what I'm doing."

"It's the one they've built ready for the new bypass, remember."

"Oh, that one!" Bob thought Kate's tone sounded facetious.

Charles had reached the roundabout. His brakelights fizzed orange in front of them.

"You can only go straight on but . . ."

The roundabout was upon them. To be more accurate, and to Bob's horror, they were on it. He braced himself as the Clio ramped up the front of the earth mound and flew across the top of the hillock, passing briefly between two wooden posts. The chassis of the car gave a metallic groan as it hit the tarmac on the other side of the roundabout.

"It's the one where they've built an archway on the top to represent the gateway to the Vendée coast," Kate explained calmly.

"But now he's . . ."

"Behind us. Yes, I know. I've often thought that these car chases in films were a waste of time. The best way to catch someone is surely to be in front of them . . ."

Bob gaped at his wife. He wasn't sure which scared him more; her driving skills or her logic.

He didn't have time to reach a conclusion. A screech of brakes behind them indicated that Charles had decided to turn round.

"That's cheating!" Kate shouted and jammed the handbrake on.

The Clio swerve-slid across the road in a cacophonous melange of molten disk, rubber and smoke. A couple of revs later Kate had the car facing back towards the roundabout, which Charles was already circumnavigating at great speed.

"Aaah!" Kate screamed, tugging fiercely at the gearstick. "I can't get the damn thing into turbo." They circuited the roundabout using the conventional route. "We'll lose him for certain."

"I wouldn't be so sure." Bob had seen a vision.

Across the fields on the left the black sky was punctuated by bright spotlights and mechanical arms that clawed the air and the ground. It looked as though a spaceship had arrived in the Vendée and was gobbling up the earth on its way to galactic domination.

"What the hell . . . ?"

"It's a combine harvester."

"And it's coming out onto the road."

The BMW broke sharply. Kate slowed the Clio, as they watched the lumbering machine lurch onto the road in front of Charles.

"I'll block him in," she said, turning the car at right angles to the road.

"But there's someone coming the other way." Bob pointed to some headlights beyond the harvester. He jumped out of the car and ran towards the BMW.

Three of them converged towards the murderer. As Bob approached Charles he recognised the new vehicle as Thierry's car and he wasn't surprised when he heard the gendarme's voice.

"Fucking British drivers. You, out!" He was pointing a small pistol towards Charles.

"OK, OK. Don't shoot." Charles scrambled out of the car and raised his arms. Thierry quickly got the handcuffs round Charles' wrists.

The driver of the harvester had jumped down from the cab and was rolling up the sleeves of their baggy overalls. Against the light Bob didn't recognise the driver until she spoke.

"You again." Betrice spat on the ground. "Why is it that I can't go anywhere without you being there?"

"I could say the same. Do you normally sit in that thing waiting for murderers to speed past?"

"No, your mate over there gave me a call." She nodded towards Thierry. "Since I was out by the garage I thought I'd come down and have a closer look. That's some car you've got there."

"And some driver," Bob said. He turned to face the Clio. Kate was walking slowly towards him. She appeared to be anxious.

"Are you alright love?" He put an arm around her shoulder.

"I'm fine." He looked at her. Streaks of oil were smeared along her cheeks. Her blue eyes shone clearer than the brightest star. "But I'm afraid the Clio's dead. I can't get her started at all." She looked at the ground sheepishly. "I'm afraid I seem to have broken this." She passed a stick of metal to Bob.

"That's our gearstick!"

"I think we might need a new one."

Bob pulled her towards him.

"I'm so proud of you," he whispered into her hair.

"The feeling's mutual."

"Looks like I'd better leave you two lovebirds at it." Betrice hiked her overalls up to reveal a pair of stilettos. "You have to wear something comfortable to drive in," she said in answer to Bob's raised eyebrow. "Kate, just promise me you won't let him out on the loose again. I don't think the women of the Vendée are ready for him yet."

"I promise." Bob felt Kate pull him closer.

Betrice marched up to Thierry and kissed him on the cheek. "*A bientot.*" She waved to them as she jumped back into the cab of the harvester and reversed it into the fields.

Thierry gestured to Charles, who was sitting in the back of the gendarme's car trussed up in enough chains to satisfy a magician's convention.

The gendarme smirked at Bob and Kate, and raised his index fingers into the night sky.

"I think that's what you Brits call 'a fair cop'!"

CHAPTER THIRTY-NINE

"FINISHED!"

Bob had just completed the final version of his paper for the conference. Just in time; the deadline was at the end of the week. He read the first sentence again to check that he was satisfied with it.

'King Lear is one of Shakespeare's most complex plays but its central theme is the concept of love.'

And that was the essential problem with everything, Bob had decided. Love. You could probably survive without it, but you could only really live if you experienced love. It could be difficult sometimes—Charles Hambleton had proved that. His love had turned to jealousy and hatred and, ultimately, murder. But it was also the most indispensable emotion of them all. Bob knew that now. And he knew that, whatever passed between them, he would always love Kate. She was, as the bard had noted 'most rich, being poor; most choice, forsaken; and most loved, despised!'

"Surprise!" Poussin poked his head round the kitchen door and waved at Bob in the *sejour*. Madame Poussin's oval face appeared next to her husband's elbow. They were dressed in their Sunday best and looked like a pair of hobbits on the way to a wedding.

"Surprise!" She beamed at Bob.

Except it wasn't really a surprise. For one thing Bob had seen them through the window as they walked up the street and past the little stone house. And for another, Thierry had told him to expect a visit from his neighbours. Apparently they had bought him a present.

"Well, this is a surprise," he lied. "Come in, come in. Would you like a drink?"

"I don't normally start this early," Poussin said. "But as it's a special occasion I'll have a glass of trouspinnette, please."

"Oh!" Bob had expected them to ask for a cup of tea; it was only half past ten.

"And I'll have the same."

Bob did a double-take. He had never known Madame Poussin to drink alcohol.

"Of course," he said calmly. "Do sit down." He suddenly realised why Poussin had told him the story about Longchamp and the dead body. Rogier had been giving his illicit harvest to local people for medicinal purposes and they would want to keep prying eyes away from their supplier. No wonder Poussin had so much life in him.

"I'm very excited," Poussin exclaimed as he sat in Kate's big armchair. "Thierry and Gautier are sorting out a little gift for you."

"They should be here any minute," Madame added, nestling herself into the same chair as her husband. Bob reflected that there was still room for about half their children.

"But why should I get a present?" Bob passed them their drinks.

"Because you're a hero!" Madame was almost breathless in her admiration. "You were even mentioned in 'Ouest France'."

"It's not every day someone we know solves a murder." Poussin handed his empty glass back to Bob.

"Well, it wasn't really that difficult," Bob said. "Especially when I realised that the first murder was Margaret Hambleton."

"What set you onto that?" Poussin started on his second glass.

"Maureen told me that she had a kitchen garden but Jasmine said that Charles did all the gardening. He must have grown some toxic plant or mushroom and fed it to his wife, under the cover of a meal at a Chinese restaurant. It was a poisonous growth, like the anger and resentment that was building up inside him."

"And all of that business with the secateurs and the airport was designed to set you up as the murderer?" Poussin held out his glass again.

"Yes. It seemed to be a lot of effort to go to. But it nearly worked."

"It's not that hard to fool Thierry." Shadows passed across the window and footsteps crunched in the gravel past the side of the house. "Talk of the devil."

"He-he. That'll be your present." Madame seemed to be more excited by the prospect than Bob was. "Have you any idea what it is?"

"It's something you really want," Poussin hinted.

"I really can't guess." Bob lied for the second time that morning. He'd been telling Kate and Thierry—and in fact to anyone who would listen—how much he needed a new laptop. He knew that Kate had met up with Thierry a couple of times, presumably to discuss the specification for the new machine. Bob didn't really care about that, as long as it had a WiFi connection so that he could browse the internet without having to lay a spider's web of cables across the *sejour*.

"Celebrating already?" Thierry grunted as he came through from the kitchen. "I'd better catch up then." He picked the bottle of trouspinette up from the glass-topped coffee table and took a generous swig.

"That stuff's not bad, but I prefer the chestnut flavour myself." Gautier appeared in the doorway. "I think Kate's ready for us in the garden."

"And I think she's well and truly over Dominic." Bob said.

"I've been trying to catch up with him," Thierry grumbled. "He's keeping out of my way. Just as well, too. If we'd known that Louise had visited the cottage that night it would have saved us a lot of trouble."

"Charles must have arrived soon afterwards and got James roaring drunk," Bob said. "Perhaps it was the only way he could have subdued him enough to actually kill him. Luring him up to the attic was a good move though. He could have been up there for months if we hadn't gone looking for the suitcase."

"I wonder why Louise didn't say anything about her visit to the cottage," Gautier mused.

"It must have been very hard for her," Kate replied. "To discover who your real father is and then have him taken away so soon afterwards must be difficult. She couldn't have known for sure whether Charles was aware of the affair. She probably didn't want him to find out through her. And now the man that she thought was her father is being taken away as well."

"He'll serve at least twenty years." Thierry rubbed his hands. "Cousin Gaston will see to that."

"Anyway, it's time for the presentation." Kate beckoned them all into centre of the garden by the small fountain that Bob had built. Thierry brought the bottle with him.

They stood in a semi-circle bathed in hot July sunshine. There was a small package wrapped in floral paper on the garden table. It didn't look big enough to be a laptop, Bob thought. Perhaps it was a tablet computer instead. They had WiFi and were small enough for him to be able to take to the beach. He started to get excited.

Gautier cleared his throat.

"Over the past year Bob you have become a real friend to us. The village of St-Sébastien has never, I'm pleased to say, had a murder of its own. The fact that you have brought one to us has been a blessing. We've had all of the excitement without any of the, err, mess."

"More's the pity," Thierry grumbled.

"In return we would like you to have this small gift to show our appreciation to you."

Gautier passed the package to Bob who began to open it.

"Kate chose it," Poussin said. "I'd have gone for a couple of dozen bottles of the chateau's finest myself, but that's women for you."

"I'm sure I'll love it." It was just about the right size for a tablet, Bob decided. Kate really was the perfect wife.

Inside the wrapping was a cardboard box. Inside the box was another box, and another, and another. Inside the final box was a key.

"Come with me." Kate took Bob by the hand and led him up the side alley. "Look!"

Bob looked. He could hardly believe his eyes. It was a gate. Not the old, wooden, half-collapsed gate but a new, shiny, stylish gate with a lock and cornices on the sides.

"This is a surprise." Bob looked up at his neighbours. Everyone seemed so pleased. Life, he concluded, was simple if you just enjoyed it on its own terms. The laptop could wait. "It's just what I wanted."

And, of course, it was *bleu*.